ALSO BY JESPER BUGGE KOLD

Winter Men

THE WALL

BETWEEN

JESPER BUGGE KOLD

Translated by K.E. Semmel

THE WALL
BETWEEN

Text copyright © 2016 Jesper Bugge Kold
Translation copyright © 2017 K. E. Semmel
All rights reserved.

Previously published as *Land i datid* by Turbine DK in Denmark in 2016. Translated from Danish by K. E. Semmel. First published in English by AmazonCrossing in 2017.

Published by AmazonCrossing, Seattle

www.apub.com

Amazon, the Amazon logo, and AmazonCrossing are trademarks of Amazon.com, Inc., or its affiliates.

ISBN-13: 9781503937284
ISBN-10: 1503937283

Cover design by Shasti O'Leary Soudant

Printed in the United States of America

For Karina, Malte, and Elvira

PROLOGUE

Berlin, October 2006

The droplets fall where the boys' wet soccer ball had thumped against the asphalt. They drip from the shaft of the knife. The knife is drawn out, and his blood flows thick and dark. His energy drains from him, both slowly and all too quickly. He hears his breathing grow heavy and erratic. Pain washes over him and pumps into his half-emptied veins, as though trying to fill them again. He gurgles hoarsely.

The recognition that his life is over gives him surprising clarity: new, unspoiled, and spontaneous, his thoughts are brief flashes of insight exploding in his head like tiny suns. Today he's himself, only inside out. Some days he is, and some days he has been, and tomorrow he will be no more. The precise language of pain tells him so.

The backyard light of his apartment building winks sharply off the broad steel blade of the kitchen knife. When it's thrust into him again, now with greater force, he hears the crunching sound of a rib. He gasps as his stomach is punctured, then doubles over the shaft.

He hangs on the knife like an animal on a spit. Two pairs of eyes, wide open in fear, look at each other. He recognizes the second pair.

He remembers the man and knows why he's about to die. He sees the sweat bead on his murderer's forehead, the broken blood vessel in his eye, the bulging artery in his neck. He himself burbles through his blood-filled mouth.

When the murderer releases the knife, he falls. He feels light, but falls heavily: not even at the end of his life can he defy gravity. The asphalt grasps him, and he watches his blood slowly pour out and trickle toward the drain like melted snow in the first spring sun.

A nearby train rattles down the tracks, momentarily breaking the silence in the backyard. The murderer takes his wallet and vanishes through the gate, but he won't die alone. In the ground-floor apartment, at the window, stands a woman. There's something about the way she's observing the scene. Her eyes give her away. They stare unblinking: he deserves this.

The muscles in his neck give in, and his head thumps against the asphalt like a ball. She quickly draws the curtains as his eyes close. With her reproachful gaze as his final human interaction, he departs this life in a fog of stillness. Time stretches, tenses like a bow, releases, and sails through the air. The hourglass gets crushed, and the shards in the fine particles of sand reveal how time passed here—until it ceased.

1

PETER

East Berlin, May 1975

The lake had always been there, fenced in by a dense forest that, in some places, stretched all the way to the water. Of course it was an exaggeration to say "always," since it had been sculpted from the landscape during the last ice age. Erosion had pulled at the terrain and carved the lake into its current form. The trees and tall reeds encircled it tightly to the bank, nearly concealing it from the world, but they had found it all the same. During the winter, the students at the international communist school Jugendhochschule Wilhelm Pieck had made tentative steps on the ice, but since the start of May, when the weather improved and the countryside regained its color, they came to swim.

A few girls on the shore shrieked shrilly when a glistening green frog hopped over their blanket. One in German, one in Finnish, one in Spanish, and a fourth in some African language that seemed to consist solely of vowels. The frog didn't notice the many linguistic variants describing a fear of *Hyla arborea*, however, and just continued to search for a sun-heated lily pad.

Peter heard Florian beside him laughing at the startled girls. The strong sun reminded Peter of his mother, but not because he wanted to think of her. Maybe it was more the way her soft voice always made her dictum sound like a piano chord in his head: *You mustn't look at the sun. You'll ruin your eyesight.* The words were always uttered softly in a gentle but tired tone of voice, as if she didn't believe them herself. They were dutiful—spoken the same way she'd heard them from her mother. The phrase was an heirloom passed from generation to generation, like a christening gown. It was the kind of sentence one carried through life, a classic childhood instruction, but as he considered it now, he could think of no one who'd ever been blinded by the sun. Helmut, one class ahead of him in school, was blind in one eye, but his blindness was the result of something he'd inherited at birth. Still, Peter wasn't eager to tempt fate. So he'd learned not to look at the sun. Instead he tried to sense it, glancing above it, beside it, around it. He fashioned its outline in his mind without ever endangering his vision.

And that's how he looked at her now, his gaze brushing innocently around her. No direct contact, no lingering that might betray him. He pretended to be watching the lake while observing her out of the corner of his eye, trying to capture shapes and details, slowly forming a complete image: her arms, shoulders, legs. Occasionally, his eyes disobeyed orders and looked directly at her; when they did, he punished them at once by turning to the other girls—who were in bathing suits that cut deep lines above their thighs.

Once again his eyes sought her out, darting quickly around the periphery of her body. She pushed off her sandals with her toes. She pulled the thin dress over her head, and her red curly hair followed through the opening in the neck. Her bikini was white like her freckled skin, which the sun had spared. She was slender, and her full breasts rested heavily in her bikini top.

She headed down to the bank. Several of the others were already in the water. She shouted something to Ejner in their language. He waved. His hands, big as barges, were raw and uneven like his beard. Ejner Madsen was older than the others and worked at the harbor in the Danish town of Korsør. He and Peter talked frequently, and they'd developed a kind of friendly rapport.

She eased into the water, and the lake grew still. The sun reflected on the dark water, where the cirrocumulus clouds were mirrored and water lilies floated and mosquito larvae climbed to the surface each evening. A few scrawny branches wavered from the trees that leaned over the water, waiting for the current that never arrived.

"She's from Denmark," Florian said.

Peter nodded. He already knew that, and he knew that her name was Elisabeth.

Then the first raindrops pattered down sluggishly, shivering the leaves with a delicate lightness. All at once the swimmers turned into hooting runners, gathering their clothing and laughing and sliding along the forest path that oozed with the transparent rain. Rain poured from the sky, and a steady aroma rose from the forest floor. He ran behind Elisabeth. The water had flattened her hair to her head. The curls were shiny, the reddish hue darker. The summer dress she'd thrown back on had grown sheer in the rain; the light cotton now merged with her body and became part of her. Her shoulders were round and strong, her spine forming a sharp line down toward her rear, where her muscles tensed beneath the fabric with every step she took.

Pellets of water dripped from them when they reached the school. The girls, including Elisabeth, went to their rooms to change into clothes that didn't cling to their bodies and reveal their figures. Peter watched her—the way her calves tightened and the gentle sway of her rear—as she disappeared up the stairwell. On the way to his room, he fantasized about stripping off the soaked summer dress that clung to her belly. Pulling the bikini top off to expose her breasts and the large, dull circles around her nipples. Pictured a droplet traveling down her breastbone, bypassing her belly button, and continuing down toward her pubic hair. He forced these thoughts away. To think of Elisabeth in this way was disrespectful.

The room was empty. His three roommates—Thomas, Otto, and Florian, all from different regions of the German Democratic Republic—weren't around. Peter unbuttoned his blue polyester shirt. When the shirt was dry, it irritated his skin when he ran his fingers across the seams, but when the shirt was wet, it was heavy and harmless. He removed it. The stiff collar stood up straight on the back of the chair. He'd never grown used to his stiff and formal uniform shirt. After three years in the Felix Dzerzhinsky Guards Regiment, he was generally accustomed to the feeling, but no other youth leagues wore uniforms. Their clothes were different. The synthetic fabric made him feel all wrong, and the uniform made noises; it rustled, and it was rigid and old-fashioned in comparison to the foreigners' colorful shirts and pants, which did not seem to irritate their skin.

He lay down on his bed, and his eyelids shut out the afternoon. He recognized Florian's footsteps, the soles' precise clop against the floor. The bed above him creaked, and he opened his eyes. Florian cocked his head and peered at him curiously, attempting to appear like a question mark. It seemed like a contradiction, because his face almost always looked like an answer. Everything was carefully measured, the distance from his nose to his eyes, the slope of his cheeks, the width of his mouth. Even his dimples appeared to have been made with a compass. Everything about him was calculated with a precision and exactness— just as one folds a piece of paper in the middle and cuts it with scissors. That was Florian's face.

"You're in love with her."

Peter already knew that, and he knew that her name was Elisabeth.

2

ANDREAS

Berlin, October 2006

His right shoe instantly absorbs water. He hears the rhythmic clicking of the turn signal, far away, like the second hand ticking around the face of a clock. The orange blinking light is reflected in the puddle of water that's filled one of the cracks in the asphalt, both illuminating his field of vision and returning it to darkness with punctual frequency. Out of the corner of his eye, he sees the scant light from the car; it glints in his eye each time the penetrating color strikes the puddle. He's paused next to the open car door, his eyes fastened on the surface of the water, which is disturbed by the impact of the raindrops. He thinks of his father.

The hum of the idling car engine and the clicking turn signal blends with the drumming rain on a mailbox. Andreas listens to these sounds until the dark-skinned man behind the wheel clears his throat. Then he hands the taxi driver a euro bill and briefly studies the small altar in the front window above the instrument panel. A rosary dangles from the rear-view mirror. He swings his backpack over his shoulder and turns to look at the white street sign. There's something reassuring—almost cozy and pleasant—about the street names in this part of the city: Kopenhagener Strasse, Dänenstrasse, Bornholmerstrasse, Korsörerstrasse.

He zips up his jacket and starts walking. To his right is an empty playground. A tire swing wavers in the wind, and a jungle gym propped in the thick sand glistens in the rain. Down the street, on a gray building with narrow balconies, he finds the number he's looking for. He walks through a graffiti-covered gate and enters a courtyard. He stops at the entrance and reads the name on the buzzer. He senses that someone is watching him, and in a first-floor apartment window, he spots an elderly woman. She pulls the curtain closed, and her shadow gradually recedes behind the pane.

He lets himself into the building with the key he'd gotten in the mail from attorneys Schultz and Donnerwitz. The walls of the stairwell are chinked and haven't seen a paintbrush in decades. At the top he finds the nameplate on a tarnished door.

He enters the apartment and drops his backpack. The small entranceway has a marbled linoleum floor that creaks slightly underfoot, as if the glue has begun to unstick. He locates the light switch and is startled by the color of the wallpaper, with its brown-and-orange flowers vining the walls. He opens a window to remove the acrid stink that emanates from the empty beer bottles gathered in one corner of the kitchen. A lonely chair stands beside a square table near the window. When he sees it, Andreas realizes how little he actually knows about his father. He pulls the chair out and sits down. He stares out the window, trying to see what his father saw whenever he sat there, but the windows are thick with rain, and outside it's pitch dark.

Berlin is a welcome diversion for Andreas, an escape, though such diversions require that one be on a path in the first place. He is the opposite. Andreas didn't want his father to die, of course, but his death nevertheless came at an opportune time. He is frustrated by his thesis, and his thesis is frustrated by him. Officially, he has been working on it for four years, but he has now run out of excuses and ways to procrastinate. So every morning he sits, staring at the pulsating, empty computer screen. He's a perpetual student who lacks motivation. The goal is far off in the distance, and he no longer wants to get there. The trip to Berlin is a welcome disruption from his daily life, which consists mostly of suppressing what his daily life ought to consist of, and this excuse could hardly be more believable.

He stands up and enters the small living room, then drapes his jacket over the back of a dining chair and watches the raindrops drip from it and onto the shag carpet, which is the same color as the turn signal in the taxi. He glances around the living room. It's a time capsule. Not only has he traveled to Berlin, but he's also traveled back to the 1970s.

Along one wall is a shelving unit made of a light-blond laminate. He picks a random book, *Die Nacht kam zu spät* by Paul Riemann-Müller, and riffles absently through it. There's a scribbled dedication: *Dear Peter.* He puts it back and takes another, a German book about solitaire with several dog-eared pages. A picture frame captures his attention. Originally it was meant to look like gold, but now it's tarnished and dull. His father stares at him from the yellowed photo: a friendly, young face. His blond hair is combed to one side, and though he's dressed in a shirt and tie, he doesn't appear stylish. His father looks very different from the way Andreas imagined he would, but he immediately recognizes himself in the space between the eyes and mouth.

As he gazes at the photograph, he feels a piercing sadness. It grows, pushing all the way through him. He's sad because his father is dead and because he never met him. When he was a child, his father was always in his thoughts. Andreas imagined that Peter could see him, as if he were a TV channel that his father could click on, but such thoughts had made him feel guilty. He had no need for a father: he had Thorkild. His mother, Elisabeth, had hardly ever mentioned Peter. Their family consisted of her, Thorkild, and Andreas, and Peter was an unknown entity whom no one ever spoke of or figured into the equation.

He and Thorkild don't share the same DNA, Andreas knows, but they share so much else: his childhood, a life—his life—but he could never fully suppress thoughts of Peter. He has always felt a certain longing, been curious. These feelings were occasionally very pronounced, while at other times they were toned down by puberty or crushes he'd had on girls. There has always been an empty place in the family album, and now he finally has the opportunity to fill that gap. Even though his father will be buried in a few days, Andreas feels he owes it to both Peter and himself to learn more about the man he was forced to live without. He asks questions, hoping that the apartment will answer some of them. Who was Peter? Did he ever think of Andreas? And why would someone want to murder him?

He tabulates the few things he already knows about his biological father: fifty-four years old, born and raised in the GDR, name Peter Körber, dead. That's it. His knowledge of the GDR is also limited. Since he was only thirteen in 1989, Germany's reunification hadn't made much of an impression on him, though what followed afterward did. The stories about Stasi—a security service that knew everything about every citizen and spared nothing to get what it wanted—and the comparisons to the Gestapo. Thorkild had explained it all to him, his voice tinged with irritation, as if the entire ideology had turned its back on him. Andreas simply hopes that Peter was never caught in Stasi's claws, never subjected to their brutal interrogations, never sat alone and afraid in one of their terrible prisons.

Something about the apartment tells him that his father was lonely. He's not sure what it is, but the apartment seems unsettled and disheartened. His eyes wander around the room. He notices immediately that everything is symmetrical. If there's a picture hanging to the right of the couch, so too is one on the left side. If there are books in the top right corner of the bookshelf, there are also books in the left corner. Everything has been arranged according to a system, with a careful exactness, like weights designed to create balance—as if anything else would bring chaos. At least he knows now that Peter was a symmetritian. He smiles. Is that a real word? Symmetritian? If not, it exists now.

There's a conch shell on one of the shelves, a tape recorder on another, and beside that an orange plastic container containing cassette tapes. It's fastened to a turntable. He spins it slowly around, and forgotten brands from his childhood suddenly spring to mind: BASF, Agfa, Maxell, TDK, and SKC. He's reminded of the sensation he felt when yet another tape he'd spent hours mixing became a tangled-up mess. He inserts a blue BASF tape into the recorder and presses Play. After a few seconds, the needle in the old-fashioned VU meter starts dancing uncertainly up and down to the music. Holding the tape cover in his hands, he sits down in the narrow leather couch beside the bookshelf.

> Today I passed you on the street
> And my heart fell at your feet
> I can't help it if I'm still in love with you

It's a woman's voice, the dusty sound of the past. The band plays proudly behind her, keeping to the background with a gentleman's discretion. A shabby tape head makes her sound like she has a lisp. The voice is untarnished, beautiful, and brutal. It is filled with longing, begging to be held, to be consoled, taken care of, and loved.

> Somebody else stood by your side
> And she looked so satisfied
> I can't help it if I'm still in love with you
> A picture from the past came, slowly stealing . . .

He looks at the photograph, and suddenly he sees his own reflection in the shiny glass. For the first time ever, they make eye contact, he and his father, and he notes the line that connects them. The bond between them is visible, and this scares him. His childhood notions of Peter come alive, and he recognizes their meaning. His longing is intense. Had it not been for his murder, Andreas never would've entered this apartment; had it not been for his murderer, they never would've gotten so close. Someone had wanted his father to die, and that is an impressive decision, actually. To choose to kill. To choose to end another person's life. To do something so definitive, becoming a murderer in order to exterminate another person. It occurs to him that his father's murderer is somewhere in the city, a man or woman for whom life would be better if Peter no longer existed.

3

PETER

East Berlin, May 1975

The school was north of Berlin, in a forested area dotted by small blue lakes. From the air, the buildings resembled letters, an alphabet stretching across the landscape, as if the architect had wished to spell something in stone, and the message was clear; the ideology was spectacular, the surroundings pompous. The complex's size was a testament to progress and greatness, and this was exactly what the students carried within them. They were part of a movement, a communist community of youth leagues that extended across latitudes and longitudes. They were part of a global political party.

Peter could see the fresh, green forest. It made its own particular crackling noise whenever a gust of wind caused the treetops to waver. A bird landed in the closest tree, some kind of sparrow, he guessed, and suddenly it annoyed him that he was unable to name other birds. This was the result of growing up in the city, where only sparrows, doves, and blackbirds had the courage to nest so far from their natural surroundings.

He now heard, beneath the window, the sound of one of the international groups on their way back from class. Totaling some five hundred students, they were divided into national and international classes, all of them facing ten months of training in communism's four key subjects: Marxist-Leninist philosophy, political economy, scientific communism, and the history of the international worker and youth movements.

There was an informant in each class reporting to the Ministry for State Security, which is how it kept its eyes and ears on everything that happened at the school. Peter was the informant in his class. He enjoyed the assignment, devising charts and systems for every type of information, developing tiny symbols and categories that described the monitored subjects and their habits down to the minutest detail. The students were unaware of his role, though Peter could tell who, like him, quietly noted the goings-on of others. Not by the clothing they wore or their body language, but by their eyes, which were always observing, inquisitive, and appraising; when their gazes met, they would nod at one another briefly and approvingly, like a secret handshake.

Every other week, Peter met with a commanding officer, Captain Meinke, in the nearby city of Bernau. The meetings always took place in the first-floor apartment of a widow who had consented to help the state. Shrouded in the scent of fresh-baked pastries and ground coffee, she would leave the apartment to feed the birds in the park so the two men could talk in peace.

"Fine and precise work, comrade Körber," Meinke always concluded, once Peter had presented yet another transcribed report.

He and his fellow students had spent more than eight months at Jugendhochschule Wilhelm Pieck. In a few months he was to begin working at the Ministry for State Security's Department XX/5. He would probably start, as was customary, by performing background checks on people. He had mixed feelings whenever he thought that his education would soon be over. Of course he looked forward to starting in one of the department's regional offices, but that meant he would never see Elisabeth again. Perhaps that was for the best. He needed to concentrate on the assignment, and thoughts of her distracted him. He always pictured her in her white bikini, her skin glistening from the lake water. Although he occasionally imagined her without her bikini, his fantasies would dissolve as soon as they began to ignite sparks. Only vulgar men had such thoughts about women.

Sometimes he tried to convince himself that he wasn't in love but that it was just a passing fancy or simple desire. They'd only spoken a few times, after all, but on the day she accidentally touched his arm, all doubt had vanished. One evening one of the Norwegian girls tried to kiss him in the café. Honored by her interest, he had vacillated a moment, but she wasn't Elisabeth, so he politely pushed her away. She'd fallen off her chair, and her soft, drunken body sprawled on the floor in a stupor.

Florian lay on the bed, his even breathing filling the room. For as long as Peter could remember, Florian had had the enviable ability to sleep through even the most impossible conditions, and today was no different. Peter was glad that Florian was at the school. He too was from a good family comprised of party members. He and Florian had grown up in the same apartment block in the Friedrichshain neighborhood. Together they had counted the bullet holes in the walls; they had gone to Kosmos and Kino International to watch the latest films from DEFA, the state-owned film studio; they'd gone to the flea market in front of the Treptower Park monument; and they'd biked to Friedrichsfelde to hand-feed the animals in Tierpark Berlin. They had worn the blue scarves as Youth Pioneers, red scarves as Thälmann Pioneers, and the blue shirts as Free German Youth. Now they were twenty-three. Although the mustache was new, Florian was otherwise still the same.

"There's a good head on that boy," Peter's teachers had always said about him. They'd said the same thing in high school, and that's how the officers had described him, too—except *boy* had been replaced with *young man*. He proudly and dutifully carried out every assignment he was given in the Felix Dzerzhinsky Guards Regiment. He was a guard at the party members' residences in Wandlitz and an honor guard at the gravesite when the country's former head of state, Walter Ulbricht, was laid to rest at the central cemetery in Friedrichsfelde.

Peter still recalled how he had felt when he was accepted into the guard regiment. He had originally planned to continue his studies after completing high school, probably at Humboldt University, but this offer wasn't something to pass up. When Peter was accepted into the guard unit, he knew his parents would be proud. Only the best young men from fine families were offered a place in it, so this offer meant that his family was elite. Though his father had made little of the news, tears of joy rolled down his mother's cheeks when he had informed them of his acceptance.

Georg Körber was a good worker, loyal party man, former medal-winning track cyclist, and now treasurer in the bicycle club.

On the day Peter was accepted, Georg had sat disinterestedly, as always, at the end of the dinner table, hunched over in that bicyclist sort of way, as if his vertebrae had become stuck in that particular position. Since the distance between the plate and his mouth was short, his posture didn't appear to hinder him. Georg Körber was like a barren island, lonely and remote, a man with a compacted will. His voice was already thick with alcohol; he must have started drinking earlier in the day because he'd already reached the point that his wife no longer looked at him. All she saw was his training uniform spilling across the chair, and when she spoke to him, she did so without letting her gaze wander too close to him, in the same way that Peter regarded the sun, and when her eyes did fall on him, it was to cut him to pieces.

Normally, Peter's mother was not the kind of woman who defied her husband, but on this day, the patriarch at the end of the table would not get to be in charge. Being accepted into the Guards called for a celebration. Peter heard her rummaging through the bureau in the living room, where she kept the table linens. Porcelain and tablecloths were pulled out, cutlery clinked, and though she said nothing, he could sense her growing frustration by the rising intensity of the noise. She had hidden a good bottle of champagne for a special occasion, like this, but it was no longer there.

Back in the kitchen, the tears of joy had turned into tears of disappointment. She had shot daggers at her husband with her reproachful glare, but he didn't notice her anger, not until she asked about the champagne.

"Of course I drank it." He faltered a moment, then got to his feet. Trying to gain control of the situation, he puffed out his chest, but his once-firm midriff spilled out under his belly button. "I'm going to the bike club."

Peter went to the window and looked down. They came in groups, from Denmark, Norway, Finland, Spain, Greece, South America, Africa, nearly every corner of the globe. Some held lit cigarettes between their fingers, some ran to their rooms to grab swim trunks that were still wet from the day before, some looked around hopefully for someone to fall in love with, and others sighed over a lost love. In order not to be noticed, Peter leaned forward cautiously without dipping his head. He watched for Elisabeth, but Ejner saw him instead. He called up to Peter, inviting him to his birthday celebration that evening in the café. Behind Ejner's broad back, he spotted her. She glanced up and waved.

Jesper Bugge Kold

From outside the café he heard the sound of voices, a birthday song in Danish. Peter smiled to himself: Danish words weren't meant to be sung—they were too ungainly. Ejner had tried to teach him a few phrases—*rødgrød med fløde*—but everyone had laughed. He'd been at the center of their laughter. Though he knew it was all meant in good fun, he still had an unpleasant feeling, but he'd played along, stuttering out the words until the Danes found a new victim for their ugly language.

They had sung another song, straining their voices to the limit, but the Danes didn't care. They were always loud, a self-assured and gregarious lot. A few of the men had beards, and they smoked a lot and spoke with great enthusiasm no matter the topic. They had names like Torben, Inger, Henrik, and Lisbeth, and they came from cities with names that were simultaneously short and long. Some of the girls were unhappy about the food. After the Christmas and Easter holidays, they returned, dragging shopping bags from home full of liver pâté, cheese, rye bread, and cans of mackerel. Though their coddled hunger dampened their revolutionary zeal, most of the Danes had the right socialist spirit.

He entered the café. Languages swirled around and above the music, with interpreters attempting to merge them into one. It wasn't just the romance of the revolution in bloom; here, all nationalities melted together in hugs and kisses. The music was loud. The Argentine Ricardo had always been one to spin the records on the gramophone, but he'd returned home to Buenos Aires to start a revolution. Yoel from Havana, a short man with a strong sense of rhythm and with a face that was one broad smile, had taken his place.

As casually as possible, Peter scanned the room. Elisabeth sat at a table with the other Danes, a few of the Cubans, and Ejner. The tall Dane spotted him and raised his hand in greeting, then called out for Peter to join them. Several bottles of champagne stood on the table. The Cubans kept rhythm on their cheeks and thighs, and the girls laughed. Night after night, they conquered the injustices of the world.

They discussed the Vietnam War, which was finally over; Angola, which, after the Carnation Revolution in Portugal, was in the process of gaining independence; and the upcoming security conference in Helsinki. They spoke of the revolution as if they were planning a party. Tonight was yet another reason for a party, because Ejner was to be celebrated.

Peter sat down, and Ejner patted him on the shoulder. "Hard to believe, twenty-eight years." He sighed and nodded at Peter, as if to emphasize aging's slow encroachment in a young man's life.

"Twenty-three," Peter said above the music.

Ejner regarded him intently and followed his gaze across the table. "You're looking at Elisabeth, aren't you?"

Peter smiled cagily at him. Was Ejner a rival? Ejner was well liked by all, and he was close to Elisabeth.

Ejner seemed to read Peter's mind. "She's a pretty girl, but I'm happily married. We're just friends." He laughed and toasted with the others, who'd raised their glasses.

Peter liked Ejner, whose enthusiasm for the GDR was infectious. He called it a model country and hoped that Denmark would one day be similar. That's why he and the others were at the school. Denmark's future depended on them.

As the hour grew late, the guests began to head home, a few at a time. When the clock struck midnight, Ejner left too, leaving only Peter, Elisabeth, and a few others at the table.

Before Ejner left, he whispered in Peter's ear. "She's probably a little drunk, so now's your chance." He winked at Peter.

One of the Cubans asked Elisabeth to dance. She said no, but he was persistent and offered her his hand. Behind the gramophone, Yoel's teeth glowed in the dim light. With a look of resignation, she drained her glass, accepted the outstretched hand, and followed him onto the dance floor. Like many of the other girls, she had learned salsa from the Latin Americans.

Peter watched her as they swayed across the floor. Her hips moved up and down, and her jeans fit snugly to her rear, which shimmied easily to the beat of the music. The last few guests stood up, leaving Peter alone at the table. The Cuban's hands clung to Elisabeth. Feigning laughter, she shoved his hands away as they tried to sneak into her back pockets. What had been a pleasure only a few moments earlier—the sight of her dancing body, the way her breasts shifted beneath her blouse—had now become the opposite. The Cuban was trying to seduce her, and she would give in to him. Peter had noticed that the girls couldn't resist the Latin Americans when they—in their halting English, with their jet-black sideburns crawling down their cheeks and their provocative dance moves—swiveled close to them. How could Elisabeth resist? He was tempted to get up and leave. To watch any longer would be masochism.

The Cuban gripped her, trying to hold on tight, but Elisabeth twisted free of his eager hands. He danced around her like a bullfighter as she tried to swat him away. She shoved his chest, and he was forced to step backward in order not to lose his balance. She used the opportunity to get away from him and hurried over to Peter. He straightened in his chair.

"You're Peter, right?" She was out of breath.

He nodded.

There were other empty seats around the table, yet she sat right beside him. "You have to protect me. His hands are everywhere."

She gestured to the Cuban with a tilt of her head. Then she put her arm through Peter's and rested her head against his upper arm. He could feel the heat emanating from her. Her hair tickled his cheek when she turned to look at him.

"You're a little strange, aren't you?"

How does one answer that? he thought, and waited for her to speak again.

"You're always just sitting there, watching, but what are you look-ing at?" She looked directly into his eyes, and then he watched her gaze travel down his body.

He gathered his courage. "You."

Elisabeth laughed, then picked up a bottle of champagne from the table and handed it to him. He put it to his mouth and held it there for a few moments, without drinking. He never drank alcohol.

Then they talked about the school, about Ejner and the differences between the GDR and Denmark. He let her go on, simply enjoying the sound of her voice. Soon he sensed a restlessness in her talk and in the way she was sitting. Not long after that, she wrapped her arm around his neck, not hard but decisively, and turned his face to hers.

"Shall we go down to the lake?"

Peter nodded slowly. He knew what *down to the lake* meant. Was that what Elisabeth had meant? She pulled him to his feet. The Cuban approached when he saw them stand. She blew him a kiss and took Peter's hand.

It was a hot evening, and they followed the little path that ran behind the dormitory. The path was dark, so they stumbled forward. The trees formed a dense, quivering darkness, and the green tree frogs sang in unison somewhere out there. Elisabeth arrived first. The moon reflected on the surface of the water, and the lake was still, but he hardly noticed. All he saw was her and her tight jeans, which tugged her panties down over her buttocks when she began to undress. Her skin glistened dully in the moonlight, and her back curved like a tenderly formed line. When all she wore was her bra, she turned toward him, grinning, and ran out into the lake. Half submerged in water, she tossed her bra onto the bank.

He could no longer see her, just hear her calling. There was some-thing teasing in her voice, and he was suddenly overwhelmed by doubt. What did she want? He stood hesitantly on the bank, unsure whether to remove his clothes. He was used to observing her, but now the roles were reversed. The bank suddenly seemed like an illuminated stage. In the café he'd been in control of the situation, but now she was in charge. He considered running back to his dormitory, letting her remain in the water, so that he would be the one calling the shots, but she had asked, and only the water covered her now-naked body. He knew what would happen, or at least what he hoped *might* happen. At the same time, he feared it.

He pulled his underwear off decisively. The night was dark, and there was only Elisabeth, and he would never have this opportunity again. He walked slowly into the water and started to swim toward her enchanting voice. Only her head was visible above the surface, her long red hair spread around her face. She swam to meet him. The water was cold, but he didn't notice. She tugged him farther out in the lake and put one arm around his neck. Her breath smelled of sweet champagne. With her other hand, she guided him to one of her breasts. She grew weightless in the water, and the bottom disappeared from under Peter's toes.

4

ANDREAS

Berlin, October 2006

It takes a while for Andreas's eyes to focus. When he wakes up and doesn't know where he is, it feels like the purest form of freedom. In that split second he is lifted above time and space. When the cellophane-like film on his eyes has faded, he glances around the bedroom. He's greeted by the same sight that greeted his father every morning for years: a white laminate wardrobe, a rocking chair, an oak commode with a clock radio on top. It's not the digital kind, but an old model that gives a little click on the hour. He pictures the numbers inside like a small Rolodex keeping track of the time. There's no radio signal from a transmitter near Frankfurt, just a simple belief that one minute takes the time it takes. It's a stable, functioning clock that faithfully slides through the seconds, minutes, and hours. He lies there waiting patiently for the small, chunky hands to display ten o'clock. It's a strange, infantile anticipation. Of course he knows what's going to happen, and it's nothing special, and yet he's looking forward to it. It clicks, and he feels a pang of disappointment. The clock turned during the brief moment he was inattentive. He smiles at himself: Andreas Jeppesen, a thirty-year-old graduate student with a tendency to the childish.

Then he recalls that time in Thorkild's car. They were on their way home, and the entire car reeked of their catch—garfish that they reeled in off the bridge near his hometown of Frederikssund, the Danish market town thirty miles northwest of Copenhagen. The stench in the trunk was thick, almost gaggingly so, but they didn't care. Thorkild took a detour with one goal in mind, and just beyond Stenløse it happened: the Ford's odometer topped one hundred thousand miles. They cheered. Thorkild rolled down the window and shouted. Like a playful pup, he stuck out his tongue, while half his body jutted through the driver's side window. Andreas looked at his stepfather, and they laughed.

Thorkild had stopped at a kiosk; this called for a celebration. They read the ice cream poster. The cheapest ones are always on the bottom of the hierarchy, and Andreas learned that one finds the treasures at the top. Hiding in the upper right corner is always the ice cream the adults don't want to pay for, the ice cream that expands in the belly so that one regrets eating it. Thorkild bought three. One for Andreas, one for himself, and one for the Ford.

He climbs out of bed. In one of the kitchen drawers, he finds a half-filled coffee can, then pours water into the coffee machine. He snaps it on, and it begins to gurgle. Although he'd never considered it before, he likes the machine's hoarse, coughing sound. The coffee machine and everything in the apartment is his now. Kurt Donnerwitz from Schultz and Donnerwitz, attorneys-at-law, had informed him in a formal letter that his father had passed away and that he'd willed everything to Andreas. He doesn't know how the attorney found him, but he recalls the feeling he had when he'd read the letter. Though he had never met Peter, the contents overwhelmed him. He opened a letter and lost his father as suddenly as he read the words. His sadness was followed by an equally crushing sensation: guilt. Andreas had never tried to locate his father. He was afraid of the person he might meet. Elisabeth had told him next to nothing about Peter, but he had detected reluctance in the tone of her spare descriptions of him. Although she never said explicitly that she didn't care for Peter, her words had transformed into questions for Andreas. What if she was right? What if Andreas didn't like his own father?

As a child he'd created an image of his father that the real Peter couldn't possibly live up to. So he'd retained the fantasy and left well enough alone. He knew that meeting Peter in person would destroy his dreams. He also didn't want to hurt Thorkild, the man who'd essentially been his father his entire life, and yet Peter's death came as a shock to him, and Andreas realized that, deep down, he'd held out hope that one day they would meet.

Now that possibility was gone. Dead at fifty-four years old, Peter can no longer meet anyone, and Andreas feels a black hole of yearning. Though it has always been there, Peter's death makes it permanent; the hole cannot simply be mended with putty or glue. A murderer, some contemptible person, has eliminated the last shred of hope that father and son might finally meet.

As the coffee machine gurgles, he gazes out the window. In the backyard he notices a bike shed and, on the roof, a soccer ball that no one can see from below. It's forgotten and abandoned.

Shortly afterward, he stands in the doorway to the stairwell, peering out. The rain hasn't ceased, but it has become gentler and less insistent than the previous evening. He heads into it. At the end of Kopenhagener Strasse is Mauerpark, a sad-looking patch of green once sliced in half by the Wall. Andreas stands in Prenzlauer Berg, a neighborhood that was once part of the Soviet sector; on the other side was Gesundbrunnen, which had been in the French sector. He starts through the park.

Through the mist, he spots the television tower in the distance. A drunkard is lying on a bench, his knees wrenched up underneath him, and a gaunt German shepherd sniffs loyally around his sleeping master. Mauerpark is anything but welcoming. In a guidebook he'd brought with him from home, he read the following about the park: *A recreational area where families with children, joggers, and bookworms make themselves comfortable when the sun is out, but when it rains, the park attracts drug addicts and the homeless.* He turns away from the park and heads down Gleimstrasse. The street is littered with hollow chestnut shells that resemble gray's sedge or tiny battle-axes, and hundreds of shiny chestnuts. He gathers a few and thrusts them in his coat pocket, slowly running his finger across the smooth surface of one. It's a pleasant feeling, heartening almost. The sand-colored section is rougher, and when he presses his nail against it, he makes a little mark in the chestnut's soft shell. As he walks, he turns them around and around in his fingers.

He heads toward Schönhauser Allee, a broad street that passes through Prenzlauer Berg. When he reaches the subway station, which resembles Nørrebro Station in Copenhagen—except that the graffiti is in German—he carefully studies the map of the train lines. The train resembles a sad caterpillar as it comes rattling down the tracks. The doors clatter, then glide open, and people spill onto the platform. In the morning, Berlin is a city teeming with busy people rushing around and avoiding eye contact. They all share the same look of despair, as if the train is moving too slowly toward an important meeting they all seem to be going to. Not wanting to stand out, Andreas simulates busyness by hustling into the coach. When the train pauses between two stations, passengers groan.

At Ostkreuz he changes to the S7 and immediately notes a shift in the atmosphere. A few stations later, the large apartment blocks begin—one block after another of giant clumps of concrete. It feels as though the city is bleaker out here. The train is dilapidated, and there's this composite smell of wood, plastic, and body odor, but everyone seems used to it. It's a lingering stench, but for the other passengers it's just part of their daily lives, one of the city's salient features. He glances around the coach and notices that people are paler here than in

Prenzlauer Berg. Even the many dark-skinned riders are pale. He sees women with shawls around their heads speaking a language he doesn't understand, people wearing clogs, and people carrying shopping bags with faded logos from long-closed grocery store chains.

He studies a sad-faced girl, who looks to be about eight or nine years old. She stares absentmindedly into space, her school bag weighing down her shoulders. She seems too fragile for these rough surroundings, and he feels an urge to embrace her. *Why isn't anyone looking after you, little friend? It's dangerous out here.* When a large group of young men raise a ruckus in the coach, he grows nervous himself. Although he makes sure to avoid eye contact with them, the girl appears unaffected by their presence. *Maybe she's the one who should be taking care of me.*

They reach the final stop, Ahrensfelde, and he starts walking up Havemannstrasse, the street on which Veronika lives. As far as his eye can see, he's surrounded by low-income housing. A sense of melancholy is always present. It's as if someone in a distracted frenzy arranged the buildings too close. They block out the sky, as if they have no interest in letting it in.

He spots a swastika on a wall. The broad red strokes were clearly painted by an amateur, not an initiate, because the swastika is backward. Drawn in a rush, the paint ran and looks like globules of blood dripping from a butcher's knife. Seeing it makes him decide that he should return home before dark. That's when he realizes that he already thinks of Prenzlauer Berg as home. Though he arrived just yesterday, he already prefers Berlin to his hometown.

Finally he arrives at his destination: a sand-colored building that, like a minor chord, sets the tone for the entire quarter. A long time passes from the moment his finger presses the buzzer until the door emits a soft, humming sound. Walking up the stairs in a state of anticipation, he taps nervously on the railing, which reverberates loudly. He's embarrassed that he, like some unthinking child, is the cause of the noise. To his relief he sees that the door on the third floor is still closed.

He hears shuffling footsteps inside the apartment. Then the door opens, and he does his best to appear relaxed.

Though he knows that the woman is not yet sixty, she looks old. She has a tired expression in her eyes; her body seems tired, too. She's wearing a dress and freshly applied makeup, but the makeup doesn't mask her profound exhaustion.

"You must be Andreas." She offers her hand, and her face slowly transforms as she smiles.

He nods.

Once he enters the apartment, they stand and study each other for a moment.

"So you're my aunt?" Since he's nervous about his German, he places the emphasis in the wrong spot, and it comes out sounding like a question. This irritates him, because he feels that his German is good; as soon as he arrived in Berlin, the language came back to him, and even though his oral examination was years ago, his *durch-für-gegen-ohne-wider-um* is lashed securely to his spine.

Veronika Körber nods indulgently, then invites him into a cramped living room with decorative plates on the walls. They sit beside the coffee table, she in a dark-brown swivel chair made of leather and he on the matching sofa. The furniture is threadbare; his mother would probably call it common. Judging by the way the furniture has carved notches in the rug, it's clear that it has not moved in years. An old-fashioned TV buzzes like an insect, and he can't help but notice that it's tuned to *Dallas*. The volume is low. JR's cheeks and white teeth fill the screen before the scene shifts to Miss Ellie's perpetually tearful face contemplating Sue Ellen, who is intoxicated by lunchtime.

Veronika's hands shake slightly when she pours coffee for him from a thermos on the table. A thin bead runs down the side of the thermos and into the joints between the table's tiles, but she doesn't notice.

"Beatrice was the one who read your text. I'm not good at that kind of thing." Smiling apologetically, she points at an older Nokia cell phone on the table. Kurt Donnerwitz had been kind enough to provide Andreas with the telephone numbers of Peter Körber's close relatives, and once he'd recovered from reading the attorney's letter, he had texted Veronika.

He's not sure if he should say anything or if he should ask who Beatrice is. He nods and sips his coffee. It's strong and bitter and no longer hot.

She lights a cigarette butt, then leans back in her chair, its dry leather creaking beneath her. "You look like your father. Same nose, same mouth. I noticed it as soon as I saw you." She exhales a thin, gray plume of smoke. "Your hair is thicker than his, but it's the same color. Have you seen photographs of him?"

"No." He's not sure why he doesn't mention the photo in the apartment.

She stands with difficulty, grabs a photo album from the shelf, and sits down next to him. He catches a sour whiff of tobacco. Her dress is frayed, as if it's been washed too often and the colors have lost their intensity.

On the TV he hears Bobby Ewing's deep voice in error-free German, and Andreas suddenly recalls Friday evenings during his childhood. Elisabeth and Thorkild watched *Dallas*, and he lay on the sofa, swaddled up in his duvet. While his parents laughed at the series, mocking it for revealing everything about capitalism that repulsed them, he asked, "Who is he?", "Is that her sister?", "Are those the bad guys?" Elisabeth shushed Thorkild, who patiently explained. On the table were two glasses of red wine and the marzipan bread's crumpled-up paper. Thorkild wrapped his arm around Andreas, grunting in satisfaction, and he fell asleep to the sound of Bobby Ewing's voice.

His father is a child for many pages at the beginning of the photo album; then he's a teenager and the album ends. She fetches a new album and tells Andreas stories, and he senses the yearning in her voice, which is frequently hesitant and faint. When she comes to one particular photograph, she pauses. They sit for a long moment, staring at the photo as Peter stares back at them. There's a striking resemblance between him and his father. Andreas has a bigger head and more facial hair. Peter's skin is smoother, and his hair is straighter.

A tear drips onto the page, and Veronika's hand is suddenly on his. Plump, warm fingers seeking consolation, her hand closes around his like a hug. He concentrates on not looking at her. What should he do? What should he say? He understands her grief. Her brother was dramatically taken from her, murdered, and Peter's own flesh and blood sits beside her. She squeezes his hand, and he tries not to move it. It's embarrassing, in a way. Peter was his father, but his grief is not as great as hers because he didn't know the man.

They riffle through the pages. Peter now appears in uniform. He looks proud, and Andreas asks, "What did my father do?"

"What do you mean?" She removes her hand and lights another cigarette.

"What did he do for a living?"

Suddenly uncertain, she leans forward on the couch. Her dress glides up, and Andreas notices her legs. The varicose veins meander like purple rivers; tributaries flow down her calves, forming a delta just above her socks. A secondary river continues underneath the cotton, where it disappears. Both her skin and her curtains have been discolored by the mentholated cigarettes she smokes, a pack of which now rests on the table. Slowly she tamps out her cigarette. On the edge of the ashtray, a polar bear regards the butt and its glistening wet filter.

The door opens. Veronika seems relieved. "This is my daughter, Beatrice," she says proudly.

A shopping bag overturns in the entranceway. Glass clinks. Plastic crinkles. A subdued voice whispers, "*Scheisse.*" A young woman appears in the doorway. Though she does nothing in particular, the energy in the room shifts.

5

PETER

East Berlin, July 1976

Serious-looking men sat in their offices immersed in conversations or bent over stacks of papers that they scrutinized down to the minutest detail. Peter glanced at them while dutifully following a man, who now turned down a different hallway. He'd been summoned to the Ministry for State Security. Peter's thoughts circled ceaselessly around the impending conversation; he suddenly noticed that his hands were clenched and that his palms were damp. To be promoted and reassigned to the headquarters on Normannenstrasse was a great honor. Only the best were assigned here, the handpicked cream of the crop. Maybe he would soon be on staff in the Ministry for State Security's Operations Department XX/5.

Once he arrived at Sonnenberger's office, the conversation proceeded as he'd hoped, and he'd just completed all of his responses, written in his inelegant right-tilting handwriting. The notebook lay on the table alongside a black Bakelite telephone and a bust of Lenin wearing a cap and a steely gaze. Sonnenberger had known the answers in advance because, even though Peter already was part of the staff, the Ministry for State Security had nonetheless investigated him meticulously. That's how it operated, and there was something comforting in its scrupulousness. It wasn't distrust; it was a form of security—both for them *and* for him.

Sonnenberger cleared his throat. Photographs of fish—his proudest catches—hung on the wall behind him. Baltic Sea salmon, carp from Lake Balaton, brill from the Black Sea. Sunlight glinted off their scales and the major's smile. A bamboo pole with a handle made of cork and small metal eyes was suspended above the photographs. The handle was worn and had probably pulled many a fish through the water to score yet another success for the frames in his office.

"Let me see if I understand this correctly, comrade Körber. You've spent the last year performing background checks?"

Sonnenberger noted his response. Over the course of their conversation, he had referred to Peter's time in the Felix Dzerzhinsky Guards Regiment and his studies at Jugendhochschule Wilhelm Pieck, proof that the major knew everything about him even before this meeting.

Uwe Sonnenberger stood, and Peter noticed that his body wasn't as large as it seemed while seated. He squeezed Peter's hand across the desk. "Congratulations on your appointment and your promotion, Sergeant Körber. Welcome to the operations department."

Afterward the major gave a brief, practiced speech about how State Security was the party's sword and shield. It was their job to know everything, and nothing in the country was allowed to happen without their knowledge. That was the only way they could maintain peace. Since the state's enemies were everywhere, *they* had to be everywhere, too. Fragments, complete sentences, and clauses were taken whole cloth from the speech Lieutenant Hufnagl had made when Peter was hired at one of the regional offices under Department XX/5 already a year ago now. As was often the case with new hires, the assignments involved performing background checks on potential informants. Candidates were always thoroughly screened before State Security made contact. The recon phase could take six to nine months, and no stone was left unturned.

First they collected hard data, like school papers, work papers, and statements from employers and party membership, as well as documents pertaining to possible run-ins with the authorities and criminal records. Then came the soft data: personality, habits, opinions, and sexual behavior. Family, friends, colleagues, and neighbors were investigated; the regional offices' archives were teeming with such reports, and Peter's job was to weed out the unfit and ensure that only the best were chosen.

A fatherly note suddenly resounded in the major's voice. "And what about the apartment we've found you here in Lichtenberg? Have you settled in?" Sonnenberger himself lived in one of the large apartments there with his wife and two children.

"Yes, thank you, comrade Sonnenberger." Peter opened the door and was on his way out of the office.

"Just a moment, comrade Körber." The major put on his glasses, which dangled from his neck on a thin nylon string. Now they rested on the end of his nose, making him look old. Peter estimated him to be around fifteen years older than himself, but his glasses extended that age gap. Behind his glasses, his eyes were insistent without being pushy; the major didn't seem like a man who ever expressed an ill-considered thought as he spoke in his slow and straightforward Thuringian dialect. The major pushed his glasses up onto his forehead, shifting his hair aside.

"This department cares about one thing: results. If you can deliver, then you are welcome here, if not . . ." He aimed his index finger at the door in a gesture that was difficult to misinterpret. As if he suddenly regretted the uncompromising implication of the sentence, he changed his tone. "You'll no doubt prove a valuable man for us."

Peter felt exhilarated as he walked through the open steel gate with surveillance cameras that captured everything, then past the sentry box that made it clear that all the blocks of concrete within were the headquarters of the Ministry for State Security and not an enormous residential neighborhood.

On Frankfurter Allee, following the spring thaw, summer had settled over the city, and the heat hung in the streets like the exhaust fumes from the East German–made Trabants. The asphalt hummed, and car tires clung to the pavement, making a kind of compressed sound. On the sidewalk, two siblings stumbled under the weight of the schoolbags strapped tightly to their backs. The heavy books tugged them backward, while their short legs—barely visible over their knee-high socks—pulled them toward home. The younger of the two boys could hardly have been more than six, but he slogged on admirably—he was *determined*. This little boy with scars on his knees was the embodiment of the worker and the peasant state; stubborn and dutiful, he was the very personification of the country. Peter was watching a reflection of himself as a child. The boy had earned his upcoming summer vacation and ice cream cones from the booths in Kulturpark Plänterwald.

Peter felt a sudden urge to walk, down the street, not toward home but downtown. First he would go through Lichtenberg and, afterward, through the neighborhood of Friedrichshain. At Frankfurter Tor, where the towers looked like observatories, the street turned into Karl Marx-Allee. Up until the June 17 uprising in 1953, it was called Stalinallee, but Joseph Stalin had been unable to witness his tanks brutally beating back the worker's rebellion because the general secretary had died in March of that year. The street was peaceful now, only filling with the sound of boots, canons, tanks, and the noxious odor of oil during the annual parades on May 1.

The striking workers of 1953 were long forgotten, but their work—the enormous, Soviet-inspired apartment blocks with their shiny slabs and Meissen porcelain—would stand forever. Every one of the city's residents wanted to live in one of the high-ceilinged apartments behind the broad window frames. The pompous buildings embraced a green circle with a fountain, which lay untouched, like a neglected construction site. Extravagant in both size and stature, the splendid buildings filled his chest with pride.

A queue had formed for the afternoon matinee in front of the boxlike Kino International; on the other side of the boulevard, Café Muskau was peddling everything from love to modern dance to artwork and coveted Russian black-market goods. The squat Kongresshalle made the Haus des Lehrers seem erect and dignified on its columns behind Alexanderplatz. An evidently reunited couple near the Worldtime Clock stood wrapped in an embrace. Beyond them, like a Sputnik on a pedestal, the television tower rose high in the air above the plaza. Everyone tilted their heads back to observe the tower with evident pride. It seemed to rise for half a mile, though everyone in the city knew the exact height was 1,197 feet; they all believed the assertion that the tower was taller than anything the capitalist world could manage. The Hotel Stadt Berlin soared up beside it, complementing the slender tower.

He sat at an empty table beneath an umbrella at Espresso Milchbar and ordered coffee.

"Sugar?"

Peter glanced up at the middle-aged waitress, who stood expectantly before him with her hands in the apron's deep pockets. Her face was slack and her skin mottled by the summer sun.

"Yes, please."

He looked at the coffee she'd set in front of him on the table. A few drops had splashed over the edge and formed a ring on his saucer. He put his nose to the rim of the cup, and the aroma tickled his nostrils. He studied the black-brown surface.

The waitress returned with a sugar bowl. He nodded politely and put two deliberate teaspoons of sugar into the steaming coffee. He stirred the teaspoon slowly, and it clicked lightly when he laid it on the saucer.

Comrade Sonnenberger had praised him, saying that he possessed the professional and personal attributes they sought in the operations department. Sonnenberger was especially satisfied with his efforts at Jugendhochschule Wilhelm Pieck, where he'd reported diligently and in detail on his fellow students. Furthermore, the fact that he was lucky enough to recruit Ejner Madsen, a Dane who worked close to the naval station in Korsør and who was on his way up in Denmark's Communist Party, showed that the department had found the right man. Peter had been selected based on the strength of his qualities, and he had no wish to disappoint his employers.

Peter had been contacted by a man from the Ministry for State Security several years earlier, back when he served as a group leader in the Free German Youth, the socialist youth movement. The man hadn't named his employer, naturally, but there was no doubt who it was. Peter was honored—his goal was to work as an informant—and a few days later he signed a letter of intent promising to work for State Security and pledging to keep it secret. During his service in the guard regiment, he'd reported on his soldier comrades, their political stances, potential unhappiness, and the like to a commanding officer in one of the district departments.

He still recalled a specific occurrence from his time in the Guards. One night they'd been on a training exercise near Gudow, a small city close to the border with West Germany. From within a dense forest, where he lay with Hagemann—one of the regiment's most respected soldiers—they could watch the roughly half-mile-wide zone that had been cleared to create visibility around the border fence. As part of the exercise, they expected an attack from a company that, on this night, was pretending to be NATO soldiers.

The two young men had watched a newspaper that the wind had carried toward them; it fluttered around, stopped, then continued its dance. One by one the pages turned, as if someone was riffling through it, right where it hung suspended in the air about six feet above the ground. Captivated by the enchanting sight of the moonlit paper, they had momentarily forgotten their mission. When it blew closer, Hagemann scooped it out of the air and began to read aloud, while Peter shushed him. It was *Die Welt*, one of Axel Springer's populist newspapers from the other Germany.

"Let it go," Peter had said, but Hagemann folded the newspaper and thrust it under his uniform jacket. At the conclusion of the exercise, he neglected to turn it over to his superior officer, so Peter reported it, of course. Though Hagemann was the regiment's best sharpshooter and could produce medals and diplomas for all his accomplishments, he was dismissed from the regiment the next day. Peter was amazed that such a capable soldier was unable to tell the difference between right and wrong. If everyone acted so carelessly, all would be chaos.

Peter did not doubt his own commitment: As a soldier his duty was to eliminate the enemy, and as an informant his duty was the same. If Hagemann read Western newspapers, then he broke the rules, and if people like Peter didn't report him, how would they maintain control?

Peter watched as three girls exited the huge Centrum Warenhaus and crossed Alexanderplatz. The tallest looked like the blonde from ABBA. A couple of boys in the whitewashed denim clothes of stiff, East German make leaned against the fountain and crushed cigarette butts under the soles of their sneakers. They shouted at the girls, who drew closer and giggled. The ABBA girl turned her head, calling out to them and whirling her blond hair. They were too far away for Peter to make out what they were saying. The boys laughed and patted each other on the shoulder, evidently pleased with themselves.

Conversations filled the air beneath the café's umbrellas: about the weather, about the upstairs neighbor installing a telephone, about trips taken thanks to the trade union's vacation service. At the neighboring table, two dark-skinned men sat speaking a peculiar language mixed with German phrases, the volume of their conversation expanding beyond the table. One moment words gushed from their lips, but in the next they came in jabbing thrusts, after which they flowed naturally once more until the two men shattered the rhythm again with another series of stammering unnatural sounds. This strange language fascinated him; it pounded like the surf against the beach. He assumed it was Turkish. Turkish men often visited this part of Berlin via Friedrichstrasse Station to get a cheap meal or to buy goods at affordable prices to bring back to Kreuzberg. They came, hoping to find a woman who would give them shelter for a pair of nylon panty hose or a pound of coffee and who might warm them up while they sent money home or reminisced about their family in Turkey. Many languages had descended upon the city from remote areas in recent years. Russians, Poles, and Hungarians had made their marks long ago, but contract workers from Vietnam, Cuba, and distant African countries like Angola and Mozambique had also found their way to the capital.

Sitting alone at another table was a man in a light-blue Windbreaker. His eyes wandered from table to table, paused occasionally, then continued with the same deliberateness as before. Then stopped. The man pulled a small notebook from his pocket. Peter knew what that meant immediately: a colleague. The man in the Windbreaker wet his pencil's tip on his tongue and began jotting a note while periodically glancing up to observe the subject of his writing. Peter followed his gaze.

A man sat on a stairwell. His beard was filthy, his clothing wrinkled, and his shoes mismatched. He seemed agitated and talked loudly to himself. The three giggling girls once again appeared on the plaza. They strolled close to the boys and sat beside the fountain.

The slovenly man stood and began chasing and kicking the nearby pigeons. He shouted that they were watching him. The birds flew off in unison toward a quieter corner of the plaza.

Without warning it began to rain. Heavy drops pounded hollowly against the umbrellas. The man turned his face toward the sky and barked something about commanded rainfall and state-controlled weather, saying that even God worked for Stasi. His neck muscles bulged and rainwater rolled down his face. Spittle flew from his lips as he bellowed. Peter shook his head. What if everyone acted like that? What chaos there'd be in the streets.

The man in the Windbreaker stood as a pair of well-meaning citizens tried to calm the man and pull him away. Just then a Barkas delivery van thundered across the plaza. Those who hadn't already found shelter from the rain leaped to one side. The van braked to a halt, and the side door shot open with a loud clatter. Two men in civilian clothes hopped out, grabbed the confused man by his arms, and dragged him to the waiting van. Moments later, it disappeared down Alexanderstrasse, water spraying from the tires. The plaza, now nearly empty because of the rain, grew quiet again. The few who remained gazed at the rainbow that had appeared above the buildings, and people nodded at one another with satisfaction once they realized the rainbow was on their side of the wall.

As quickly as the rain had started, it ceased. Peter breathed the aroma of rain. Summer rain was cleansing, and in a city like Berlin, the air needed to be cleansed now and then. As he drained his coffee cup, he could smell the wet asphalt. Then he started home.

When he let himself into his apartment in Lichtenberg, the door shoved a letter to the side. He hung his coat on a hook in the entranceway and picked up the letter. When he saw the sender's name, he swallowed a lump in his throat: Elisabeth Jeppesen.

6

ANDREAS

Berlin, October 2006

"I hate it out here." Beatrice walks ahead of Andreas down the stairwell. "Did you take the train?"

"Yes," he replies.

At the front door of the building, she turns to face him. "We can go downtown together."

Out on the street, he's struck once again by the feeling that he's being squeezed by the endless rows of gray buildings. The air is saturated and lethargic. It's difficult to breathe being surrounded by so much concrete, and there's no oxygen coming from the few trees jutting out of the pavement.

"It's a dreary place," he says gloomily.

She sighs. "There's no color out here, just life in gray, and I grew up here," she says wistfully, shifting her chewing gum to the other cheek. Without another word, she points at a playground, which someone in a municipal office had decided to squash between the concrete blocks. There are no children.

They start toward the station. "Marzahn and Ahrensfelde were once places everyone wanted to live. It's hard to believe, isn't it? A place reserved for the finest citizens," she adds in a scornful tone. Then she continues. "Look at my mother. She lived well in the GDR, but she's not doing so well in Germany, and she still lives in the same apartment."

He nods and tries not to make eye contact with a group of young men lounging on a street corner. A ghetto blaster, blaring a Rammstein song, vibrates on the asphalt around them. One of the youths, his face tattooed, whistles at Beatrice while seated on a moped; she ignores him as if such catcalling is a common occurrence.

"Hard to believe the East Germans actually thought these prefabricated concrete apartments were the future." She points at all the boxlike concrete blocks. "It's exactly the opposite here now. The only people who live here now are drunk Russians, Vietnamese, and people from the Balkans."

She adds, "Along with East Germans who don't have the means to move. Everyone else fled when they could."

"You know a lot about the GDR," Andreas says. He wants to hear more.

"Maybe it's how I hold on to my social inheritance." Her smile forces her cheeks upward.

"Can't Veronika move?"

"She doesn't want to. For her, Ahrensfelde is still the GDR." She pauses and looks him in the eye. "Don't misunderstand me. It's not like she dreams of returning to the old days. All she wants is for things to be better again."

She starts to walk. "That won't happen out here, but she's happy as long as she has cigarettes, has coffee in her thermos, and can watch something good on television."

A drunken man calls out to them in some Slavic language. Beatrice pretends not to notice and just walks a little faster, as if she's used to the area's unpleasantness. Andreas is relieved to reach the station. Beatrice tells him that she visits her mother once a week to buy her groceries: prepackaged meals and cigarettes. Her mother doesn't walk so well anymore; a janitorial job ruined her knees and hips.

"Are you doing anything now?" Andreas asks. He doesn't want to return to the apartment and sit alone among his father's things.

"Actually, no," she says. She responds slowly, as if waiting to hear his suggestion.

"Want to get a cup of coffee?"

She hesitates.

"You're the only person I know in the city, Beatrice."

She laughs. "Don't call me that. Only my mother calls me Beatrice. Call me Bea." She smiles broadly.

They board the train, and she sits opposite him. He senses that she doesn't wish to speak during the ride. This is a tendency he's already noticed: Berliners don't talk while riding the train. They keep to themselves. It's as though they're charging their batteries before emerging into the world and using their voices. He watches her on the sly; her eyes are large and blue, with small, dark slivers that break up the color. Her eyebrows are blond and practically invisible, so fine that he can only see them when sunlight bursts through the window. There's something brittle about her face, except for her mouth. Her mouth is wide for a woman, which makes her nose seem too narrow and delicate for the rest of her face. She's dressed in black. Her nylons are nearly frayed through, and there's something shabby and coarse about her outfit. She has an average figure, borderline gangly, and she's wearing flat-soled sneakers as if she's trying to make herself appear smaller. When they stood on the platform, he noticed that she was only an inch or so shorter than he.

Her shoulder bag, an army-green canvas affair, is lying in her lap. She drums on it with her fingers while staring past him. Then she begins to rummage in her bag; he glimpses an iPod, an empty bottle of nail polish, and a tattered paperback. He tilts his head a bit to read the title on the cover: *Tipping the Velvet* by Sarah Waters. She removes a pack of nicotine gum, then digs out a knotty gray lump from one corner of her mouth and deposits it in one of the empty slots in the pack. The wrapper crinkles when she opens a new piece. She pops it into her mouth and continues to chew her restlessness away.

They get off at Hackescher Markt, then cross an expansive plaza filled with restaurants and cafés and kiosks. He takes in the colorful parasols, the aroma of coffee, and the young, well-dressed people standing shoulder to shoulder and sharing earbuds. Street hawkers sell homemade jewelry from their kiosks and blankets. One of them says hello to Bea, who clearly knows him. He looks Latin American; at his stand, wristwatches gleam next to multicolored pearl necklaces and wide tin bracelets and leather leashes. A man with skin as dark as night is blowing soap bubbles that turn into miniature rainbows before bursting in the wind. Andreas almost can't believe it's the same city that Veronika lives in.

They pass a Starbucks. People by the window are sitting in tall, un-ergonomic stools, writing on their laptops. On the sidewalk next door, orange plastic chairs that are wet with rain surround several round tables. In one window—which doesn't indicate whether it's a shop, café, or movie theater—is a bust of Laurel and Hardy with apple-red cheeks and bowler hats, and in the other is an old television surrounded by film spools. The sign above the entrance reads in curvy neon letters: Café Cinema. Bea pushes open the door.

"This is where I work," she says.

Andreas looks around the cramped, oblong room. There's a bar at the far end, and Bea hugs the blonde behind the counter. Dangling lamps faintly illuminate the wooden tables with flickering candlelight, making the customers forget that it's still only afternoon outside. The furniture is dated, and along with the faded clippings in glass frames on the wall, it tells stories from the old days. Behind a wrecked piano, the wall is covered with film posters, German titles he's never heard of. He scrutinizes them to find one he recognizes, but gives up.

"Would you like a coffee?" Bea asks.

He asks for a beer instead, though he's not sure why. He's never been a café-going type; he becomes uncomfortable. All the exotic names and coffee varieties make him feel like an outsider, and whenever some teenage barista asks him whether he would like a double shot, macchiato or Americano, he never knows how to respond. Maybe that's why he'd rather have a beer. He's not required to choose.

They take a seat by the window. The place is unassuming and pleasant. "I often come here, even when I'm not working," Bea says, "though the darkness in here doesn't fit my easygoing nature." He can't tell whether she's being serious, but her cheerful laughter convinces him that she is.

"Did you know this is the oldest café in the neighborhood?"

He looks at her, confused. "It's my first time in Berlin. So, no, I didn't know that."

She laughs again, mildly. "Oh, right."

She fills him in on the café's history, and he listens to her voice, which is as soft as the lining of a jewelry box and stands in stark contrast to the four-letter words she uses.

A tall girl approaches to say hello to Bea, who stands. The two women kiss each other's cheeks. He watches Bea, already feeling as though he knows her. She's close to smiling during the entire conversation, and her hands flutter up and down to emphasize her words. She sits down and apologizes for the disruption.

No worries, he's quick to tell her. Then he asks, "Where do you live?"

"In Kreuzberg. I'm studying social science at Humboldt University and work here to finance my studies. I've also got a scholarship from BAfög, which helps a bit," she explains. "What about you?"

As he tells her of his own studies, he feels like a broken record. He doesn't know her well enough to tell her the truth: that all his years at the university have been wasted.

"What about your love life?" she asks. He considers a moment. Should he tell the truth or his version of it? Then he hears himself explain.

"I can no longer recall whether we were in love. Maybe we were. We were together for two and a half years. In the beginning we would go out to restaurants, to the movie theater. We moved in together and talked about having kids, but in the end we just ended up on the couch, watching TV like an old married couple. Our relationship stopped evolving, maybe because we were numbed by the flickering light of the TV screen. The love just trickled away like dry sand through our fingers." Andreas looks at Bea and awaits her reaction. She stares at him with her round eyes, and he goes on. "We broke up during the commercials between two programs. I've forgotten which one of us actually took the initiative for once, but it didn't matter: We were in agreement."

It's been six months since then, and he still misses Lisa.

Bea gives him a sympathetic glance, and he feels momentarily insecure. Has he told her too much about himself? Has he exposed himself? Has he laid it on too thick? Her facial expression removes all doubt. His little story has made an impression on her. She smiles as if to console him, and he feels a close connection between them. He likes that they are here together, he and his cousin, his new cousin. He'd like to get to know her, and he needs her help because there are a number of decisions he must make concerning his father's death. He's the executor for a dead man in a country he doesn't know. How is he supposed to make decisions about a man he never met? He doesn't know what Peter enjoyed doing, what he liked and didn't like. This makes him sad.

He asks guardedly, "Isn't Veronika his closest relative?"

"We can't ask her to be the executor," Bea says, picking up on his meaning. "She's just not capable of it."

Bea offers to help because Peter was, after all, her uncle. Andreas is relieved, and they agree to meet the next day.

She stands up and fetches a cup of coffee and another beer. The bust of Laurel and Hardy sits in the window, their backs turned; he wants to touch it, to feel what it's made of. Though he's close enough to reach it, he suppresses the urge and shakes off the memory of Lisa, while Bea exchanges a few words with the young woman behind the bar.

He thinks once again of his visit to Veronika's. There was something sad about his aunt, something incomplete, as if God's creative juices had ceased to flow when Veronika came into the world. For a moment, he forgets that he doesn't believe in God, and he allows himself to be pulled along by this stream of thought. Veronika has suffered in her life. The atmosphere in her apartment is thick with her hard life and the grief she feels over her brother. A life filled with disappointment. Andreas feels bad for her. She dodged his questions when he asked what his father did for a living. There was something about her behavior, as if she felt he was confronting her, but why? Bea could probably tell him.

He watches the two women behind the bar. They laugh at something Bea says. He studies her as she effortlessly foams milk for her coffee. The whir of the machine reaches him through the music, which plays softly under the ceiling. With her coffee in one hand and his beer in the other, she returns to their table.

She sets the beer down in front of him. He drinks slowly from the bottle and then positions it perfectly on the wet ring it had made. She starts talking about the music. Ani DiFranco is one of her favorites, but Andreas doesn't know her. Bea's telephone rings. She speaks quickly. He notices her chipped nail polish. When she ends the call, he tries to catch a name, but all he hears her say is good-bye. He wants to ask her if she has a boyfriend. Because she'd asked him, it doesn't seem wrong or pushy, yet he decides not to. Girls like Bea always have boyfriends, and now she'll probably go see him.

She tilts her head to one side and purses her lips. "I need to get going, unfortunately. I'm going to see my . . . sweetheart. It's kind of new," she adds, as if apologizing.

He nods, understanding, and they finish their drinks in silence.

She gives him a hug outside the café, and he feels that he has to say something.

"I would like to meet the doctor," he says impulsively, which surprises him.

"The doctor?"

He convinces Bea to briefly tell him about her and Veronika's visit to the hospital and how the doctor told them of Peter's death. Remembering him, her face grows sad. Her tone of voice reminds him that it's only been a few days.

"I would like to meet him," he repeats, without knowing why he feels this need.

"But you know how he died."

"I would just like to hear it from him."

7

STEFAN

East Berlin, July 1976

The needle rasped across the vinyl record. A ball of dust had grown behind it, and Bruce Springsteen's *Born to Run* was transformed into white noise that brought Stefan to his feet. One of the half-empty beer bottles on the small Formica table tipped over and slowly poured its contents onto the carpet. Ulf picked it up as Stefan carefully brushed the delicate needle off with a hand broom. He slowly rotated the record between his two index fingers before thoroughly cleaning side one again. He set the needle in the groove, and the intro to "Thunder Road" began to boom through the loudspeakers. Ulf jammed along to the refrain on his imaginary guitar as the smoke from Stefan's cigarette spiraled toward the ceiling. They had no plans for the afternoon except for listening to records and sharing the rest of the Radeberger beers on the table.

Ulf had what everyone envied: an uncle in the West who brought cigarettes, chocolate, LPs, and nylon stockings for his mother and sister. The last time, Uncle Arno returned with a curling iron, Bruce Springsteen's *Born to Run*, and Pink Floyd's *Dark Side of the Moon.*

The records were sent to Uncle Arno from the United States, and he convinced Ulf that he was the only one in the entire GDR who now owned both.

He heard a gentle rapping at the door through Clarence Clemons's saxophone solo. Stefan's mother put her head in. "Can you go down and see where Alexander went? He's been standing in line for two hours."

At the sight of Ulf, her eyes changed expression. Stefan read her glance instantly, as if it were spelled out. *When will that boy cut his hair? When will he get a job?* He knew what she was thinking, and yet her kind nature caused her to hold her tongue. Ulf had practically lived with them since elementary school. She'd open her door to him whenever Ulf's parents were fall-down drunk—consumed by mutual hatred for each other—and laid waste to the house, throwing everything that wasn't nailed down. She was his embrace, his warmth, his refuge. After supper she always left a covered plate of food in the kitchen in case Ulf came over. Now he was twenty, the same age as Stefan. It wasn't that she didn't trust Ulf; it was more an inner disquiet. She couldn't help but drag him into those thoughts and worries a mother has for her son, and with Ulf that amounted to three sons.

They found Alexander standing in front of the butcher's shop. From a distance Stefan noted that his brother's hair had grown long during the summer, and he recalled that time after summer vacation when Alexander was sent home from school with a note in his backpack because his hair fell past his ears.

Ulf said good-bye to them and crossed the street to catch a tram. Finally, it was Alexander's turn. The butcher's apron was splotched with red stains, and his hands were smeared with blood. Behind him, his wife was slicing pork. She handed her husband some slices, and he packed them into crinkly paper. When they were younger, the brothers had secretly stared at the enormous breasts that had caused her apron to swell, but time had sunk its teeth into her and gravity now dragged them downward; the boys had found other, younger breasts to admire.

On the way home, they mostly discussed girls or politics. The brothers' parents always spoke apologetically of the state, as if it was *their* fault it repressed its own people. When they discussed the party, it was with regret, and though they poked fun at the head of state, Erich Honecker, their mother would still hang his portrait on the wall today. They believed in communism, just not in their leaders who practiced it. *They* were corrupt and greedy and masked their greed behind rote ideological phrases. The Wall was a constant reminder of what country they lived in.

Worker and peasant state, they snorted. The workers and peasants were hostages on a playground run by a bunch of avaricious men. Stefan's family watched Western news, even though it was verboten. Although authorities kept an eye on which way antennas were turned on the rooftops, many families turned their antennas anyway. When Stefan's parents saw an antenna turned toward ARD or ZDF, they knew yet another East German had been successful in conquering the Wall. No one said anything, but the entire Lachner family smiled in their characteristic, wide-lipped way, visible in every photo in every album on the bookshelf.

They despised the state for transforming their country into a prison, but they couldn't vocalize their feelings, especially today. Aunt Karin was coming for a visit. So today all their views had to be bottled up or tucked away at the bottom of a box in the attic. Though the cupboards were crammed with aversion and drawers teemed with defiance, they weren't a disobliging family. They simply couldn't see any connection between the ideology and the reality, and they couldn't understand why Aunt Karin was an informant for Stasi. For this reason, no one else in the family invited her to visit anymore, but Stefan and Alexander's mother, with her butter-soft heart, still sent invitations with Karin's name on them.

They handed her the package from the butcher. She removed the meat, sautéed it, and let the cubes crumble in the sizzling, red *soljanka* soup already bubbling aromatically on the stove.

Their aunt arrived at six o'clock and immediately started questioning Alexander about his studies, then Stefan about his work at the chemical plant. There was something admirable about the way Alexander spoke to her. Though his tone was always a little mocking, he never let on that the family knew her secret. *Knew* was maybe an exaggeration since they'd never had their suspicions confirmed, but they nonetheless regarded it as an established fact. There was something about the way she asked questions, the way she observed them all with barely stifled contempt for their life and the way they chose to live it, and Alexander had a lot of fun with her. When she spotted the portrait of Honecker, she tilted her head and, like a schoolgirl with a crush, smiled at the leader of state. They all saw it, and every single one of them felt their suspicion was confirmed.

Then Alexander began to enthusiastically recite the story of the Hecht family, whom he'd heard of in his medical studies. Using an old cement mixer, they had constructed a catapult to shoot the father, the mother, and their three children—ages four, six, and eight—over the Wall near Ackerstrasse. The father had calculated the angle so that they would land on the sidewalk on Bernauer Strasse, and from there they would start their new life in the West. Alexander's father gave his son a disapproving smirk, and Aunt Karin listened, indignant, her eyes wide, while everyone around the table suppressed the laughter that would have caused them to spray soup all over the table.

After supper, Stefan and Alexander went to their room. Their father sank deeper into his recliner, while the two sisters slowly wore him out with childhood memories and chatter about acquaintances who'd moved to Erfurt and girlfriends who'd married men named Jürgen.

Not until he'd heard the door close did Stefan dare put his Springsteen record on again, this time on side two. He'd concealed the records between books on the shelf in the hope that Ulf would forget them. Stefan had more use for them than his friend. As the needle scratched across the record, Alexander tapped a Karo out of his cigarette pack. Stefan looked up to his brother for his courage and intelligence. Alexander's sharp wit was his driving force, and Stefan envied his intellect. With the possible exception of finding a girlfriend, nothing seemed difficult for him. Stefan had just met Nina, an eighteen-year-old hairdressing student from Biesdorf. A sweet cloud of perfume followed her, as did her soft, curly hair. He didn't even care that she wore glasses. Something fluttered in his chest whenever he thought of her.

"What's that record called?"

"*Born to Run*," Stefan said. "Do you like it?"

"*Born to Run?*" His brain once again occupied, Alexander grew quiet. His attention wasn't on the music, and it wasn't on Stefan, but on a thought turning in his head. He squinted.

"One day, little brother . . ." With a sudden gravity in his eyes, Alexander looked at him as the cigarette smoke spiraled from his lips into his nostrils. "One day you and I will make our escape."

8

PETER

The thrill he'd felt following his meeting at the Ministry for State Security was suddenly forgotten. All he could think about at that moment was the little envelope with the Danish postmark. He glanced at the sender's name again. Elisabeth had changed pens between the letters *b* and *e*; the line was thicker, darker, bluer. The envelope itself was light. He weighed it in his hand and guessed that the letter could be no more than a single page. He felt a strong urge to tear it open immediately, but he would wait a little while longer. To look forward to something and yet have the courage to delay your pleasure was a sign of self-control.

He thought of Elisabeth often. A scent, a sound, or a word could bring her to mind. Until recently, his daydreams of her had been untroubled. Then he began seeing another woman, and his dreams were mixed with guilt—and now he held tangible evidence that Elisabeth still thought of him.

Peter had met Martina at a dance club that served inch-thick bock-
wurst and meatball sandwiches while bands enticed men and women
out onto the herringbone parquet floor with their music. People came
from all over the city, even from the other side of the Wall: workers,
soldiers, civil servants, and cheating spouses afraid of being discovered
and concealing themselves in the corners, lipstick on their cheeks.

Peter went there with Florian. Florian wanted to dance and Peter
watched the girls dance and kept an eye on his friend's beer. He and
Martina both seemed out of place among the dancing couples, and that
established a clear connection between them across the room. They'd
seen one another on his first visit, and they'd been a couple ever since.
That was three months ago.

She lived in Kopenhagener Strasse in Prenzlauer Berg, taught at the
Yuri Gagarin Polytechnic School, and was a member of the Democratic
Women's League of Germany, and her parents read *Neues Deutschland,*
the party's official newspaper, so frequently that their hands were black
with ink. In short, Peter had done a thorough background check on her
and determined that she and her family were clean.

Peter went into the living room. He'd been overjoyed to receive the
letter, but now he was suddenly afraid. He sat at the dining table with
the envelope in his hand, studying it. Though she'd written his name
and address with a sure hand, his own shook. Why would she write to
him unless it was to deliver good news? Why take the trouble unless
she wanted to share something with him? Maybe she'll be coming to
the GDR soon? What would he do with Martina if Elisabeth came?

He'd knocked three times under the table, at first in anticipation,
but now he did it again, this time in fear, for good luck or, at the very
least, to ward off any bad news. It was a ritual he'd inherited from his
paternal grandmother, though she had always added an extra knock, a
fourth and harder knock, as if that last one was meant to go beyond a
mere invocation. She'd collected a surplus of knocks, thousands—a kind
of motoric tic for use in emergencies. She had married a good man and

had four children who were still alive, and she herself had survived two wars. Her tic had worked right up until the day the truck came roaring along, and all the little knocks had merged into one giant crash.

He tore open the envelope, unfolded a single sheet of paper, and began to read.

After he'd read the letter to the end, it slipped from his hand. He stared at it, dumbstruck. He tried to make sense of it, but struggled to comprehend the consequences. A son? His son? Peter counted on his trembling fingers. The boy must be five months old now. That's how long he'd been a father, and he was only discovering it now. It was her duty to tell him, she wrote. She knew he would never be allowed to leave the GDR, that he'd never be able to see Andreas. Why tell him, then? And why did it upset him? After all, he hadn't wanted a child.

9

ANDREAS

Berlin, October 2006

Andreas was born at Rigshospitalet in Copenhagen. When Elisabeth had come home from studying in Germany, her belly had started to expand. She never even considered having an abortion. She wanted the child. No one understood the decision, but she wasn't going to change her mind. The young, aggressive left-wing activist was going to be a single mother. Was she rebelling against her parents or protesting mainstream society? And why wouldn't she say who the father was?

During a political protest, Elisabeth—in the late stage of her pregnancy—chained herself to the fence at the newly opened Barsebäck Nuclear Plant, and it was there she met Thorkild. They fell in love as the Swedish police attempted for several hours to locate bolt cutters to clip the chains. Thorkild was the union rep at the Burmeister & Wain shipyard and, like Elisabeth, active in Denmark's Communist Party and the popular movement against the European Economic Community, and both rejected the Soviet-critical Maoists in the Communist Workers Party.

Thorkild wanted complete honesty in their relationship, so he convinced Elisabeth to write Peter a letter informing him about his son. At first she'd refused, but Thorkild was persistent. He didn't want to begin yet another marriage with untruths and nondisclosures. On the day Elisabeth mailed the letter at the post office on Jernbane Avenue, he proposed to her. They were married in January 1977, when Andreas had yet to turn one. Elisabeth had just turned twenty-three, and Thorkild was thirty-two.

They bought a house in Vanløse and told their friends they were only renting it. In their social circle, where no one believed in the right of ownership, one wasn't supposed to own a house. Publicly, then, Elisabeth and Thorkild had rented the villa for twenty-nine years, but the equity told quite a different story from the one their former party comrades knew.

Elisabeth's sister Irene had been a nun, a servant of God who believed in something larger than herself. She'd placed her life in the hands of the divine, while Elisabeth had placed hers in the hands of a revolution that never materialized. Elisabeth had once been zealous in her convictions, believing she would go to her grave for them, but that was no longer the case. Her convictions were harmless now; they were streamlined, adapted to voters and not the other way around, and she was a member of the city council as a social democrat. Elisabeth still considered herself a leftist. Her communist background was a repressed memory, concealed behind a thirty-year mortgage, retirement savings, and interest deductions.

Thorkild had also softened with age, but given the right cue, he could still go on for hours about the solidarity at Burmeister & Wain where the workers were organized. Their crowning achievement was— even if it was many years ago—the founding in 1865 of The Workers' Building Society, which would later build the workers' district known as Humleby in Copenhagen. When he told such stories, the old fire returned to his eyes, and he read good-night stories every night to

Andreas in the same spirit. Thorkild had not read childish fairy tales to his son in the soft intonation of a doting father, but rather, with the tone of a union rep, his voice thick with indignation, as he impressed the family's convictions upon the child.

There was something teddy bear–like about Thorkild, though he wasn't fat or hairy. Everyone liked him. He always wore Wrangler blue jeans, a comb poking up from his pocket, fine-toothed on one end and thick-toothed on the other. He once tried to grow a beard, and they'd laughed at him until he began to laugh himself. His laughter came from deep within his belly. Thorkild loved Elisabeth, and she loved him, and together they were a perfect match.

Thorkild's life had stalled, but not in a negative way. He was fine with the fact that Elisabeth was the one with a career who went to political meetings night after night. Meanwhile, he took care of Andreas.

When Andreas was a boy, Thorkild was much more of a father to him than any of the other fathers were to the other kids in his class. It was almost like an act of defiance: no one could say he was not Andreas's father. Andreas and Niels were the only boys in the class who didn't know their biological fathers. Niels's father had died on an oil rig in the North Sea when Niels was just a bump pushing his mother's belly button out. Niels got Svend instead. It was better to avoid some fathers, and Svend was one of those.

Elisabeth hadn't actually wanted Andreas to know that Thorkild wasn't his biological father, but Thorkild had insisted: the boy needed to know, and you got farther in life when you were honest. When Andreas was a few years old, they told him the truth. Andreas continued to call Thorkild his father. Thorkild had never asked him to, but it seemed natural, because that's how Andreas viewed him. Thorkild had always been there for him and never let him down.

Thorkild's honesty backfired on occasion. During his first few years of school, the other kids called Andreas "German Pig" and "German Boy" or other long-forgotten nicknames from the postwar years that were suddenly popular again once Thorkild told everyone about Andreas's origins at one of the class's first parent meetings.

Andreas looks at his watch. For a moment he considers calling Thorkild. A sudden loneliness gives him the urge to talk with his stepfather. It's Wednesday, so Thorkild is at the Open University. Elisabeth knows that Andreas is in Berlin, and she knows why. Still, she was strangely silent when he told her of Peter's death. Thorkild was the one who smoothed things over. "She doesn't want to stir up the past," he told Andreas. For Andreas, Peter has never been part of the past, and now, even though he's dead, he has suddenly become the present.

Near the river Spree—with its canal tourist boats, it looks like just about any big city destination—is the Charité hospital. Its buildings are scattered across a large area, except for a colossus that towers unattractively above the city. The name is misleading. Not the meaning so much, but the fact that they chose a French word for a hospital in a city where everything else has a German name. An old king was enchanted by the neighboring country's culture and language, and so the hospital is named for the French word for *charity*.

Once inside he immediately feels the word *hospital* resting on his diaphragm, reminding him of when he was a child and how the word *police* automatically made him feel guilty, even though he hadn't done anything to be guilty about, but the word *police* was linked with guilt, just like the word *hospital* was linked with pain.

Berlin's police had contacted him the day before and told him they'd put more people on the case. Andreas had trouble gauging whether this was true or simply something the police said to reassure Peter's relatives that they were doing their jobs properly.

He reports to the reception desk. The woman behind the counter immediately hands him a form through the bisected window. When he attempts to explain what he's there for, it's as if she doesn't want to understand him. Swiftly and aggressively, she yanks back the form and ignores him for a few moments. Then she asks him to have a seat. When he turns toward the waiting room, she sighs.

He sits down. He has plenty of patience; he knows full well that doctors in hospitals are busy. He grabs a magazine off the table. He flips through the pages, then puts it back. He wishes that Bea was here with him, but she's at a university lecture.

He watches the receptionist, how she greets all the patients with a smile. Perhaps it's because he's not here for an examination but something else—something she doesn't understand—she seems to think he doesn't deserve a smile, but it doesn't matter; it's only a dutiful smile. When she catches him looking at her, she turns away immediately. He's been waiting for three hours. His grumbling belly chases his patience away. Drumming his fingers on the armrest, he considers leaving.

Wooden clogs clap against the floor. Finally. She points him out to the doctor, as if she has found him guilty of something. There's something reproachful about the receptionist's narrow wrist poking out from her smock. He pictures her biking home later, frustrated by her day. She'll shout at a driver, snarl at a pedestrian, and scold a husband who has forgotten to buy cat food. In the evening she'll lie in bed, tossing and turning, unable to sleep, because she'll still be irritated at Andreas.

The doctor approaches him. He pulls Andreas aside so that the other patients can't hear their conversation. He lowers his glasses from the top of his head as if donning his professional countenance.

"My name is Volker Dietmaier. I was the one who received your father."

Andreas nods. He hears the gravity in the doctor's voice, and all at once his words become momentous. The man standing before him was the last person to see his father alive.

"Was he dead upon arrival? Here, I mean." His own voice sounds hesitant and weak. He doesn't want to cry, but the heavy atmosphere of the hospital presses down on him. Swallowing loudly, he keeps his tears at bay by thinking of Bea.

"Yes. He died quickly." The doctor scrutinizes Andreas, as if considering how much to tell him. "If you'd like to know whether or not he suffered, then the answer is no. He died almost instantly."

Andreas latches onto the word *almost*. How much pain is contained in *almost*? The doctor has contradicted himself, because either Peter died instantly or he didn't, but Andreas remains quiet out of respect.

He looks at the doctor, who speaks with the authority of his profession. "Maybe your father had enemies. Perhaps someone held a grudge."

This last statement sounds like a question, but Volker Dietmaier backtracks. "On the other hand . . . it didn't look like revenge."

"What do you mean?" Andreas asks.

The doctor clears his throat. "If someone had wanted revenge, he probably would have been stabbed many more times than the two wounds that killed him. Deaths motivated by revenge are typically more violent."

Outside the hospital, Andreas gets a call on his cell phone.

"We've arrested the culprit, a homeless man. There was still blood on the sleeve of his coat." The policeman pauses as if to build suspense. When Andreas says nothing, he goes on. "He knew your father's name. He said it himself." Then he makes a sound that's impossible to misunderstand: it is beneath him to catch this kind of amateur. He had looked forward to solving a case involving an autopsy and DNA analysis, but instead he'd been pulled into this trivial matter.

"The motive is simple: robbery. Your father was at the wrong place at the wrong time and had a wallet in his back pocket."

The line goes silent. The policeman's cliché rings in Andreas's ears. What's he supposed to say? Is he supposed to praise the work of the police? Is he happy? Relieved? He doesn't know. He simply doesn't know how to react. The man breathes loudly into the telephone, as if he'd just now run down the homeless man and is trying to catch his breath.

"He had your father's wallet on him. Would you like to come to the station for it, or should I send it to you?"

After the call, he starts toward home, feeling dejected. He got nothing out of the conversation with the doctor, but what had he expected? That Volker Dietmaier had heard Peter's final words? Andreas can't allow himself to be disappointed, and yet he feels it welling up in him. How could a doctor who had treated his dying father have helped? The case is closed. He'd imagined that it would take weeks—maybe months or years, an exhausting length of time—to track down the culprit, but now it's over. The murderer has been apprehended. He wants to direct his anger at the man who killed his father. Why take another's life? Before sticking the knife in his father, he'd made a decision, however incomprehensible it might seem. If the murderer wasn't a random person, then it was someone who intended to kill his father. Andreas feels overwhelmed at the thought. Where does he go from here? Meeting the doctor has only made him sadder, and the swift resolution of the case only confuses him further.

Andreas has been at Peter's apartment for an hour when Bea arrives. When he opens the door, he sees that she's carrying a shiny black crash helmet under her arm. Every now and then, she borrows her friend's motorcycle, she explains. Andreas pictures the boyfriend. Tall and muscular, maybe an upgraded rockabilly look—though without overdoing it—his slicked-back hair shining black like the enamel on the motorcycle's gas tank, his tattoos spreading across his muscular forearms. Not showing them off, but as if they've always been there. He makes Bea laugh, and she's proud of him. One day Andreas will meet him, but even now he knows he doesn't want to.

In the entranceway, he tells her about his conversation with the policeman.

"Murdered by some insignificant vagrant." Bea snorts. "He chose the wrong victim. Peter drank all his money."

"Did he drink a lot?" Andreas asks hesitantly, not certain he wants to know the answer or that he wants to reveal to Bea that the murderer knew his father.

"Big time," she says in English, which sounds comical emerging from her mouth.

Something about this information makes him sad. It underscores the loneliness he's sensed here in his father's apartment, and it explains the many empty bottles on the kitchen floor. He imagines his father: gross, slovenly, and reeking of piss like the winos he rides past every day who squat in the little plaza behind Nørrebro Station in Copenhagen. How they sit, sprawl, or lie on or behind the benches—their world is colored green, because their misty-eyed stares see it through the beer bottles they're always drinking. Maybe Peter was also like that, just in another plaza in another city? It's depressing to think that his father might have hit rock bottom at the end of his life.

"Can I make some coffee?" Bea asks.

He'd like to say yes, but doesn't feel that the decision is his. The apartment is as much hers as it is his. He nods, and they go into the kitchen. She looks for the coffee, and he points at the can on the top cupboard. She hasn't been here in a long time, she says apologetically, and he hears hint of guilt in her voice.

The coffee machine whirs as the final drops fall into the pot, what appears to be sludge. She hands him a full cup, and they return to the living room.

"It probably tastes awful. Do you use milk?"

He nods.

She returns to the kitchen and comes back with a carton. The coffee tastes horrible, and they agree that the coffee machine belongs in a time capsule. They drink it anyway.

"Was Peter ever married?" Andreas asks.

"Not *married* in the traditional sense," Bea says, then tells him about Martina and Kerstin. This was once Martina's apartment, she explains. She points at the conch on the shelf. "And that's all he had left of Kerstin. She's probably suppressing her past in Freiburg, Stuttgart, or Bremen—somewhere in the West. All I know is that she abandoned him when the Wall fell. I think it broke his heart."

Bea keeps talking, but Andreas is no longer listening. He's busy thinking of what he's going to say next. He interrupts her.

"I don't think your mother wanted to tell me what Peter did for a living." Andreas looks at Bea as if he'd asked a question. Her face glows, and Andreas notices that even when she doesn't smile, her dimples appear as pronounced, tiny divots in her cheeks.

"Did you ask her?" she says, without looking at him.

"I asked her yesterday."

"And?" Bea peers over the rim of her cup, which she holds to her mouth with both hands. Her eyes are fastened to his, and he nearly forgets what he wants to know.

"Then you came in the door." He clears his throat. "Will you tell me?"

He sees how suddenly uneasy she has become on the otherwise comfortable couch. It's clear that Bea would prefer not to discuss it. No one wants to tell him; it's as if his father's job was a disgrace, and it slowly dawns on him what he might discover.

He's wrong about Bea. She looks directly at him, and there's something courageous in that gesture. She dares to say what Veronika wished to keep silent.

"Prepare yourself to learn something that you probably don't want to hear."

"Okay," he hurries to say, trying to brace himself.

She drains her coffee cup, then takes a deep breath and holds it a moment. There's determination in her eyes, and her pupils contract.

"You don't know what your father did for a living?"

He shakes his head.

"After reunification, Peter worked as a security guard." She looks down. "Before reunification, he worked for Stasi."

The truth has been emerging slowly ever since Andreas came to the city, and what he'd feared has now become a reality. Deep down he'd known it. Something in Veronika's evasive response to his question about what Peter did for a living said it all, and yet the truth still shocks him, still hurts. In Andreas's childhood fantasies, Peter had been a revolutionary who'd bravely fought the East German state. Instead he'd helped the state that brutally subjugated its own people. He'd been a henchman for a horrific ideology. Andreas has several questions and has had them ever since meeting Veronika, but it's not the right time. He won't ask, because he doesn't want to hear the answers just yet. It's as if he's been drained of himself. His entire existence is suddenly cast in doubt. The world that he'd imagined for his father snaps apart when he hears the word *Stasi*.

Bea studies him. Without even noticing she's doing it, she bites her nails and awaits his reaction.

He sighs, then shrugs. What can he say? "Jesus, this is all so strange."

They say nothing for some time. He's suddenly irritable. His fantasies of his father and himself, which had been strong these past few days, have disintegrated. He hears his stepfather, Thorkild, telling him about Stasi when he was thirteen, and the words ring hollowly in his head as he recalls his emotions back then: a thirteen-year-old boy who got a bellyache worrying about what would happen to his father if he was arrested by Stasi. He couldn't have imagined that the opposite was true, that Peter himself worked for Stasi. His worldview suddenly flips its axis, and the truth feels almost like a kind of pain. Couldn't Peter have just been a postman? A factory worker? A bookkeeper? Bea shouldn't have told him. He didn't need to know. She should have shielded him from the truth.

He stands abruptly and grabs the funeral director's brochure off the dining table. "Let's get this over with." He tries to sound determined, but it doesn't come out that way.

Bea clarifies all the words in the brochure that he doesn't understand. His German is good, one might call it sensible—if language could be described that way—but things go faster with her help, and right now he wants to be quick about it.

He feels frustrated. "Burial or cremation?"

"Your father didn't believe in anything. Well, except for the State, once." She tries to make it sound like a joke.

Andreas shoots her a slightly irritated look. "So, burial." He makes a sloppy X in the box.

Up until a few minutes ago, he'd wished to learn everything he could about Peter—to research his life, leave no stone unturned, and gather all the details he could about the man responsible for bringing him into the world. Now it no longer means anything. It doesn't matter. Peter worked for Stasi, and he needs to be laid to rest as quickly as possible so Andreas can return to Copenhagen. It's all been a misunderstanding, Veronika, Bea—all of it. Peter's death has whacked Andreas's life off-kilter, and now he must go home to restore his equilibrium, but there is no balance, not here and not at home.

As they complete the form, Andreas grows increasingly angry. His disappointment is vast and turns to frustration, which he now takes out on Bea. He'd like to stop himself, but he can't control it. It's so unlike him; he doesn't act like this normally. Suddenly everything has been flipped on its head.

"I've got to admit that I'm getting a little annoyed with you," she says suddenly and loudly. "You can't judge Peter if you didn't know him. How can you? And how can you judge us for liking Peter?"

He's so surprised at her outburst that he's left speechless. Neither of them says a word. He's hurt. Something else too, something larger, something worse. He feels powerless. All his dreams of his father have been crushed, ruined, obliterated. Before today he could imagine his father to be anyone at all, but no longer, and there's a finality to that realization.

"I think you should go."

She laughs hesitantly. "Do you mean that?"

He doesn't look at her directly, but senses her gaze on him. The moment lasts too long and transforms into something else, something unrecognizable. His silence is his answer.

She stands up and says softly, "Okay."

He hears her grab the crash helmet from the hook.

10

PETER

East Berlin, July 1976

Elisabeth frequently appeared unannounced in his thoughts, as did Andreas, but his thoughts about the child were vague. Since he couldn't imagine himself as a father, he pictured Elisabeth with the little one instead. She's nursing the child clutching at her breast, who is as aromatic as a newly washed article of clothing. Once he received her letter, he saw pregnant women everywhere: with prams or scabby-kneed boys or walking hand in hand with pigtailed girls. He hadn't ever noticed them before, but now it was as if every female in Berlin were pregnant.

He started recalling his childhood. As a child, Peter had been taught to believe in a society in which everyone was equal. The family history didn't begin until 1949; his parents never discussed anything that happened before that time. It was like West Berlin on the East German map: a black stain, nonexistent. All that mattered was the future.

In his youth, his father, Georg, had been a tremendous cyclist who'd won medals for the GDR. Peter had spent hours in cold velodromes waiting for his father with his sister, Veronika. He'd never taken them to a horse race in Hoppegarten, a football match, or the track-and-field stadium. For Georg, life was all about cycling: man's struggle to propel the bike forward in a race against time or his opponents. Before the children were born, cycling had brought him to tracks in Czechoslovakia, Poland, Hungary, and the Soviet Union, and he had always returned home with medals around his neck. Later, he became a sportsman without a sport. He still wore the bike club's blue training suit as if always about to head off to a race; it had been custom made for his body, but had since grown too tight. Peter recalled how the boys in the street would laugh at his father each morning when he rode off to the factory, his racing bike groaning under him. Whenever the bike tires struck a pothole, his entire body would heave above the creaking bike frame, and his belly would touch the crossbar as he stretched toward the handlebars. The bike was designed to travel at high speeds, but not with Georg Körber in the saddle. On the day his father sold his bike, Peter and the bike were both relieved, but even without his bike, Georg visited the club every single day.

Peter recalled when the Wall was built. Back then it was all very strange, but he'd grown used to it after a while, and it had become just another building like all the others. It was constructed in the middle of the night. On August 13, 1961, at 2:00 a.m., it had sliced the city right down the middle. The city was already been divided, but that night it was torn irrevocably in half. Nine-year-old Peter and his family lived a few miles from the border with West Berlin, and they'd been startled awake by the noise. His father had turned on Radio GDR 1. Music played quietly until the press statement was read aloud. Gazing out the apartment's windows, they could see that the broadcaster was telling the truth: trucks, tractors, cranes, and troops were rolling through Friedrichshain, and Russian T-34 tanks were a menacing presence at all the main thoroughfares. Drum after drum of barbed wire fence was emptied, and by the time the sun set the following day, the border had been secured, sewn shut like stiches used in an operation. Almost every crossing between the two halves of the city had been closed; 192 streets and roads were sealed off and train lines and telephone lines cut right down the middle. West Berlin was locked in, or rather, locked out.

Georg had welcomed the Wall. He'd been furious when the well-educated fled in droves from the country that had provided them with their education. The Wall, he said, would create stability in the country and secure the future.

Eleven days later Günter Litfin was shot while trying to swim across the border in Humboldt Harbor. Some officers from the transport police who were responsible for the train stations and railways had discovered the twenty-four-year old Litfin in the water, and they'd killed the young man by firing a bullet into his neck. One of the girls at Peter's school was Litfin's cousin, but she hadn't heard the news. A boy knew the story from Western media, and when he told her, she'd started sobbing. The girl was allowed to go home, and the teacher reported to State Security that the boy's parents watched Western TV.

Back then, Peter had felt bad for the girl, but now he saw it differently. Maybe children are softer and more lenient? After Litfin, others, such as Peter Fechter, Heinz Sokolowski, and most recently Herbert Kiebler—all men who held twisted views of life in GDR—had, in a fit of insanity, overcome their fear of death to try to reach West Berlin. Some were secretly hailed as heroes, which only people who didn't know any better would do.

Department XX was assigned to fight these types of people. The department was divided into several subdepartments. Department 5, to which Peter was assigned, monitored political dissenters, underground groups, and other possible dissidents; another department kept watch on the church, one watched Free German Youth and other youth organizations, and one scrutinized media and cultural life. Many had their own specialties. Some people questioned the methods the departments used, but Peter didn't see anything wrong with them. The formula was in fact very simple: all people would commit some kind of crime at some point in their lives, and it was the department's job to help them. It was up to him to persuade those who didn't want help that they needed it, and those he couldn't persuade had to be gotten rid of, because they would hinder the progress of the state. Luckily, many wanted the project to succeed.

State Security used a number of informants, and the state's job was easier when the broader population wanted to assist them. Some offered their apartments for secret meetings, some reported on their neighbors and colleagues, and others were active in infiltrating enemy circles. In every shop, factory, apartment building—even in the military and in every field of study—there were watchful eyes and ears. All informants provided small or large bits of information, and when they were added together, the bits formed a whole that portrayed an image of the enemy.

On the table in front of Peter lay yet another operative investigation. Service location: Berlin. Service unit: XX/5, Operative Investigation, Reg. nr. XX 1436/76. He opened the file. The purpose of an investigation was to confirm or remove suspicion from a person regarding activity harmful to the state. If such activity was confirmed, an operation—that is, an active investigation—was set in motion. It was very simple: One checked to learn of any harmful intentions, and then one investigated in order to prove those harmful intentions. If everyone followed the rules, his role was superfluous, but his job was necessary. That the department continued to grow was proof enough of that for Peter.

In the file was a black-and-white photograph of a well-dressed man. His facial skin was so smooth that it appeared nearly polished. His hair was cut short and precisely. Only his nose marred his otherwise attractive face; it was cracked down the middle as if made of two disparate parts or as if the man were a former boxer, but he wasn't—because if that were the case, it would be noted in the file. The man was from a good laborer family and was a former sergeant in Free German Youth, a member of the Society for German-Soviet Friendship, a party member, and apparently a loyal supporter, and yet, he and his family had applied for a travel permit. The Declaration of Helsinki in 1975 had raised many people's expectations, and many had submitted similar applications. Did they really believe that a better life awaited them in the West? Why did it seem so alluring? Was it true that one only desired what one could not have? Naturally, the application had been rejected, and his attempt to flee—even if it had been legal—would have consequences. First he would be dismissed from the municipal office where he worked, and then his wife would be dismissed from her job. The couple's willingness to cooperate with the state would determine what happened after that.

This kind of assignment excited him. There was something intoxicating about this power, this control, and something honorable about protecting the state. In time he hoped to become an operative outside the office, to get assignments out in the city and use the technological equipment his colleagues talked about: video surveillance, listening devices, invisible ink, and smell tests. He only needed to be patient. Sonnenberger trusted him, and if he continued to be so meticulous with his assignments, another promotion would surely follow.

In the evenings, when he left work and returned to the apartment in Lichtenberg, he often sat alone at the table and ate. State Security men in other apartments on the street would be seated at their own supper tables, some with wives, some with children. He had a child himself, Andreas, and yet he sat there alone. He tried to suppress the thought. What good was it to have a son if he could never see him? It was best not to think of him.

Peter and Martina were meeting Veronika and her new boyfriend, Wolfgang, at Kino International tonight. He felt a growing irritation as he walked over to the cinema. Until she'd met Wolfgang, Veronika had always been punctual, but now she and Wolfgang were always late. That's not how Peter and Veronika had been raised.

Martina was already waiting at the entrance. He watched her from a distance. He liked to observe her while she waited for him. This tension, followed by a thrill that could be released only by him, made him feel loved. She glowed in the summer's evening light. Her short, slightly boyish hair was tousled along the sides and pulled back in a little pigtail. She wore a turtleneck underneath red overalls, and her suspenders were pressed tightly against her breasts. He let her wait a bit. She watched for him patiently. He enjoyed this moment, and then he enjoyed seeing her light up when he finally went to her. She kissed his earlobe, embarrassing him.

"Not here."

They waited in the wood-paneled lobby, where they had a view of Café Moscow across the street through the large glass façade. The theater was impressive—with lavish décor, an enormous hall, and floor-to-ceiling wood paneling—but he couldn't enjoy the architecture tonight, because Veronika and Wolfgang were late. Peter had bought four tickets to *Nelken in Aspik*. They could hear the film and the music starting up in the theater. The film would begin any minute, and they would miss it.

He looked at his watch for the third or fourth time. At least he could enjoy the placement of the lamps on the ceiling. As a child he'd discovered that he liked finding patterns in things. Disorder made him irritable. Symmetry created harmony, just like his own name. His first and last name had the same number of letters. First name, pause, breath, last name. A symmetrical perfection.

When they finally arrived, Peter glared at his sister, but Martina laid a calming hand on his forearm. Veronika shrugged as if the delay meant nothing, and the two women greeted each other warmly. Wolfgang, who still had crumbs in his beard following dinner, shook Peter's hand and patted his pockets.

"I don't have my wallet," he said, a hint of an apology in his voice. "Can I pay you back?"

How could Wolfgang invite Veronika to the movies without bringing any money? Peter could say no. He could say that he wouldn't pay for them. The volume increased in the theater.

Peter patted his shoulder. "Of course."

11

ANDREAS

Berlin, October 2006

The cemetery is a tunnel of green and gold. It resembles Assistens Cemetery in Copenhagen except the signs are in German and there's a botanical garden for the deceased. The gardener himself is buried there, and no one has assumed his duties. The graves and paths are covered with a thick layer of fiery maple leaves, as if the autumn wants to call attention to itself. Everything is untended in a lush and pleasant way. There are no tailored suits or Hermès ties in this graveyard; it's a place where it's okay to leave your shirt untucked or let your shoes go unpolished.

Andreas goes by himself, and it feels wrong. He and Bea haven't spoken since he asked her to leave. The chapel is empty except for the rows of chairs and a palm tree that's taller than he is. The bark is ribbed, and its leaves are too green. The tree is too fresh for this place and is jarring next to the dull coffin. He chose the cheapest casket, and now he regrets that. A shiny black box would have put the palm tree in its place, but instead this bland wooden coffin looks like a form of defeat, but isn't death always defeat? A few clay pellets have fallen out of the flowerpot and now lie on the floor in their own brown dust. A wooden cross hangs on the far wall, illuminated from within. The rest of the room seems clinical, like a dentist's office waiting room, just without the racks full of old magazines.

He sits down tentatively. A woman clears her throat behind him, and he recognizes the female funeral director. He notices that she's wearing practical shoes with thick crepe rubber soles. She sways on her feet, and he imagines that she could stand for hours in those shoes. She's in charge of the funeral. Like any good funeral director, she possesses the ability to express the gravity of a situation at a moment's notice. With a sympathetic air, she introduces herself, even though they met earlier in the week, and then guides him to the first row, reserved for the closest relatives of the deceased.

Then other people begin to arrive, and it occurs to him that some may be relatives that he hasn't met, maybe an uncle or an aunt, a cousin whom Bea forgot to mention in her grief.

Bea's helping to support Veronika, who seems old and despondent—maybe she *feels* older now that her younger brother is to be buried. An older couple has already sat down, and he recognizes the inquisitive woman from the first-floor apartment. The man seems irritable, like he's here only to fulfill an obligation.

Andreas stands and takes Veronika's arm. He shoots Bea an apologetic glance. He hadn't meant to act the way he did, and he can tell that she understands. He guides Veronika into her seat. She clasps his hand, and that's how they sit: Veronika in the middle, holding Bea's and Andreas's hands all the way through the songs, which Andreas let the funeral director choose. They're all too strident; the tone makes him uncomfortable, and he hears his own voice squeak through verses he doesn't recognize. Throughout, he must guess whether the next note will be higher or lower than the one emerging from his mouth, but he nonetheless feels he must continue to sing. Anything else would be rude.

The woman in the practical shoes is the only person singing along with confidence. While everyone else fumbles hesitantly through the melodies, her voice rises above the group, with a clarity and assurance the others lack. He makes eye contact with Bea, who smiles at him through her tears. It's not until he sees her crying that he realizes just how much Peter meant to these people. He studies them. Their faces are distorted in pain, in varying degrees of loss and longing. They may be strangers to him, but they knew his father; they knew him well enough, in fact, to feel he's worth crying over.

Veronika leans toward him and whispers through her tears. "You couldn't have asked for a better brother. He always wanted the best for me." It almost sounds like an apology, though she has nothing to apologize for.

He sees that only the first few rows are occupied. There are no other family members. Peter's family consisted of Veronika and Bea.

He's now uncomfortable at Veronika's touch. Their single encounter doesn't justify the close contact, but does their blood relation? They are family, after all. Still, they're strangers. Until a few days ago, he didn't even know Bea and Veronika existed, and now they have suddenly been added to his family tree. All at once he feels like he's part of some bad soap opera, and once again he thinks of *Dallas*. Just like on that series, unknown family members have surfaced in his life. Luckily, they don't appear to have any hidden motives. They aren't after oil; they're not out for power—in fact he was the one who sought them out. Soon he will leave them again. All he has to do is get this over with so that he can return home to Copenhagen and put it all behind him. His thoughts shame him, and he tries to find the right funereal expression.

The coffin rests in the center of the chapel on a raised platform with wheels. He recalls the last time he saw a coffin. It lay in a hole in the ground at Bispebjerg Cemetery. Andreas was twenty-five years old when Aunt Irene was buried. The sexton had been meticulous; the grave was a perfect rectangle. At home they'd never called her Aunt

Irene; instead, they called her Aunt Irrelevant. She'd been a nun of the indignant variety, but the only place her faith had gotten her was that neatly dug grave.

There had been three sisters, each with her own set of beliefs: a nun, a communist, and a lawyer. The two remaining sisters, Elisabeth and Birgit, scowled at each other from either side of the grave—Elisabeth with Thorkild and Andreas, and Birgit with her husband, Arne, and their three kids whose names he always forgot. Aunt Irrelevant seemed suddenly relevant, and it wasn't until that moment that Andreas understood how much his mother had loved her sister.

Every time Elisabeth sobbed, Birgit sobbed too, as if they were competing to see who grieved the most. The scene grew painful to watch.

The final song ebbs away. They don't have enough people to carry the coffin, so the funeral director wheels it out to the waiting hearse with professional care. As they'd agreed, Andreas walks behind the coffin. His sneakers squeak on the floor, embarrassing him. The others follow him with bowed heads. Outside, the treetops absorb the street noise; the city seems remote. One by one the guests approach him to shake his hand. Frau something or other, Herr this or that—everyone expresses their deepest condolences.

They watch as the shiny, polished car crunches slowly down the gravel path. They remain standing. No one says a word. Several people cough, either because they are uncomfortable with the silence or are raising a cigarette to their lips.

A large bald man exits the chapel last. He walks toward them.

"My name is Grigor Pamjanov." His voice is deep and confident. "My condolences."

He offers his hand, and Andreas's own is buried in a huge, soft mitt. The back of the man's hand is covered with dark hair all the way up his wrist before being split in two by his expensive watch. It's not merely a device to measure time but a symbol of how much this man has succeeded in life. Thorkild always said that you can tell a lot about a man by looking at his watch, car, or wife. His stepfather would have called Grigor Pamjanov a Gucci type: the type who reads thrillers, drives convertibles, and goes on packaged golf tours—and he would get all that just by looking at the man's watch.

"I'm sorry Peter died in this manner," Pamjanov says. He smiles, revealing his teeth, and adds, "Any day I'm not in a grave is a good day."

Though his German is correct and his pronunciation impeccable, he has a thick accent, the remnant of some Slavic language. He's a large man. His body may have once been toned and slender, but it has gone slack, and his belly now pushes against his down vest. "Canada Goose," the tag reads. His clothing clearly isn't just *purchased*, but carefully selected without regard for price. He dresses like a young man, like someone who feels pressured by his wife's age on her birth certificate. His tie is tight, and the knot looks as though it's causing his face to swell. He talks like a military man and tries to appear friendly and relaxed.

He stares at the ground. "Sad, sad."

They nod in unison. Neither speaks. An older couple approaches to say their good-byes with a few well-intentioned words. They shuffle slowly off, and suddenly Pamjanov shifts his tone. When he asks whether they've ever eaten a genuine Russian meal, the solemnity in his voice is gone.

Bea glances at Andreas and shakes her head for both of them.

"Then I invite you to do so." He thrusts out his arms, as if he's going to embrace them, but stops when he notices them hesitate.

"I knew your father well," he says to Andreas, trying to get him to accept the invitation. When Andreas doesn't respond, he continues. "I insist. I'm flying out tonight at eleven o'clock. Meet me at Oblomov at seven."

He starts down the path without waiting for a response.

They watch him go.

"What just happened?" Bea asks. They both laugh, and their laughter seems wrong.

12

STEFAN

East Berlin, May 1977

His mother adjusted his tie one final time. She had already done so several times—proudly tightening it, brushing the lapel on his suit, and pinching him softly on the cheek through his beard, and he let her, because today was her day, too.

People were dancing, and the entire time he'd kept his eye on Nina, who was now dancing with Alexander. Her dress swung girlishly to the music, and her buoyant perm—which smelled like the large storage halls at chemical factories—fluttered behind her. He looked at her with pride and was bursting with love. Now she was his, and after the party they would move in together, into a two-bedroom apartment in Prenzlauer Berg that they had been assigned by the Housing Administration.

Stefan couldn't help but notice how Ulf's gaze kept seeking out Gisela Rahn, who ran the hair salon where Nina worked. It was understandable—all men looked at her. Her hair had a reddish tint to it, and her cleavage made her dress tight. The turquoise fabric was so tight on her bottom that you could see the lace of her panties; she edged closer to the men on the dance floor, rubbing her body against them promiscuously. Meanwhile her husband, Jörg, a wizened type with small round glasses that seemed ill-suited for his fine clothes, watched with visible despair, but he was used to it, because this was how Gisela always acted. The same scene played out at every party Stefan and Nina had been to. Late in the evening, they would embrace, hot and heavy, and he was certain that they went home and made passionate love, with his glasses hopping on the nightstand right up until the children knocked on the bedroom door.

Stefan and Nina had been married in the huge cafeteria where he worked. Chemiewerke Coswig was a mastodon of a chemical factory that produced artificial fertilizers and animal feed. They'd sat at a long table decorated by their mothers and had eaten dinner. The beer had flowed in a constant stream and continued to do so, and now people were drunk and dancing. Games were organized, and although he considered himself too grown-up to participate, Nina had laughed along, and so had he.

Ulf handed him a mug of beer, and Stefan smiled. Nina crossed the floor and kissed him. She still had rice in her hair. Family and friends had showered them with it in front of the town hall, and according to tradition, he was supposed to count them. For every grain of rice he found in her hair, they would have one child, but they weren't planning on having children anytime soon. Not until they had made it to West Berlin.

Outside, he smoked a cigarette with Alexander and Ulf, and they regarded the factory's two chimneys. During the day two columns of smoke spiraled out of them, touching the sky like slender cosmonauts, much the way Laika, Yuri Gagarin, and Sigmund Jähn had.

The two brothers sucked silently on their tobacco, casting glances at one another, waiting for Ulf to return to the party. Despite their friendship, there was no reason to involve Ulf in their plans. In this country you never knew who you could trust, so it was better to be careful.

Alexander didn't need to say anything, because even without words Stefan could sense that his big brother was seething. He hadn't wanted Stefan to get married. It made their escape more difficult. Alexander said that he, like a virgin waiting for marriage, would hold off on finding a wife until he reached West Berlin. He claimed that was why he had no girlfriend, but Stefan knew the real reason was that Alexander was awkward around girls.

Mostly it was Alexander who discussed fleeing, but Stefan wanted to go along, and he wanted Nina to come, too. He had yet to tell her of their plans, and he knew her view on the matter. They still didn't have any idea how they would get to the West, but they knew that others had managed it. It had to be possible somehow. For that reason they would take their time, turning over every stone to find the safest method. Each of them knew that their very lives would be on the line no matter what plan they chose, but they were ready to run that risk. Anything but this country. Every minute, every hour, every day, Stefan could feel his freedom becoming more and more restricted. The state was everywhere and into everything. The freedom they'd been promised had been transformed into a prison with borders.

In the meantime, they had to keep a low profile, though Stefan found that difficult. Results were everything. Five-year plans, production increases, agricultural effectiveness, numbers, statistics, and lies. Every last thing was colored by the party, painted in whatever color the party leaders wanted. Viewed from the upper echelons, everything looked rosy, and the GDR mission was a success. If he could, he would scream of state repression, friends who couldn't find work, the goddamn informants who were listening everywhere, Wolf Biermann being thrown out with the bathwater, the lack of free choice, Erich Honecker—but doing so would only get him into trouble. Instead he did it on the sly, dropping small hints about his true feelings or changing his tone of voice, and he believed that several in the factory's cafeteria agreed with him. He wanted to get away from all of it, away from the fact that he couldn't speak his mind without fear of reprisal and away from all the people who stared through a telescope. They simply had to leave.

One evening a few months after the wedding, he and Nina took an evening stroll, passing near the Wall at the end of Gleimstrasse. He glanced at the floodlights slicing the city's darkness in half, keenly aware that their freedom lay over on the other side. They passed a few dilapidated storefronts with only a few goods displayed in the windows. As they strolled, Stefan considered how they lived in a city of paradoxes. The shops where foreigners could purchase luxury items that normal people didn't have access to—jeans, fine soaps, leather jackets, gramophone records, alcohol, and cigarettes—blatantly conflicted with the state's ideology. The state wasn't for the people; it was all a lie. The people were merely a tool serving a few men's deranged dreams, and these men lived in seclusion with their families in the tony suburb of Wandlitz. According to rumors, the party elite inhabited a parallel world secured by a six-feet-high wall surrounded by barbed wire and an electric fence. They lived safely in their luxury villas, went pheasant hunting, and bought good French wine in their special supermarket. They ate and drank until their waistlines were tight and their belts needed more holes. Their Citroën CX limousines sped them the eighteen miles into Berlin, and in the Palast der Republik, they sat on their thrones shielded from the people, carrying on conversations on behalf of the people. They were hypocrites, all of them, and that's what Stefan and Alexander would tell the world once they managed to escape.

It began to rain as they walked. Nina sneezed. In the West, rain poured down just like in the East, and on both sides of the Wall, people were sick with the flu, the same virus. The city was wet and gloomy, and the fallen chestnuts were like small, shiny nuggets on the sidewalk. He knew she would keep the secret, but what if she didn't want to come along? He'd dreamed of getting out for so long, but he'd never leave

Nina. What would he do if she put him in that quandary? There was only one way to find out.

It was time. He turned to Nina and whispered the words through his next breath, quiet and secretive, telling Nina about their plan that wasn't yet a plan.

She looked sensitive and delicate as she stopped and turned to him, her curls tamped down by the rain. In that moment he loved her even more.

Confusion swirled around her face. She looked at him with frightened eyes. "I don't dare."

"We can't stay here," he said, trying to infuse his voice with confidence to get her to understand the necessity of their flight.

"We can. We must."

"It's not because I don't want to, Stefan." Nina fell silent.

The chestnuts in her hand glistened, and she stared at them. They walked toward home in silence. For the next few days, she only talked to him about everyday, practical matters. He knew she was intentionally avoiding any talk about fleeing the country. He knew deep down that he couldn't live without Nina—just as he knew he couldn't stay.

He spent the next several months trying to convince her. Though he'd initially been worried about her reaction, he decided it simply required more strenuous effort on his part. He enlisted Alexander to help him, but when Nina won a weekend trip to Wernigerode in a drawing among the city's hairdressers, Stefan could tell that she was relieved.

"It'll be good to get away from Alexander and all his ideas," she said.

13

PETER

Peter and Martina eventually began to talk about moving in together. Peter entered the conversation with an expectation that they would move into his apartment in Lichtenberg, but Martina refused to move to that part of the city. She was stubborn, and he couldn't convince her that it would be a nice place to live. Peter suddenly appeared to be at a crossroads: either he could put his foot down and risk losing her or he could bend to her wishes. Since he wanted to be with her, the choice wasn't difficult, and in April he visited Major Sonnenberger to tell him he wanted to move in with Martina in Prenzlauer Berg.

Sonnenberger was initially skeptical, because most of his coworkers lived in Lichtenberg or Hohenschönhausen. The Ministry for State Security secured their apartments, and they'd given Peter a good place to live, Sonnenberger pointed out. His men typically didn't live in Prenzlauer Berg's rundown apartments. They were for the workers, artists, and students.

"What about marriage?" the major asked. Before Peter could respond, he continued, "I'm married, but as you've probably heard, my wife is very ill. We don't know how long she'll be with us." The major slumped, drooping his head. Peter didn't know what was wrong with the major's wife, and no one ever said. He didn't ask, because he knew that any additional details would just make him uncomfortable.

So Peter returned to the question. "We'd like to get married."

Although he had never asked Martina, he couldn't imagine that she would turn him down. Theirs was a quiet love, so quiet that he often questioned whether it really was even love, but whenever he watched her while she slept, all his doubts vanished.

"It would be good for you to settle down with a wife and, who knows, maybe a few rug rats. She's a good girl."

Sonnenberger had never met Martina, but Peter knew that they'd checked her. State Security didn't let any of its employees marry without its approval, and that was what the major had just granted him.

Even in their first meeting, Peter had sensed that Sonnenberger had tremendous respect for him, and he used that now to press for permission to move in with Martina. In Prenzlauer Berg, he argued, he would be close to some of the dissident groups. Opposition to the state was often found among the workers, artists, and students. If he lived in the heart of their world, no one would suspect him, because everyone knew that State Security employees were secluded in their ghettos in Lichtenberg and Hohenschönhausen. Once he had painted the picture of himself as the department's Trojan horse, Sonnenberger softened.

"We've never done this before, but I trust your judgment."

The decision was, however, not up to Sonnenberger alone. In July he reported that Colonel Kreider had given his approval, and so in September Peter moved in with Martina. As a teacher, Martina was entitled to an apartment; the municipal administration had made the residence available to her the year before, when she was hired at the school in Pankow. The only things harder to obtain than an apartment were travel papers and a car, so she'd been happy.

When Peter moved in, the apartment was modestly furnished, since Martina's salary didn't allow for luxury living. One of his privileges as staff of State Security was that he had access to products that were unavailable to other citizens, and thanks to his good salary, Martina could furnish the apartment however she wished. So they outfitted the apartment in a modern style with a laminate shelving system for a Stern TV, a floral-patterned sofa, a Formica coffee table, brown floor lamps, and orange wall-to-wall carpets beneath it all. The portrait of Erich Honecker was hung in the living room on a nail hammered through the thick burlap. In the kitchen, the new coffee machine brewed silently, while Gisela May's alluring voice emanated from the speakers of the Stern radio. Peter bought them a black Bakelite telephone with a rotary dial, but since their families didn't have telephones, they didn't have many people to call.

He noticed right away that Prenzlauer Berg was very different from Lichtenberg. The buildings were Altbau from the Wilhelm period, and the red brickwork was in a state of disrepair. The streets had holes on their knees and cuts on their elbows, and had only been patched in a few places. The electrical unit was overloaded, so if he turned on the stove and the coffee machine at the same time, the fuses blew. Even the people were different. In Lichtenberg people kept their heads up, but here, people shifted their gaze to the sidewalk to avoid making contact with others. Many of them looked exhausted. Then there were the artists, with their unkempt beards and tousled, greasy hair that fell past the collars of their denim jackets.

One evening after work, Peter sat at the dining table, wondering how to begin a report. He bit down on the end of a sharpened pencil and immediately felt tiny slivers in his mouth. He tried to catch them with his tongue. He could barely register Martina's quiet singing in the kitchen as she cleaned up their dinner dishes.

Peter was supposed to write a comprehensive report about all the residents in his new building, and no detail was too inconsequential. He'd suggested the assignment to Sonnenberger himself, because the more he thought about it, the more it made sense. If every employee wrote up a report on their neighbors, the Ministry would have a great deal of information on people who might someday harm the country. Just as he'd done when he'd given Peter permission to move in with Martina, Sonnenberger had made an exception. Normally he would have informants carry out such an assignment, but Peter had insisted. Since he lived so close to these people, he might as well devote some time to analyzing them. Besides, there were people here who might eventually demand greater scrutiny.

He set to work systematically. He would start with the ground floor and move up through the building. He asked himself questions: Had anyone displayed any suspicious behavior? Had he heard anyone express critical views or in any way speak negatively about the party? Did anyone talk about fleeing to the West? Of course not, because no one talked about that kind of thing beyond the four walls of home. Since he knew them only superficially, he tried to imagine who might dare to conspire against the state. He quickly ruled out all the elderly residents.

Irene and Sven Krause lived on the first floor. They were only in their midfifties, but they acted like old people. Irene always supported Sven's arm when they went out, and both ambled around with the slightly hunched gait of people getting on in years. On several occasions he'd watched the newspaper boy put the party's official newspaper, *Neues Deutschland*, in their mail slot. Irene was always peering vigilantly out the window whenever Peter put the key in the main door, and every time she acted as though it was a coincidence. Whenever she disappeared behind the double curtains, Peter thought she was undoubtedly an informant for State Security.

Mr. and Mrs. Schnellhardt and their irritating dog also lived on the first floor. The little poodle always seemed to be freezing cold, and Mrs. Schnellhardt often carried it in her arms. The couple seemed arrogant, and he didn't even know their given names since they weren't etched on the brass doorplate. Despite their attempts to hide their origins, they were simple workers.

Jürgen and Margaret Floh on the third floor also belonged to the group of older residents. They were quiet, working-class people who kept to themselves. He also quickly ruled out Artur Polk on the first floor, a punctual man in his midthirties who left his apartment at the same time every day and returned precisely at quarter past five. Judging by his attire and demeanor, he was a clerk of some kind or perhaps even one of Peter's colleagues. He carried a brown leather briefcase, and his slender hands didn't show signs of manual labor. Peter had the impression that Polk had lost his wife, because he wore a wedding band on his ring finger.

It was then that Peter saw that he'd taken the wrong approach. It wasn't his job to rule out anyone—it was the opposite. His job involved describing these people, their habits and comings and goings in the minutest detail. Then he would leave the rest to the experienced staffers in the evaluation department. If his report was comprehensive, they would be able to determine who required additional attention. He crumpled up his two pages and started over. Once again he began at the bottom and moved up through the building, but this time he imagined himself interrogating every resident in the building.

He began to write again: Bottom floor, first apartment . . . He left nothing out, including everything from the way Franz and Gudrun Colbach left their shoes on their "Welcome" mat to how Gisela Matuschyk's thick perfume wafted from her door on the third floor every time she had gentleman visitors—which was quite often. Peter took an entire page to describe an encounter he'd had in the stairwell with Gregers Eichner that had convinced him that the man was an alcoholic. As he wrote he imagined Eichner's two boys in the yard—their pants rolled up to just below their knees, the leather ball wet from splashing in puddles and echoing against the walls—and Irene Krause behind the glass, trying to puncture the ball with her gaze. Luckily, there were good people in the building, and not all of them were Bohemian types, unlike the people in the other blocks in the quarter.

He described an encounter with Greta Riemann-Müller, who lived across the hall from Peter and Martina with her family on the top floor of the building. Greta and Paul had never had children; Paul was married to books, and he'd become one of the country's most treasured writers. The books he wrote reflected a long and industrious career, and his works were read far and wide, from Karl Marx-Stadt to Rostock, from Magdeburg to Cottbus. He always seemed distracted, lost in thought, whenever Peter ran into him on the stairs. Greta would speak while Paul usually hummed some refrain or other that Peter didn't recognize.

One day Peter ran into Greta on the landing, and she told him Paul's story. The next book had been in the works for a long time, and tears formed in her eyes as she explained how the book would never be finished. Paul had written his last book; he just didn't know it yet. Every day after his morning coffee, he sat down eagerly at his typewriter. He was practically bursting with ideas, and his rapid-fire typing didn't ease up until around lunchtime. She would hear him humming in his office, something he only did when he was inspired. What he didn't realize was that, although his imagination was thrumming with ideas, it was always the same idea. A blood clot in his brain had ruptured his memory, and every day he wrote the same six pages. Although his memory was no longer sharp, this one idea had become stuck, as if stenciled onto his cerebral cortex.

Early on, Greta had tried to show him the pages from the day before, but he was always adamant that they were quite different from his new idea. This new idea was better and more profound, he proclaimed. This pattern had continued every day now for three years.

Then she'd tried to explain to him that he suffered from memory loss. Occasionally, she said, it seemed as if he understood, but by the next day, he'd forgotten again and sat back down at his typewriter, enflamed with an urge to create. She no longer had the heart to try to dissuade him. Paul was happy, and he wrote and wrote.

"If there's anything I can do . . ." Peter had said, shaken at the notion that a person could lose control over his own memory in such a way.

"No, thank you. You've enough to worry about," Greta said as she let herself into her apartment. Peter heard humming inside.

One of the quarter's many artists lived on the second floor. Like the Dutch painter with whom he shared a name, Jens Rembrandt was a painter. Peter often encountered him in the stairwell, dragging canvases and an easel, his woolen sweater stained in every color of the rainbow. He rarely shaved, and he wore his scarf in a nonchalant, indifferent way that irritated Peter. A cigarette was constantly in his mouth, like an extension of his lower lip, and it would bob up and down whenever he said hello. He only ever seemed to remove it when it had burned all the way down to the filter.

Peter didn't like artists, who seemed to feel compelled to complain about the system—some loudly, others in more subtle ways, and those who didn't speak out protested in their own way by their *lack* of critique. People like Wolf Biermann with his songs and Christa Wolf with her books were dangerous. Everyone could see that. Rembrandt may be an emerging Biermann, and Peter had the chance to stop him. Although Peter had never spoken to him, he devoted three whole pages to the young painter on the second floor.

Sonnenberger was very satisfied. Valuable material, he said about the report. Although Peter hadn't spent much time in the building, he'd caught a glimpse into the lives of individual residents and their habits and quirks.

"That's why you're in this department," Sonnenberger said, waving the extensive report.

In August, Veronika and Wolfgang were married. Peter's father, Georg, had been soused and unpleasant at the wedding, causing Peter to recall an incident before Veronika met her new husband. The family was sitting at the dinner table, and Veronika was crying quietly, having just been dumped by some boyfriend. At that point she was not yet twenty, and she was inconsolable, despite her best attempts to stifle her tears. Though her mother tried to comfort her, Georg had sat at the end of the table, his penetrating eyes revealing his disgust. In his eyes she was a weakling. No one, man or woman, should indulge in such an emotional outburst; tears were only for children. He moistened his lips, sliding his tongue from one side of his mouth to the other, and let loose a torrent of rage that caused his temples to throb. Although he didn't shout, his voice was sharp, and his tone was clear.

"I might as well just kill myself. Nobody wants me here anyway," Veronika said, burying her face in her hands. Their mother watched in horror, not because of what she'd said but because she feared Georg's response. To everyone's surprise he stood without a word. They heard a clatter and a rustle in the bathroom. Then Georg returned to the kitchen, pausing next to Veronika.

"Here." He slammed a bottle of pills down hard on the table. "If you want to kill yourself, you'll have to ride your bike out to the woods, because you're not doing it here."

They finished their meal in silence. Not long after that, Veronika met Wolfgang.

14

ANDREAS

Berlin, October 2006

He walks in from the funeral and sees his backpack in the entranceway, packed and ready. He still hasn't decided whether he'll take the train home to Copenhagen or fly, and he hasn't decided whether he should say good-bye to Bea. He feels obligated, and he would like to see her one last time, but that will also make his departure more difficult. He can't lie to himself: he's attracted to her.

He walks around the apartment. It's his now, but he's unsure what he should do with it. In a way he's begun to like it, the old-fashioned furniture, the heavy blankets, and the woman's voice on the cassette tapes. The apartment is steeped in the past, and it belonged to his father. He punches the button on the tape recorder. He takes his father's conch shell off the shelf and sets it on the couch. As its ocean sounds whisper in his ear, the woman begins to sing.

He puts the conch back on the table. What would he go home to in Copenhagen? Nothingness. A vast, swampy marsh of superficial friendships and trying to score a kiss at a bar on a Friday night while crossing his fingers behind his back in the hopes that more would follow. No one is waiting for him now that he and Lisa have broken things off. She kept the apartment in Absalonsgade when they split up, and he'll never feel at home in his little one-bedroom apartment. He can't stand the street noise, the rickety buildings, the people. He knows he'll never be finished with his thesis and that he has no more ambition, but that seems to be the only thing that people care about—setting goals, fighting, contributing to a community and society. So he plays along; he *pretends* he's doing his part, just so he will be left in peace. Everyone asks whether he'll move on soon, finish his studies, earn his degree, and get a job, but he doesn't dare tell the truth: *hell no*!

That answer had been precisely why Lisa had left him. He'd never understood why she loved him and then he gave her a reason not to. When they used to walk together, he'd caught himself wondering whether passersby saw them as a mismatched couple: the beautiful young woman with the sparkling eyes and pouty lips beside the unkempt-looking Bohemian university student. It was hardly a surprise that she'd finally realized she deserved better. Lisa wanted more out of her life, and he could hardly blame her.

Andreas tries to picture Peter. He must have been ambitious. Wasn't that pretty much a requirement in that kind of job? Andreas knows very little about Stasi or what Peter actually did for them. Maybe he was just a small cog in the wheel, some low-level employee or office mouse? Andreas realizes what he's doing—judging, evaluating, categorizing—everything that he rejects. He hates it when people measure each other by their jobs, because what does a career actually say about a person? Don't people only reveal their true selves in private?

Still, he can't separate the man from his job, and he feels cheated in some vague way. He found his father only to lose him again. Were he to go home now, it would mean excising his entire existence, as if his father were a pernicious tumor that must be removed.

He recalls how people cried at the funeral. In a sense, it makes him happy to know that his father meant something to people. If Bea and Veronika and the others in the chapel that day thought he was worth loving, why can't Andreas bring himself to do the same? Who was this man, who was both well liked and feared at the same time? Andreas can remain in the city and try to find out, or he can go home. He feels uncertain and suddenly fearful. He's standing on the rickety ledge of a decision. *Should I stay or should I go?* The woman on the tape sings that she's falling to pieces, and he has the same feeling. How can he reconcile with a father he knows worked for Stasi? If he leaves and thereby rejects his father, he'll never learn what kind of person Peter really was. On the other hand, if he stays and investigates his life thoroughly, he might discover that Peter had hurt other people, that he had been a bad person in the employ of the state.

But how can he go home without knowing who he was? Doesn't he owe it to himself to resolve that question or to at least try? The tape player clicks when the tape ends, and he makes his decision.

The restaurant where they're meeting Grigor Pamjanov is in Karlshorst. When he meets Bea near the station, Andreas notices that she has changed her clothes. As they hug, he absorbs the heat of her embrace. Though she is lanky, there's a softness to her.

"I'm staying in Berlin."

"How long?" she asks.

He shrugs. He doesn't know, but he'll stay as long as Thorkild continues to loan him money.

They cross a broad street. The slick tracks split the street in half, and the trams resemble yellow moving boxes as they glide past, filled with people using their sleeves to form peepholes on the steamed-up windows. The autumn air sends a cold blast down the street, causing the overhead wires to vibrate. Karlshorst looks like a typical German city, its streets lined with squat houses painted in pastel yellow, green, and blue—all almost too pale to actually be considered colors at all.

As they walk, Andreas tells Bea of the doubts that nearly sent him back to Copenhagen.

"I think I'll stay a while and research Peter's life, try to get a better sense of who he was." He turns to Bea to gauge her reaction before continuing. "I'm hoping that you and your mom would be willing to help me. I might even try to talk Grigor Pamjanov some more."

"What are you hoping to accomplish, exactly?"

"I think . . . I think I just want to confirm that my father was, despite everything, a good man."

"Yes, he was," she says, turning to him and smiling.

This newfound purpose relieves Andreas, providing him with a decisiveness he hasn't felt in a long time. He would like to say that this purpose raises his spirits, but perhaps it's more accurate to say that it's because he's made a decision on his own. He's decided to dig into his own life.

The decision is his and not the result of others' expectations, and he is aware that this is a new way of thinking for him. During the past few years, he has been stuck in the past, but the past can remain in Copenhagen. In Berlin he can reinvent himself, wash the slate clean, and start over. It's a liberating thought.

Bea nods. "Of course. You're his son, and you deserve to know who your father was."

"First there's something I would like to know." He tries to sound normal. "How was it possible for you to like him even though you knew what he did for a living?"

Before she responds, she takes a deep and calm breath, as if the question irritates her. "I was nine years old when the Wall fell. I never knew Stasi-man Peter. He was just Uncle Peter. He was nice when the Wall was still standing." She smiles.

When they enter the Oblomov, Grigor Pamjanov calls out to them from across the room. He stands up, the porcelain on the table clinking, and greets them with exaggerated warmth. They sit down and glance around the intimate restaurant. White lace decorations rest atop thick red tablecloths that nearly touch the floor. The chairs are upholstered, and there's a samovar against a coarse brick wall. Above that hangs a portrait of a Russian ice hockey team, all smiles, with missing teeth and gold medals around their necks. In white letters in the bottom right corner, "1984" is written. The thick curtains have been cinched tight on the windows facing the street.

Pamjanov smiles at them. "Everyone believes one must go to Café Moscow to eat Russian food, but they don't know Alexei."

The host approaches to take their orders.

"Alexei here makes the best borscht outside of Russia." As he speaks, he holds the host's hand for an unnecessarily long time. Though the man is smiling, Andreas can see how uncomfortable he feels, and he can tell that Alexei is searching for an excuse to let go, but just as he'd done with their invitation to join him for dinner, Pamjanov insists.

They confer briefly in Russian, and Pamjanov orders without consulting them. Relieved, the host pulls his hand out of Pamjanov's grasp and reaches for his notebook in his apron pocket.

Pamjanov leans confidentially across the table and switches to German. "Did you know that Vladimir Putin was stationed in the GDR, in Dresden? He worked for the KGB. That was before he became our new czar. He ate here whenever he was in Berlin. Isn't that true, Alexei?" He tosses that last observation over his shoulder toward the bar.

Alexei nods eagerly. Andreas tries to determine whether he's enthusiastic about Putin or just trying to satisfy a good customer. Alexei goes behind the counter, then begins to open a bottle of Vedernikov.

Pamjanov turns to Bea. "I've heard a great deal about you. Peter always talked about his little niece, but now you've become a grown woman. Look at her," he says to Andreas, as his eyes wander unabashedly up and down her body.

Andreas can tell she's offended. Pamjanov's straightforward style is intimidating, but she acts nonchalant. Though his manners are vulgar, he clearly considers himself a man of the world.

"He always wanted me to send these postcards. They were meant for you," he says to Bea.

"I never got them. From Peter?"

"Yes."

"Strange." She looks down as if she's lost interest in the conversation. When the waiter sets the appetizers before her, she jams her nicotine gum demonstrably beneath the edge of her plate and begins to nibble on her food.

"Well," Pamjanov says. It's evident that he's used to controlling the conversation. "Were you pleased with the funeral?" he asks Andreas.

Andreas just manages to reply in the affirmative before Pamjanov continues. "It is said that you can measure a man by the number of guests at his funeral."

"So you didn't like Peter?" Bea says, her voice tinged with hurt, as if he's offended her.

His response is swift. "Absolutely. Peter was a good man. Not many people knew that. He wanted his loved ones to be happy, but his methods weren't always the best."

Several dishes are placed on the table, and Alexei pours wine. Pamjanov tastes it knowingly and continues, saying, "Many banged their heads against the Wall when it stood, but Peter didn't run into it until it was gone."

"What do you mean?" Andreas asks.

"The fall of communism was painful to many people, including Peter." He swirls the wine around in his glass expertly as he talks.

They are silent for a while as they eat.

"What about you?" Bea says after she has finished her meal. She sounds a little impertinent, but Andreas seems to be the only one to notice the challenge in her voice.

"I got by. Business is business." He smiles.

"Even during communism?"

"With the right friends, you can earn quite a bit of money. Even during communism." He laughs hollowly, then raises his glass so that his expensive watch appears from under his shirtsleeve. "Some of us were privileged. In my position I could travel wherever I wanted, and I did."

"And what position was that?"

"Business is business."

Bea shoots Andreas a peevish glance, and the silence is interrupted when Alexei removes their plates.

Pamjanov clearly dislikes the silence. "Let's not discuss the past anymore. Sentimentality is something you should flush down the toilet or into your gullet. Prost."

They toast dutifully. Andreas doesn't want Bea to spoil the atmosphere, because he still hopes to learn something more about his father from this man who knew him.

"Did you live in East Berlin back then?" Andreas isn't even sure what *back then* means and just hopes that Pamjanov will tell him more about Peter.

"For a while. You're probably wondering how I knew your father. We met through work. At first we just talked about work. Then we began playing chess and drinking tea, though I tried to get him to drink vodka. After that we became good friends." He looks at his watch and he wipes his mouth with his cloth napkin.

"Can you tell me more about Peter?" It sounds to his ears like a childish question.

The Russian rests his elbows on the table, scrutinizing Andreas intensely. Then he begins. "Peter loved his family. He was very fond of his sister and of you," he says to Bea. "He was a methodical, dutiful man. He believed wholeheartedly in the state and loved his job, and he was good at it. He noted everything, remembered every detail—he kept everything in order. If I arrived late to one of our appointments, he was irritated. He wouldn't say anything, but I could tell." He drains his glass. "And there was something about him that women liked, something impossible to put your finger on. Maybe it was his understated charm or the touch of innocence in his face. When people spoke, he listened, and of course women love that." Pamjanov nods proudly, as if he himself were a master of this art, but Andreas isn't so sure.

"I'm afraid I have a plane to catch," the Russian says, and—as if to brag—adds, "to Cairo." He signals to Alexei, who immediately brings him the check. Pamjanov presses a stack of bills in his hand and pats him on the cheek.

"*Spasiba.*"

He removes a business card from his wallet. "Call me anytime. I'm heading back to Moscow in two weeks."

Then he hands Andreas a wad of bills. "For the taxi."

Before Andreas can refuse, the Russian is on his feet and leaving the restaurant.

Bea stands behind him. "What an idiot." She sighs. "I thought he'd be able to tell us a lot about Peter, even things I didn't know, but all he wanted to talk about was himself. *Look how much money I have. Look, I'm flying to Cairo now.*" She makes a face.

They head out onto the street, and Bea continues. "When I can't find anything positive to say about a person, I look forward to seeing them nourish the plants."

Andreas laughs and suggests getting a beer. She declines, telling him that the funeral wore her out, and he realizes he's exhausted too, and annoyed. Pamjanov was withholding something. He'd talked for hours, but told them nothing. The whole point of the dinner had been lost in all his bragging about his travels.

Maybe his disappointment is really directed toward himself? Is he wasting his time by playing detective like this? Though he has only been in the city a few days, he already feels restless, but he must be patient. He can't unfurl an entire life in such a short time. It'll take a while to get to know Peter, and the faster Andreas comes to terms with this, the less disappointed he'll feel.

He's convinced of one thing, however: Grigor Pamjanov knows more than he's letting on, and one day Andreas will give him a call.

15

PETER

East Berlin, February 1978

His hand inched slowly up the cord, fumbling for the switch. When the nightstand lamp chased away the night, he squinted. Outside it was still dark. He could hear Martina breathe, a soft whistling each time she exhaled. The rhythm of sleep. He observed her. Her face was unperturbed. The bed sheets had left deep marks in her cheek, like on a minted coin. Her mouth was open, and her breath felt like a moist brush against his skin. She had a cold sore in one corner of her mouth. The duvet was pulled up over her slender neck. She wasn't pretty—a thought that astonished him with its sudden appearance. He gently touched her small ear and the swollen hole where she wore her amber earring. She rolled over and wrapped her legs around the duvet. He pulled his hand away. They'd made a pact. He wasn't allowed to watch her while she slept or to speak to her in the morning. In exchange, she wasn't allowed to ask him about his duties in the Ministry for State Security, where she knew he worked.

He'd always wondered what she saw in him. Now, the opposite question had begun to emerge in his head. Staring at her, he questioned his love for her and what it meant. He wanted very much to love her and, for a moment, strained to do so, because the love he felt seemed all too faint to him. He ran his index finger cautiously across her soft cheek. Then he made a decision. A vast sensation filled him; it lay deep within and rang like an echo through his body. He looked at the clock. Though it wasn't even six, there was already something irrevocable about this morning.

He stood up and studied her back in the gleam of the lamp; he listened once more to her breathing and removed a clean shirt from his dresser. One of her hairbands was on the bathroom floor, her brown hair coiled around it like ivy. He imagined her short ponytail, which swayed from side to side whenever she was happy.

He let the water run in the sink until it was hot. When it was just the right temperature, he washed up. He dressed before the mirror in the entranceway, then combed his hair. He'd hung the mirror high, too high, as if it would stretch his body and make him taller. He was five feet eight inches. If he only was a few inches taller, he would be happy. Or a few inches shorter, so that his unhappiness would have a target, but he was the kind of height a person couldn't be satisfied or unsatisfied with: an ordinary height.

When the machine had stopped brewing, he poured the coffee in a thermos and set it on the table. He enjoyed the silence, interrupted only by the light whistle of the thermos. Martina's bare toes creaked against the linoleum floor, and he noticed her sour breath as her lips brushed his cheek. She never spoke in the morning. Her language was reduced to facial expressions: smiles, shrugs, quick embraces. It was as though she didn't have enough voice to spare and was saving it all for the classroom.

The toaster crackled. He watched her as she pulled her legs up underneath her on the chair, yanked her nightgown down, and rocked tiredly back and forth like a small child. She rested her head on her knees. She gave him a deep, warm look, which confirmed the decision he'd made in bed: it was time to propose to her. He kissed her on the cheek, donned his winter jacket in the entranceway, and headed out the door.

A horse-drawn carriage clattered slowly down Kopenhagener Strasse. An odor rose from the horse's mane and flanks, and steam spiraled from its flared nostrils. An arching cloud of dust rose from the bed of the carriage, which contained a cargo of briquettes. During the winter the city was enveloped in thick brown coal smoke, and the penetrating stench clung to his clothes. On Schönhauser Allee, a coal deliveryman was busy filling bicycle bags from a heavily laden handcart. The threadbare leather bags swelled from the weight, and the deliveryman's mouth narrowed to a sharp line each time he swung a bag across his shoulders.

Peter climbed aboard the tram, which sliced through the yellow-brown smoke-saturated fog. When he arrived at the Ministry, he stood outside Sonnenberger's door.

"Peter, come in here a moment." Sonnenberger took a deep, audible breath and chewed on the earpiece of his glasses. "I'm not obligated to tell you this, but I'll do it anyway." He moistened his lips and stared out the window, as if something had caught his attention in the building across the street. He tapped one foot absentmindedly on the floor, and the thump of the sole against the carpet made a soft, pulsating sound. Peter tried to read his expression, but couldn't. He turned to face the same direction as the major.

Sonnenberger cleared his throat. "We're launching a surveillance of Wolfgang Dewald, your brother-in-law."

The last part was unnecessary, of course, but Sonnenberger hadn't wanted to let the name hang in the air. The name created a void, a gap between the words, which he clearly didn't like. He was usually not the kind of man who allowed others to sense what he was thinking, apart from when he spoke of his wife's illness, but in this case, Peter could tell that more was coming.

"We're instituting an operational review of Mr. Dewald." Once again he lifted his glasses to his mouth.

"May I ask on what grounds?" Peter asked impassively.

Peter couldn't imagine Wolfgang planning anything that would bring him into disrepute with the state, but then again, he'd noted how Wolfgang always laughed loudly whenever Russian athletes lost or made mistakes, and Peter once spotted a large hole in one of Wolfgang's socks. When Peter had pointed this out to him, Wolfgang replied that it was his own little anarchic rebellion. Though it was innocent—perhaps even a little childish—many of his actions revealed faint traces of opposition to the state.

"Your brother-in-law has been involved in painting slogans hostile to the state on public buildings." Uwe Sonnenberger peered at him quizzically, clearly wanting to gauge Peter's reaction.

"Well," Peter said.

Wolfgang wasn't an enemy of the state, but he believed that he was. Someone must have convinced him to engage in this pointless little rebellion, and his actions, grounded in stupidity, had been found out. Peter could warn him, tell him to be careful, but that would have to be Wolfgang's own headache. Peter would have no objections to his arrest. It might even be a good thing for Veronika. He'd seen the way they argued loudly and how much frustration permeated their marriage. He felt sure that Veronika was unhappy with her husband.

To indicate that he had nothing against the operation, Peter smiled at the major.

"I would like to ask a favor." Sonnenberger paused.

"Yes." Peter noticed the bite mark on the tip of the earpiece of his glasses.

"If it comes from you, Wolfgang will have no cause for suspicion. You'll give them a telephone, and we'll establish a connection that we can listen in on."

"I'm happy to do it, naturally."

"It's your sister, of course. We'll also be listening to her."

"If Wolfgang has committed a crime against the state, this is what we must do. Besides, Veronika has nothing to hide." Peter didn't feel bad for his brother-in-law. Wolfgang knew the rules, and he'd broken them. There must be consequences.

"Good. So it's settled, then."

Peter could hear the relief in Sonnenberger's voice. The conversation had gone better, it was clear, than his superior had hoped. Peter saw nothing wrong with the assignment. If State Security was correct, then it was obviously in Veronika's best interest as well.

One week later the telephone was installed, and his sister was delighted. The couple had suddenly risen in status. State Security staff knew that whenever they installed a telephone, they would have to listen in on a great deal of unnecessary chatter, whenever family members, friends, or neighbors wanted to borrow the new phone, but even in those cases, of course, they might discover something useful.

Shortly after their conversation, Peter was promoted to an operative. Sonnenberger considered it a waste of Peter's talent to have him working on individual reviews. His skills needed to be put to use in the field. People in the department all said that Peter possessed a highly developed sense of observation, and the major agreed that he was a valuable colleague, and Peter had no reservations about his work for the state. Why would he? Had the state given him any grounds to believe otherwise? Dissidents saw visions, things that existed only in their minds, and only because they inwardly wished that such things existed. Why? Did they really believe that better times awaited them on the other side of the Wall?

He began to work with informants. They were indispensable, so whenever he met them in covert locations—apartments, parks, or a discreet corner of the city—he treated them with respect. They would become close. Peter was the only one who knew their secret identities as informants for State Security, and that created a mutual interdependence. The best informants were stable citizens, honest and loyal and quick to adjust, but those with weak characters could also be exploited.

Now he sat in a cover apartment in Weissensee, across from an unstable citizen by the name of Gisela Rahn. Mrs. Rahn had been careless, and her affair with a local baker had come to the department's attention by way of an informant. In the beginning she had refused to cooperate, but one sentence had brought the gravity of the situation home to her: what if you lose your job at the hair salon? That same day, she signed a letter of intent, and she'd been a valuable informant ever since.

Mrs. Rahn presented a detailed report on a case that immediately aroused Peter's interest. A young woman by the name of Nina Lachner worked in same hair salon as Mrs. Rahn, and her husband, Stefan, often picked her up. The three of them often had a cup of coffee in the backroom after work, and Stefan had made known his unambiguous views about the State. Mrs. Rahn was a friend of the family, which explained why Stefan wasn't afraid to talk. The workers were the foundation of the country; they were regarded as heroes, and not even God or film stars or rock musicians could match their status, but Stefan had miscalculated, and everything he said had reached State Security's ears. Then Stefan had suddenly gone quiet. The informant at the chemical factory where he worked had nothing to report for several weeks, either. Another informant, Stefan's friend, Ulf Kramer, explained that Stefan spent all his time with his brother, Alexander, and that they no longer wished to be around him.

One day when there were no customers in the salon, Nina had confided in Gisela Rahn. Although she hadn't said it directly, the message was clear: Stefan wanted to reach the other side, and she had made it obvious that she'd follow her husband wherever he went.

Peter found all this suspicious, and, in an effort to make sense of what was behind the silence, he decided to begin monitoring Stefan

Lachner himself. He wanted to know who the man was, what he looked like, and how he acted. He attempted to think like a dissident. If he could understand them, if he could understand their driving force and the rationality behind their actions, then he would be better at his job, but no matter how hard he strove to understand them, he couldn't do it. How could they express views about something they didn't understand? They didn't know anything about political correlations or what made a country tick, and yet they somehow formed opinions—the opinions of the ignorant—and defied those who actually understood. Even Peter, who had additional insight based on the strength of his education, didn't feel qualified to have any opinion on the subject. One had to trust those who possessed the knowledge.

From another informant in the building where they lived, Peter knew that Stefan's brother, Alexander Lachner, came and went from the couple's apartment at odd hours of the day. When he pieced all the tiny scraps of information the informants had gathered together, it was clear that it was time to act. Sonnenberger agreed.

A super in the building produced a key to the couple's apartment. They had arranged for Nina to win a lottery among the city's hairdressers. The prize: an all-expense paid weekend trip to Wernigerode. While the couple was away, microphones were installed throughout the apartment. They meticulously pried the covers from electrical outlets and affixed microphones within. Then they screwed the panels back in place once the technical units had completed their work. The entire operation took less than an hour, and that same day Peter paid Gisela Rahn fifty marks for a job well done.

16

ANDREAS

Berlin, November 2006

Andreas thinks of Peter so much that he begins to dream about him, with lifelike scenes of a father and a son. In them the city doesn't appear like it does now; a sepia film covers it, like a filter from the past. They play soccer on a field, feed swans beside a lake, and bike along a canal. Peter doesn't look like he does in the photos: he's the man from Andreas's childhood fantasies. With his masculine jaw, kind eyes, and upper lip that tugs into his mustache whenever he smiles, he shares a striking resemblance to Tom Selleck. Other people appear in his dreams as well. He's certain that he knows them, but they have no faces.

Andreas and Bea sit in her apartment in Kreuzberg. She's told him all about the women in Peter's life, the trips she'd taken with Veronika and Peter, and the people Peter knew. Not until she mentions her own father does he dare to ask about him.

"Where is your father?" Andreas instantly regrets his question. It came out wrong, intrusive and thoughtless. Maybe it's not something she wishes to discuss—maybe it's even painful. Why did he ask? Does he have the right to know? How can he take it back? He can't, but perhaps he can clarify. "I mean . . ." He doesn't know what to say. "Do you have a father?"

"I have a father. Wolfgang." She pauses. "But I've never met him."

As she begins telling him about Wolfgang, he hears the pride in her voice. When she was little, she didn't know anything about him, just that he'd fled to the West in 1980, the year she was born. Veronika never mentioned him, and Bea didn't understand why, but as soon as the Wall fell, she grew more courageous and asked about him. All Veronika said was that he'd fled to the West and was now dead to them. Then she would follow that up with a strong embrace, which Bea always thought lasted unnecessarily long. Veronika squeezed the urge to ask more questions out of her, until her questions were gone. Gone too were the images of Wolfgang in their photo albums, along with every trace that he'd ever lived in the apartment.

"How did he escape?" Andreas asks.

"No one knows."

"Over the Wall?"

"He must have. Or through one of the border crossings." Holding her hands up to her mouth like a funnel, she whispers, "And I think Peter helped him."

"You're kidding. That's crazy."

The tiny dimples on her cheeks become visible.

They sit in silence. Why has Andreas never met his father? Why has Bea never met hers? What kind of forces are in conflict within them? Why are blood relations so important? He notices her smiling dreamily. She's thinking of him now, no doubt, the father she has never met. Right now she and her father are united in her thoughts, just as he'd often been with Peter during his childhood. Ever since the Wall fell, Andreas has dreamed that Peter would turn up one day at their garden gate. Parked on the street would be a Mercedes or some other car indicating how well he'd done for himself following reunification. The shiny metal would gleam in the sunlight, and so too would his smile beneath his mustache. He'd missed his son. From opposite ends of the sidewalk, they would run toward each other and fall into a never-ending embrace.

"I wasn't even born when he fled. Mom was pregnant with me," Bea says, making it clear that she wants to discuss Wolfgang with him.

"Did he know she was pregnant?"

"That's what she says." Bea smiles. "But he writes to me."

Bea has thought about him quite a bit. What he looks like, what he does for a living, whether he's married, whether she has any half brothers or half sisters somewhere in Germany. Every now and then, she gets a postcard from him, one to two each year, never sent from home but when he's on trips, and never on birthdays.

She fetches a box. The words "From Dad" are written on the lid. She opens it and shows him a postcard. Venice is divided into small squares. Andreas recognizes the Campanile di San Marco, the Bridge of Sighs, Piazza San Marco, Rialto Bridge, and a gondolier in a red-and-white striped shirt, then recalls how a gondolier once put his straw hat on Andreas's head. His name was Giuseppe, Luigi, or Aldo, and Thorkild snapped photographs of him. That's what Andreas remembers, the photos. Not the trip, not the Hessian hills, getting carsick, or watching the doves on Piazza San Marco. It was the photographs.

"When I was growing up, people gave my mother funny looks because he had escaped. Just about everyone considered those who fled to be cowards. Had it not been for Peter, things would have been much worse for her. He protected her from the worst of it. They had a strong bond." She pauses as if she this is the first time she's ever considered this fact. "Maybe Georg, their father, brought them closer during their childhood. He was tyrannical." She seems surprised at her own observation about her grandfather. More than a minute passes before she continues.

"I don't have my father's address or anything. I know his name, and I've researched all the central registers, but I doubt that he goes by Wolfgang Dewald anymore. It's like he doesn't want me to find him, which I don't understand. He always writes how much he loves me. Always writes that we'll meet someday."

Andreas doesn't know what to say. When she talks about Wolfgang, she sounds like a little girl. He wonders what Wolfgang gets out of writing her. It seems a pathetic attempt to win her sympathy, and it doesn't seem to do Bea much good. He seems to be using her to relieve his own guilt for having abandoned his family.

Andreas nods, now seeing Peter in a different light. If he assisted Wolfgang in his escape, then he can't be a horrible person, and he clearly looked after Veronika and Bea, taking them on vacations and such. At the realization that Peter sacrificed himself for his sister's family and put himself in danger to aid his brother-in-law, Andreas feels the knot in his belly slowly unraveling.

Andreas is captivated as Bea tells him more about the GDR. "Every aspect of life was controlled and marked by regulations, but if you learned how to wriggle in and out of the system, things went more smoothly. Paperwork simply needed the right signatures." She paused, then continued. "In their spare time, people were interested in only three things: soccer, fishing, and photography. The East Germans were like the Japanese back then; they took photos of everything. Nothing remained undocumented, and every one of them was produced on yellowish-white ORWO paper." Her voice sounds different when she talks about the country that was. It's not longing, but different, heavier and more hopeless.

In her telling, the country comes alive, and he tries to imagine Peter. Rule-bound, correct, dutiful—quite the opposite of Andreas himself, but Peter lived in another time, another country, another culture. The entire mindset behind Stasi is incomprehensible to him. Stasi was built entirely on manipulation and fear, with a complete disregard for human rights. The people were repressed by a state that claimed to be protecting those very same people. Despite his best efforts, he still can't comprehend how Peter could have served as a henchman in such a repressive system.

Bea knows next to nothing about Peter's days at Stasi. "Stasi was a spiderweb of secrets. Even those on staff didn't know what their colleagues in other departments were doing. All I know is that Peter worked quite a bit, but I have no idea what he did all day." She stopped, as though trying to remember Peter back in those days. "Later, after the Wall fell, he worked for a security company called Sonnenberger Security. After work, as far as I know, he went to the bar, and then he went home to bed."

As Bea talks, they begin to organize the pieces of Peter's life, and Andreas can create a complete picture of who his father was. As the stories come out, they make lists of people they can speak to, people who might know something about Peter. They jot down who was at the funeral, figuring that anyone who attended must have known him.

They visit Veronika in her grim neighborhood, but she acts as if she suddenly knows nothing. Maybe it's grief, or maybe she's afraid that Andreas and Bea will learn something that will destroy her memories. Veronika is always guarded around Andreas, he can tell, and every time he asks about Peter, she dodges him with her standard response: "Peter never told me."

At one point Andreas asks Bea about the woman on the tapes, but she doesn't know anything about them. They ask Veronika about them.

"Look at the handwriting here on the case," Andreas tells her. "It's not a man's handwriting. I've seen other documents with his handwriting. This can't be Peter's."

Veronika finally discloses something helpful: the tapes belonged to Kerstin. So Bea and Veronika tell him about Kerstin Hopp.

It's not important, Bea says, but Andreas has to know: who is the woman singing on the tapes? Bea's friend works in a record shop in Kruezberg. Just ask for David, she says.

Andreas heads down there one day while Bea's at the university. Everything in the store is displayed according to an overwhelming floor-to-ceiling principle. There are plastic-wrapped records arranged on racks, scores of T-shirts on coat hooks, and one entire section dedicated to Doc Martens shoes and boots of all kinds.

Andreas riffles disinterestedly through the records and recognizes no names. All the covers look like horror films. He edges past a shaved man with a bodybuilder's physique. Like centipedes, his tattoos crawl from his hands and up under the sleeves of his black T-shirt. Andreas walks hesitantly around the store, and the man behind the counter asks if he can help him with anything. It turns out to be David. In the backroom David locates an old tape recorder. Someone left a cigarette on the speaker, and the plastic has melted there. The tape head is stuck tight and clicks loudly when David presses Play.

Briefly David searches the archive in his mind, past the heavy drawers with punk, metal, and ska, and behind the band Joy Division he finds the answer: Patsy Cline. There's no doubt about it. His mother always listened to her when she was cleaning.

David looks her up on his computer: Patsy Cline, born Virginia Patterson Hensley in 1932 in Winchester, Virginia. Her biggest hits include "Walkin' after Midnight," "I Fall to Pieces," and Willie Nelson's "Crazy." Died March 5, 1963, in a plane crash in Tennessee. Andreas thanks him. David tells him to say hello to Bea, and Andreas can't help but wonder whether they were ever a couple. They seem to be each other's type. Maybe Bea kissed his beard, and maybe David still imagines her naked?

Bea's in the apartment when he gets home. She let herself in. There are some papers on the dining table, an application that Bea printed out for him. As a relative, Andreas has the right to read his father's case files at the Stasi Records Agency, the organization that safeguards Stasi archives.

They fill out the application together. They must be patient, they read, because it could take months before they get a response of any kind. Fearing what he might found out, Andreas's hand shakes as he signs his name, and the envelope lies on the table for three days before he summons the courage to mail it.

17

PETER

How did one propose to a woman? As he saw it, there were only two possibilities: the romantic method or the practical one. The first required him to be romantic, of course. He tried to imagine a scenario, maybe on the bank of the Weissensee with the sun's rays glistening on the sparkling water in the background. He could buy a bottle of wine and put on his finest clothes. The more he thought about it, the more he realized that the practical variant—where the question sounded like a confirmation of the inevitable: "I think we should get married"—would make him less vulnerable. He couldn't actually imagine her rejecting him though.

He understood why he'd waited. It was because of his father. At Veronika and Wolfgang's wedding, Georg had ruined the party. Intoxicated, he'd accidentally overturned the gift table, and his speech to the bridal couple had turned into a whiny ramble about his own wasted life. His bicycle career long forgotten, he was a nobody, just another cog in the state's machine. During his dance with Veronika, he had tripped over his own wobbly legs. They had fallen heavily to the floor, and Veronika broke her hand, so the guests went home. Maybe Georg would drink himself to death before his and Martina's wedding?

Martina was stable and practical. Though he didn't burn with desire for her, he would have a peaceful life with her, and she would allow him to concentrate on his work. She wasn't passionate like Elisabeth, but he decided he loved her enough to marry her.

He frequently asked himself what Elisabeth had seen in him back then. Why she had invited him to the lake? Why she had made love to him? And why she had kept the child when they were no longer together? He couldn't find any explanations, but she'd created a lasting memory in him and a pent-up longing for a son he never would meet. Because he knew he would never see Andreas, he felt a keen desire to have children with Martina.

One day he left work early intending to surprise Martina. On the way home, he bought a bouquet of flowers. When he walked into the building, he heard voices in the stairwell. There were footfalls on the stairs above him, followed by soft murmuring. Perfume wafted into his nose as he passed Gisela Matuschyk's door. He came upon the artist Jens Rembrandt on the landing between the second and third floor, carrying a lamp. When he noticed Peter, he stopped; his cigarette fell from his lips and smoldered at his feet. He was unshaven, and he stared fearfully at Peter. Rembrandt hesitated a moment. Overcoming his sudden confusion, he took a few tentative steps down and refrained from saying hello as he sidled past. Peter paused to examine the burning cigarette, then kicked it down the stairwell with the toe of his shoe. Filth. A luminous streak trailed after it down the shaft of the stairwell like a comet. Rembrandt was practically running toward his door now, the cord clacking loudly against the lamp shade. Not until the man disappeared in his apartment did Peter realize that he knew that lamp: it was Martina's.

Confused, he continued up the stairs. Their apartment door was open, and someone was puttering around inside. In the entranceway he nearly tripped over a cardboard box. Martina was in the living room. The sofa was covered with clothes—her clothes—and the dining table was covered with stuffed bags.

He closed the door slowly behind him, and she glanced up. He was immobile, paralyzed by a thought he'd never considered. She didn't appear alarmed when their eyes met; rather, her expression was stubborn, determined. A long moment of silence followed. She would have to say something. She was the one who needed to explain herself. He waited, feeling empty and numb. He let go of the bouquet, and when the flowers struck the floor, the silk paper rustled.

Though her face was unperturbed, he sensed some uncertainty beneath the surface. For a moment she hesitated, as if trying to make a decision. Then she picked up a heavy box, its weight causing the veins in her forearms to bulge.

"I'm leaving you."

She walked past him. Not long after that, he heard a door slam one floor below.

Martina moved in with Jens Rembrandt. Her conscience demanded that—or so she said—she offer the apartment to Peter. He knew they'd expected him to refuse. How could he live in the same building as the woman who'd just left him?

But Peter stayed. He'd begun to like this part of the city, which was more lively and less blocky than Lichtenberg. Besides, Stefan and Nina Lachner lived on Gleimstrasse. If he moved away, he would have to take himself off the case.

In the beginning he was sad. He couldn't understand why she had left him. She hadn't ever expressed any unhappiness with him, and then suddenly this. He'd hoped that they would learn to love each other.

Though he missed her, he eventually began to wonder if she'd just been a shield against loneliness. His sadness was soon replaced by relief. The marriage would have been a mistake.

Chance meetings in the building were few, but when they did run into each other, they were silent. They hurried past each other without a word, like strangers, then immediately closed their apartment doors and exhaled a sigh of relief. Peter hated being the rejected lover, the abandoned, the unwanted.

18

STEFAN

East Berlin, April 1978

"We're not getting anywhere." Alexander's face was drained of energy, and his voice had sounded unusually somber.

Stefan cracked open a beer and handed it to his brother. Alexander had grown increasingly sulky recently. The enthusiasm that had once enlivened him was fading. Stefan was now the one who had to carry the burden of planning their escape if they were ever to get out of the GDR. Alexander mustn't lose the courage, not now. Stefan needed his help, too.

Their frequent deliberations over the course of a year hadn't brought them any closer to a solution. It seemed impossible; they couldn't simply scale the Wall. Many had already made reckless attempts without proper preparation—based on nothing more than complete faith that will alone was enough to get them over—and such attempts would only get them killed or imprisoned.

Alexander took a sip of his beer and sighed.

"I've thought of something." Stefan waited until his brother looked at him before going on. "Maybe we need help."

"We've discussed that. It's too dangerous to involve others."

"But I have an idea."

"You don't mean Ulf?"

"No. Of course not."

"Good. The only way he can keep a secret is by not knowing it."

Stefan began to explain his idea. If only they knew how others had escaped, maybe they would find a solution. Unfortunately, that information wasn't easy to find. Once an escape route was discovered, Stasi closed the hole and did their utmost to keep the news of it quiet to avoid encouraging others to make their own attempts, but he and Alexander still might learn from others' efforts.

"We'll also learn something by seeing what mistakes people made," Stefan said. "So we can see what we should and shouldn't do."

"I know that."

"Do we know anyone in West Berlin?"

Alexander shook his head dejectedly.

"Ulf has an uncle in West Berlin. Arno." Stefan knew that his brother wouldn't like the suggestion, but he went on. "Ulf doesn't need to know."

"But only if we can keep Ulf out of it. I don't trust him."

Stefan nodded.

"How do we get in touch with him?"

By the time the silver-gray Mercedes slowly rolled around the corner, Stefan had been waiting for two hours. The driver took his time parking the car in front of the building where Ulf lived with his family. Ulf had told him that his uncle was planning to visit. The car gleamed among the oppressive gray of the tall buildings all around. There was no doubt that it had come from West Berlin.

A man in a light cotton coat with a loose belt climbed out. His hair was combed back, and he was deeply suntanned. He hoisted a couple of shopping bags from the trunk.

Stefan gathered his wits for a few moments. Then he exhaled heavily and walked toward the man. "Arno Kramer?"

"Who wants to know?"

Speaking quickly and precisely, Stefan explained the connection to him. If Arno refused to help them, Stefan and Alexander didn't know what else they could do. They'd tried everything. As he spoke, Arno cocked his head to one side and studied him. After a short period of consideration, he agreed to meet Stefan in nearby Volkspark Anton Saefkow in three hours.

Stefan waited on a bench, watching the old gasworks on Dimitroffstrasse. The air above the facility was thick and dark where the three large nineteenth-century smokestacks stood in a row. They'd once been positioned outside of the city, so they had all the room their unwieldy shapes demanded, but the city had grown up around them and now they seemed ungainly. The three fat brothers, they were called. They reminded him of the brothers Grosicki from the building where he grew up. He recalled them waddling down the stairwell; they would lean backward, clutching the railing, as though fearful that their own weight would pull them forward and cause them to roll down the steps like beach balls.

Arno arrived an hour late. Stefan was concerned—it didn't bode well if Arno was unreliable—but he apologized and explained that he'd been invited to stay for dinner. Stefan was relieved. His voice was soft and kind, without the touch of arrogance people from West Berlin generally used to let East Berliners know how superior they were.

Arno wanted to help. He knew a journalist at *Die Welt* who could get what Stefan was asking for. Stefan was well aware of the Axel Springer building, where *Die Welt* was housed, and GSW Immobilien GmbH's building right beside it, from which a large news ticker sent daily propaganda over to the eastern side of the Wall, much to the chagrin of the state. In 1968, the state constructed an entire complex of twenty-three- to twenty-five-story buildings on Leipziger Strasse to block the news ticker and put an end to the free press.

One week later, on the same bench, Arno supplied Stefan with the Western newspapers he'd received from his journalist friend and then smuggled across the border. They included every article covering successful escapes out of the GDR.

"What would it take for you to help us?"

"A roll in the hay with your sister." Arno laughed warmly.

Stefan hesitated. "But I don't have a sister."

"Well, then, I don't want anything." Arno patted his shoulder. "Just let me know if there's anything else I can do for you."

Stefan and Alexander threw themselves into the task of reading all the newspaper clippings. Peter Fechter was the nightmare scenario, someone for whom escape had ended in catastrophe. He and a friend had attempted to scale the Wall near Zimmerstrasse back in 1962, but he was shot. Though his friend made it to the other side, Peter had bled to death not two yards from West Berlin, obstructed by the Wall. While his whimpering was heard by dumbstruck bystanders on the west side of the wall, the East German border guards just watched him die.

They read about people fleeing through tunnels they'd spent months digging; some had been successful by crawling into the sewage system and crossing over onto the subway track, then stopping a train to West Berlin. Others had built a hot-air balloon, constructing the burner from old gas cylinders and parts of a stove, but every time there was a successful escape, State Security increased surveillance.

The Wall had gradually been fortified with a security fence, barbed wire, alarms, floodlights, manned control towers, and dog patrols, so no one could get over it that way. This meant they would need to sneak through a border crossing, and in order to do that, they would need valid papers.

After deliberating intensively over all their options, they chose one that seemed to involve the least risk. They would transform themselves into West German citizens who were only visiting East Berlin for a day. Arno had agreed to smuggle passports, false driver's licenses, and one-day visas to them, and they would produce Western items from their bags: Colgate, Rexona, and Nivea cream would convince the border guards that they'd come from the other side. With the help of Western television, they learned words and phrases that were only used in West Berlin and studied Western behavioral patterns in TV broadcasts.

Nina overcame her fears once she realized the two brothers did not intend to give up on their plans. Though Stefan still doubted whether she would really go through with it when the time came, he sensed her opposition weakening. He understood that she found it difficult to leave her mother, who had been alone since her father's death, but he reminded her at every opportunity that their lives would be changed for the better. They would live freely, and they could have children who would grow up free. The state wouldn't rule their lives, threatening them with prison for speaking out. Although it would be hard, she would have to sacrifice her mother for freedom.

Over the course of the next few months, Arno procured clothes for them, bags from West German stores, West German cigarettes, and even a pack of West German condoms. The paperwork would be more difficult, but Arno assured them that it would work out. Stefan was impatient, but if everything went according to plan, they'd celebrate Christmas on the other side of the Wall. He was invaluable to them, and Stefan occasionally wondered what Arno got out of helping them. One day he put this very question to him. Arno explained his altruistic worldview. Stefan didn't know what he meant, but he greatly appreciated Arno's strange words. "We're not all selfish crooks here in the West, even though that's what your government wants you to think."

"Soon it won't be my government anymore."

Arno laid a hand on Stefan's shoulder and smiled.

One day when Stefan came home, Nina was waiting for him in the kitchen. She was quiet, but he could tell that she wanted to talk. There was coffee on the kitchen table, and Nina sat in her chair, as if she'd been practicing what she wanted to say. He sat down opposite her. He noticed a trail of tears in her mascara. He extended his hand toward her cheek, but she pulled her head away.

"What's wrong?"

She shook her head like a child.

"Tell me."

"I'm pregnant."

19

PETER

East Berlin, March 1980

Nina gave birth in March 1980. There were new sounds in the apartment, and the tone of the surveillance reports changed. Before the birth there had been terrible arguments about how she could get pregnant after they'd agreed to wait on children until they were in West Berlin, but life in the two-bedroom apartment in Gleimstrasse was calmer these days. Peter himself listened in frequently. Stefan and Nina spoke lovingly to the child and to each other, and their voices fell to a whisper whenever Petra slept. Despite Stefan's opposition to the unexpected pregnancy, he seemed to have welcomed his daughter with genuine love. When Peter was listening in, the child's crying made him think of Andreas. His son was four years old now. Though he'd never seen him, he missed him, an incomprehensible emotion given that he'd never met him, but the Wall would always be there—as well it should—and if that meant he would never see his son, then that would be his sacrifice.

Stefan and Nina's escape had been planned to the minutest detail, and State Security knew everything. Surveillance of the couple's apartment had revealed that Stefan, Nina, and Alexander would attempt to escape to West Berlin by pretending to be West German tourists, and to that end they had procured Western passports and papers, items, and clothes. They had been admirably thorough, and had it not been for State Security listening in, Peter was certain that they would have succeeded.

Peter heard Stefan and Alexander trying to persuade a reluctant Nina to make a go of it with the baby. When she finally acquiesced, they set a date for May. In April the couple was arrested, and Peter organized the arrest himself so that he could be sure all went as planned. State Security would take care of the child. That's what he'd told Nina Lachner anyway, though he knew it was a lie. The girl would be raised in an orphanage or, in the best-case scenario, with some family—if anyone wanted her. They'd used a delivery van with the words "Centrum Warenhaus" on the side to pick them up. The driver zigzagged through the city so the couple couldn't determine where they were being taken in the windowless vehicle. After an hour's ride, they arrived at Hohenschönhausen prison. The team that was supposed to retrieve Alexander Lachner at his residence returned empty-handed. Stefan's brother had gotten away, and Peter was furious.

They interrogated Stefan Lachner at length, trying to get him to reveal Alexander's hiding place. They grilled him at all hours of the day and night, but Stefan wouldn't talk. Peter frequently participated in the interrogations, but even he couldn't get him to betray his brother.

One evening on the way home following yet another unsuccessful interrogation, Peter spotted Wolfgang outside a bar in the company of a woman. They didn't notice him, and on a sudden impulse, Peter followed them. They stopped in an archway, and Peter watched them kissing hungrily, then saw her bury her hand deep in Wolfgang's pants. Shaken at what he'd just witnessed, he hurried home.

The next day he sought out Sergeant Gülzow, who he knew oversaw the surveillance of Veronika and Wolfgang. Gülzow let him read the reports. Over a period of four months, Wolfgang had called three different women. The notes describe Wolfgang whispering into the receiver each time, the women speaking to him in amorous, infatuated voices. Assignations were arranged, promises made.

Peter understood what he ought to do: report Wolfgang to Sonnenberger. Of course he couldn't demand that he be arrested on account of infidelity, so he was forced to resort to a white lie. He didn't consider it a transgression of his authority; it was a necessity. Wolfgang was cheating on his sister. He had to be stopped, and Peter was the only one who could do so. If he told Veronika directly, she would be crushed. It would be yet another blow in a long series of defeats. So he resorted to using official channels.

The next day Peter visited Sonnenberger in his office.

"Wolfgang told me, confidentially, of course, that he's going to attempt an escape. He didn't tell me how, but he's going to do it three days from now, on Tuesday."

Sonnenberger looked confused. "He said that?"

"Yes," Peter lied. "He views me as his confidant."

The expression on Sonnenberger's face changed, and Peter could tell what he was thinking. His yearlong surveillance of Wolfgang hadn't been wasted after all. "Well, then, I guess we'll have to get on it."

20

ANDREAS

Berlin, November 2006

Like a door-to-door salesman, Andreas begins to knock on the neighbors' doors. The neighbor across the hall, Greta Riemann-Müller, has only good things to say about Peter. He was always a friendly and helpful man, she says, always very kind.

"He was so good with Paul before he moved to the nursing home." She chokes up when she talks about her husband. She brings out a few books, which she shows him proudly, along with a photograph of Paul shaking Erich Honecker's hand.

None of the other neighbors seem to know Peter at all. They greeted him in the hall, but they never stopped to speak with him. He always reeked of alcohol, says a young woman with a child in her arms. Andreas notices that several become uncomfortable in his presence. Andreas figures that this is because they never took the trouble to get to know Peter, and Andreas is their bad conscience rapping on their door. Before he died, Peter meant nothing to them, but now they're irritated that the man's son is making them feel like they failed him in some way.

He knocks on Sven and Irene Krause's door, the elderly couple who was at the funeral, but she has nothing to say now.

"Did you know Peter at all?" Andreas asks.

But she shakes her head, backs into her apartment, and slams the door.

Andreas has spent entire evenings rummaging through every cabinet and every drawer in search of clues, anything that could tell him more, but he has found nothing of interest. He's alone in the apartment quite a lot. Then he thinks about Lisa. He tries to keep thoughts of her at bay, but they're too insistent. They're lying in bed. He pictures his hand sliding up her back. It rests on her naked shoulder, and he feels the warmth of her skin against his fingers, and he's never going to remove his hand. It should always be right there. He tells her what he's thinking, and she turns and smiles. He misses being looked at like that, misses her smiling at him.

To be alone is not unusual for him. As an only child, one learns such things, and now the city is his companion. He begins to take strolls around Berlin, exploring new parts of the city each day. It's like being intoxicated or dizzily infatuated, like champagne bubbling up to the rim of the glass.

Time has been hard on the city, but it has nonetheless aged gracefully. From the dilapidated to the bourgeois, the endless concrete blocks to the beautiful Altbau buildings, Berlin is a study in contrasts. In some places, Berlin's a shabby hag with missing teeth. Elsewhere it's a boastful playboy, a middle-aged man with leather tassels on his shoes, a well-dressed matron in high heels with an expensive handbag, or a ripped bodybuilder. She's a punk, she's a yuppie, she's a hippie. She's cool and uncool at the same time. She's pure and aromatic, but the side streets need a shower, washed hair, and a clean set of clothes. He walks everywhere but is particularly drawn to the city's underbelly.

He doesn't want to return to Denmark. Lisa has ruined Copenhagen for him. Everything about it reminds him of her—why can't he just forget her?

He calls Thorkild. "Can you pay the rent again? I'll pay you back."
"Of course. Are you okay, Andreas?"
"I'm okay."

Andreas can't fully grasp or manage his love of Berlin, but another threatens as well, and it's something he doesn't want. It has come on slowly. Is it love when you think of another person more than you think of yourself? He thought he could control it, master his emotions, but he's given up. Though he can never have Bea, he wonders whether maybe he loves her precisely *because* she's unobtainable. He suppresses the emotion and tells himself he's an idiot.

They've agreed to meet at Café Cinema before Bea starts work. He gets off at Alexanderplatz. Though the plaza has been decorated with synthetic Christmas ornaments, it somehow smells of spruce. Winking lights in the form of small, plum-shaped bulbs displace the afternoon's growing darkness. There's something oddly beautiful about these illuminated evenings, and Andreas imagines the lights on the Wall erasing the darkness in the same way when they flooded the sky. On the plaza in front of the large Galeria shopping center, hot dog vendors manage their entire operations under their orange umbrellas. They are out-shouted by salesmen hawking candied apples, pretzels, and Christmas cakes from wooden booths arranged around the plaza. Andreas walks by nativity scenes, men and women carrying shopping bags stuffed to bursting, and fathers with tired children drooping on their shoulders. He watches as the heat-seeking are sucked into Galeria, crossing those who've been spat out now that their money is spent. He hurries across the plaza at Hackescher Markt, where more street vendors shiver patiently in the cold.

The café is a Christmas-free zone where guests can enjoy a reprieve from the season's all-embracing pseudo good cheer, says Bea, setting a beer down in front of Andreas. The Ramones' "Merry Christmas (I Don't Wanna Fight Tonight)" blares through the loudspeakers.

Bea has managed to track down a telephone number for Martina Dietzsch. She's written it on a sheet of paper and places it proudly on the table. Martina still lives in the city, in Pankow. He wants to wait, but she convinces him to call her at once. Even though the crinkled paper in his hand is a breakthrough, he has begun to fear this kind of moment. What if she'll talk to him? What if she won't? Will she say things that may be best left unsaid? The questions run laps in his head.

Bea watches him in anticipation as the phone rings. When Martina picks up, Andreas introduces himself.

She's quiet. The line buzzes faintly.

He asks if he can meet her in person.

"It's been so many years." Her voice is hesitant, weak.

"I just want to find out who my father was."

"I'm sorry. I can't help you." She hangs up.

Andreas is disappointed as he heads home. That same evening he calls Grigor Pamjanov.

"Hello." He's clearly drunk. A woman laughs in the background, and Pamjanov sounds distracted. Andreas speaks up, and the Russian returns his focus to the conversation. Yes, yes, Grigor knows everything. For some reason he switches to English, maybe to impress the woman. Something makes Pamjanov sound naked, as if Andreas has caught them right in the middle of the act. He imagines the all-too-young wife, or maybe a prostitute, sitting astride the huge body spilling across the bed. She rides him slowly, while the Russian sweats on the telephone. As though to put an end to the conversation, Pamjanov mentions Ejner Madsen, a Dane Peter had once told him about. The last he'd heard, Ejner Madsen had settled in the GDR. Then he speaks to the woman, who lets out a long moan. Andreas hangs up.

21

STEFAN

East Berlin, April 1980

A fist hammered against the door. Nina was already sitting up in bed when Stefan opened his eyes. He put his hand on the nightstand and feverishly pawed for his watch: 6:22 a.m. Then he realized it was Saturday. Who the hell would wake them up on their day off? The insistent banging left a marked stillness in its wake, and in that stillness he now heard Petra beginning to stir in her crib.

He pulled on a pair of pants and went to the window. The street below was calm and impassive. A delivery van was parked in front of their building, a Barkas B1000, from Centrum Warenhaus. Fumes billowed from the exhaust pipes. A heavy fist pounded against the door again, making the mail slot vibrate. Petra's wailing pierced the apartment.

"Open up. This is State Security."

Their eyes met, and without a word, they said the same thing: it's over, finished, good-bye. He took Nina in his arms so that he would remember the heat of her body. He knew that it would be a long time before he could hold her again. He buried his nose in her hair and inhaled deeply, filling his lungs until they ached. He must remember all of this: her touch, her aroma, her voice. Someone had reported them, but no one knew of their plans, so who could it have been? He didn't know the answer, but it was clear that life as he'd known it was definitively over.

His shoulder grew moist from Nina's tears. Together they went to the crib to gaze at their child. Petra had grown quiet now. Lying on her back, she was jerking her arms and legs. Stefan kissed his fingertips and touched them softly to Petra's forehead. He kissed Nina's wet cheek. Then he opened the door.

Four men dressed in civilian clothes rushed into the apartment, pushing and yelling, forcing Stefan and Nina back. A vase fell from a bureau and shattered, and the shards crunched under the soles of their shoes. Petra cried out. The men had evidently decided their roles ahead of time, as three men advanced on Stefan and one on Nina. The man who held Nina's hands in an iron grip behind her back was panting audibly, as if he was hyperventilating or was sexually aroused.

Stefan's blood surged through his body like a strong current. He glanced at his fists, and turned to the man closest to him and studied his jaw. He looked once more at his hands, then at Nina. He saw the tiny network of veins in her eyes. She had marks on her wrist from the man's hard grasp.

He studied his hands again. They were great big mitts. They could break, flay, and crush. *I am a man. I must defend you; I must defend Petra. They will hurt you. They will hurt us.*

Though her mouth was closed, he heard her words resounding in his head: *Don't do it. I beg you.* And they were her words, and in them he heard her love for him.

Two of the men clutched his shoulder, hard. The other man was clearly ready for the anticipated counterattack, but Stefan was like a declawed animal, tamed by his love for Nina. He wouldn't fight back. It was pointless, and they already had Nina.

As he let himself be guided into the hallway, Nina was suddenly caught between being sensible and a surge of maternal helplessness.

"What about my baby?" she cried.

"We'll take care of her." A man they hadn't noticed until now stood in the doorway. Though what he'd said was meant to be reassuring, it sounded false. Any defiance she had left in her subsided. All hope was lost. That was the actual meaning of the man's words.

The man—who Stefan assumed was a kind of commanding officer for the operation—acted as if he knew what would happen next, as if he could foresee their future. Though he looked young, he had an air of authority. He gestured with his hand, and his subordinates went into motion.

They guided Stefan and Nina down the stairwell to the delivery van and its ticking engine. The inside of the van was parceled into small cells, and they were put in separate units. Stefan sat on a hard seat, next to a man who smelled of tobacco. His handcuffs tightened around his wrists. They drove for what seemed to him hours. Gentle brakes, sharp ninety-degree turns, U-turns, potholes. Outside he could hear the city: the roar of a busy street—probably Karl Marx-Allee, Dimitroffstrasse, or Prenzlauer Allee—and he recognized the sound of an Ikarus bus accelerating, then the rattle and whine of an S-train train moving over the worn, shiny tracks. The sounds of his city, the city he'd grown up in, and the city where an uncertain future awaited them. What would happen to Nina? What would happen to Petra? He was inconsequential; his girls were what mattered to him now, but he was the one who'd brought them all into this mess. Just him.

The sounds faded. The vehicle stopped. "Out." The uniforms outside shouted at them.

Tobacco Breath shoved him in the back. "Get out."

He turned to catch a glimpse of Nina, but they held her in the van until he was gone.

22

ANDREAS

Berlin, November 2006

It turns out there's only *one* Ejner Madsen in all of Germany, and he lives in the village of Stralsund. Andreas rents an Opel Corsa, and Bea accompanies him. She enjoys a little "land air," as she calls it. North of Berlin, they drive through huge tracts of forests, past lakes of all sizes, past fields and endless heaths. The landscape is flat here, as if a large rolling pin has leveled everything. It's a long trip. They chat and listen to music on the scratchy car radio, which gets no help from the broken antennae.

He's glad that Bea's with him. She's the exact opposite of Lisa, and her foreignness fascinates him. She was born in the GDR, her mouth is too broad, and she laughs too loud when she tells lewd jokes. Plus she's not afraid to use dirty German invectives that make Andreas blush. Her clothes are threadbare, like the country she grew up in; she's tall, lanky, and boyish in appearance. Her breasts are nearly imperceptible beneath her shirt, unlike Lisa's, which were neither too large nor too small but filled her blouse in such a way that turned him on. Still, he's attracted to Bea, and he knows that it's much more than sexual attraction.

"I'm feeling kind of guilty, Andreas. I mean, I haven't been much help to you since you came to Berlin."

Andreas doesn't know how to respond.

"You know, new lover and all that," she says apologetically. She begins to hum.

He has a sudden urge to tell her what's on his mind. No more secret desires or checking out her ass on the sly. He steals a glance, trying to determine what would happen if he told her. He feels he's got to tell her. If he doesn't do it now, he never will.

He looks back at the road. "I'm in love with you."

"What did you say?" She stops humming.

He snaps on the turn signal and crosses into the passing lane. "I'm in love with you."

"You don't mean that." Her voice is suddenly tense.

"Yes, I do." For some reason he can't explain, he smiles. He has said what he wanted to say, but he can't gauge her response. Something in her tone of voice makes him uncertain. He looks down at her hands, which lie in her lap. She taps soundlessly against her thighs with her fingertips, and he figures that he's made her uncomfortable. He senses her restlessness. She reaches in her purse for a piece of nicotine gum.

"What the hell, Andreas. Haven't you figured it out yet?"

"Figured out what?'

"I'm a lesbian!"

He signals to the right and shifts the Corsa back to the inside lane. "No," he says softly.

"My girlfriend's name is Alice."

He looks at her, and suddenly they sputter with laughter that seems to go on for minutes. Neither one of them can stop. Their glee fills the car, and they carry on until the car is drained of air.

"Why are we laughing?" Bea stammers.

Andreas shrugs, and that makes them laugh until tears roll down their cheeks. He's relieved that he told her, and he feels a hint of pride, too. Though part of him, deep down, didn't believe he could do it, he had done it. He was brave and told her how he felt. The result is far from what he'd hoped, but his sense of self has changed.

How had he overlooked all the signs? Or maybe he just refused to admit it? The way she often made remarks whenever she saw a beautiful woman; her love of Annie Lennox, Ani DiFranco, and Skunk Anansie; and her little asides and comments. He wishes she had told him outright. Then he could've saved himself the trouble of all these emotions. She tries to get his attention, but he stays focused on the white stripes vanishing beneath the car.

After almost three hours of driving, they reach the waterfront town of Stralsund. The harbor's in disarray, and the enormous shipyard—once the pride of the GDR—is now in and out of bankruptcy.

Ejner's neighborhood is a dilapidated patchwork of crumbling façades, pothole-riddled streets, and prefabricated concrete apartment blocks with roofs made of cheap asbestos cement sheets. The stairwell reeks of something indefinable—like a hamster cage, or maybe someone using it as a toilet. There's a bent teaspoon on the stairs, along with a ball of tinfoil, and Andreas begins to regret the trip.

Ejner's flannel shirt is unbuttoned underneath his leather vest, his beard is thick and unkempt, and his hair is long. He offers Andreas a pale, liver-spotted hand. Because of his enormous, ungainly body and the stench of the apartment, Andreas has no desire to enter, but he and Bea nonetheless follow the Dane inside.

They sit in the living room, and in a rusty voice, Ejner tells them he used to live in the Danish harbor town of Korsør; he worked down at the harbor and passed on information to the GDR about the naval station, NATO exercises—anything that might be of interest to Stasi, for whom he'd been working since 1975. In the mideighties, he decided he'd had enough. Because he was a member of the Danish Communist

Party, he was monitored by the Danish secret service, and he started to fear that he'd be outed as a spy.

"I moved here when I got divorced."

"Why Stralsund?" Andreas asks, suddenly realizing how long it has been since he's spoken Danish.

"I could find work here. I'd stayed in contact with Peter, but he wouldn't help me, even though he owed me. We were friends, and I'd always helped him, but he told me they had more use for me in Denmark, that they would lose an important contact if I left, but I had to get away, and the GDR was where I wanted to go. He kept pressuring me, telling me that I was too valuable and should stay in Korsør. They sent others to convince me to stay too, but I insisted, and that was it. I never heard from him again." Ejner removes a pack of tobacco from his leather vest.

Andreas feels bad for him, but he's mostly thinking of Bea. He never should have told her that he was in love with her. It's best if he puts that episode behind him as quickly as possible. Otherwise it'll ruin his relationship with her, and he doesn't want that.

As they return to the car, Andreas glances up at the apartment. Ejner lives a lonely life in the middle of overcrowded apartment blocks. He is unemployed, with no future. His story is a sad one, and Peter was an accomplice in his decline.

Andreas can't get comfortable in his seat. His seatbelt is cutting into him. Should he have helped Ejner? Should he have given him some of the money he'd borrowed from Thorkild?

Ejner stares out the window. He raises his hand to wave, and Andreas does the same. Then he turns the key in the ignition, and they head back to Berlin.

23

STEFAN

East Berlin, April 1980

"Remove your clothes."

Stefan stood in his underwear before a uniformed man who sat behind a desk. Another stood next to the wall. A third was posted at the door. On the desk were an ink blotter, an ink pad, some papers, and a telephone with a blinking red light. The man behind the desk glanced up at Stefan in what looked like an attempt to appear friendly, but there was something false about his smile, which couldn't hide the contempt in his eyes. He asked his first question with a sigh. Stefan answered mechanically—that one and all the questions that followed—and the man wrote the answers down on a form. Stefan's mind was elsewhere. None of this had happened. Suddenly he saw himself from a bird's-eye view, nearly naked, his dark body hair curling over his skin, on his back, on his chest as if to shield him from this humiliation. The soles of his bare feet pressed against the cold floor and brought him back to reality. *This is the lowest a person can sink.*

"Pull your underwear down."

Stefan hesitated, and the order was repeated, more sharply this time.

He pulled his underwear down to his knees, slowly, a silent protest, and let them drop to his ankles. The sight of his white cotton underwear filled him with an overwhelming sadness. He had the material to make a white flag; all he needed was a pole to hang it on, then his surrender would be complete. He struggled to keep his tears in check. The man behind the desk glowered at his genitals, and smiled. They were here to bend him, break him, and humiliate him, and they were enjoying themselves. Stefan wondered how their food tasted when they came home from work. What did they say to their children when they told them about their day?

The man next to the wall stirred. "Bend over, and spread your cheeks."

The man was so close that Stefan could smell his uniform, which mixed with the scent of the plastic gloves. The man bent Stefan over and shoved a hooked finger into his anus. He moved it in circles before pulling it out.

"Pull your foreskin back." The man stood now in front of him, Stefan's limp member in his gloved hand.

I'm not here. This is not happening.

"Are you listening, Mr. Lachner?"

Stefan hesitated. "I demand a lawyer."

"This isn't an American television series," said the man behind the desk, laughing. Then his face became somber again. "Mr. Stefan Lachner." He let the words hang in the air. "Forget your name. You will no longer need it. From now on, you're prisoner number 243. Get dressed." He pointed at a stack of clothes on a chair beside the door.

The cell was cramped. There was a cot made of dark wood beneath the barred window. It was raised a little on one end as if to help the prisoner know which direction to rest his head. His new home consisted of a mattress upholstered with faded floral fabric, a nearly flat pillow, a low desk, a footstool, a washbasin, and a toilet in the corner. The two-tone walls were white with a yellow-brown stripe right down the center, and the marbled floor was clammy and cold. When is a room large enough to call it a room? He sat down tentatively on the hard mattress and buried his head in his hands. Not this.

He thought of Petra. Her naturally sweet, perfumed scent; her toes that were like small, blond hazelnuts; her warmth that could envelope him, Nina, and the entire apartment. When would he see her again?

As evening fell, he was still thinking of his daughter and how she could sleep in the same position all night long. The guards had instructed him—or rather ordered him—to sleep only on his back, with his hands along his sides on top of the blanket. He doubted if he could. He always fell asleep on his belly. At 10:00 p.m., the merciless lightbulb on the ceiling was snapped off. The mattress bored into his back. He tried to bend one leg, then the other, but he couldn't get comfortable. *Where is Nina? Are they treating her the same way? How many nights will this last? When . . . ?*

A hundred-watt bulb tore him out of his reverie and back to his cell. It penetrated the entire room and made his eyes twitch.

"Prisoner 243, adopt the correct sleeping position! On your back! Hands on the blanket!" The shout echoed in his skull. He tried in vain to get to sleep.

The next morning, a guard came to fetch him. The huge cell door slammed shut with a bang, vibrating in Stefan's ears as they started to walk down the hall.

Stefan was guided roughly down several frighteningly long corridors. The prison's halls were endless, stretching through time and space. They were built to make prisoners feel small, and it worked—Stefan felt smaller, both inwardly and outwardly, as he walked on the linoleum floor's seemingly infinite patterns. All hope was lost here. There was no mercy.

They eventually stopped at a door. The guard knocked three times, pausing between each one. "Come in."

"Prisoner number 243 ready for interrogation!"

"Thank you. Sit down. My name is Emil Brank."

The man who sat across from Stefan appeared to have a steely resolve. His eyes looked welcoming, but Stefan didn't dare believe in their sincerity. His hair—which couldn't seem to decide whether it was ash-blond or red—was combed back, except for a lock of his bangs that broke jauntily to one side. His ears were large, and his earlobes stretched down toward his strong chin.

Stefan glanced around. This room was longer and wider than his cell and furnished with a table, two upholstered chairs, an architect's lamp with weak springs, and heavy curtains. The only decoration consisted of framed photographs of Ernst Thälmann and Felix Dzerzhinsky on the wall, and a plastic plant on top of a filing cabinet.

The man studied Stefan at length. He seemed to be asking himself what kind of hooligan he would be dealing with now. Stefan stared back in an effort to appear defiant. He knew what they wanted. He was supposed to admit that they'd planned to flee the country, He was supposed to apologize and repent for his traitorous actions, and he was supposed to tell them how they'd intended to escape, but he wouldn't let them break him. If he and Nina managed to get out of here someday, which he doubted, they still had the passports and the papers that Stefan had hidden in a secure location. Though their chances of escape were slim, he wouldn't make the man's job easy.

"What is our crime?"

"An escape attempt."

"We didn't attempt to escape."

"No, you didn't get that far." Emil Brank smiled at him as if they'd been friends for years, then got right down to it. The questions came in bursts, at first with deliberate pauses to allow him to reply, but gradually in rapid-fire succession. Brank sat motionless and stiff in his chair. Whenever he smiled—and he did so often as if to underscore the relationship between them—the skin of his cheeks stretched tightly. Question, answer, question, answer, question, answer. Stefan grew hot. He heard himself talk and yet didn't. He knew how he wanted to respond, but wasn't sure that what he'd told himself to say was what came out his mouth. Emil Brank occasionally nodded encouragingly, almost appreciatively; sometimes he shook his head, evidently displeased.

The interrogations continued for weeks, and Stefan lost all sense of time; it felt like months—years—had passed since his former life. Every day he was brought to this little room. Emil Brank always modified the conversations, turning up the heat, turning it down, rewording his questions, catching him off guard with a supplemental query. Stefan tried to tell the same story at every interrogation, always denying everything—even though the truth gnawed at him. The sentences were a tangle of ribbons, streams of words intoned without variation.

They fetched him at night, in the morning, afternoon, and evening—there was no pattern. He never saw another prisoner as they guided him down the corridors. When another prisoner was being moved, he was ordered to turn away and stare at the wall. The guards clearly wanted to ensure that the prisoners never caught a glimpse of each other, deepening their sense of isolation. His only company was Emil Brank, and Emil Brank was always the same, regardless of the time of day. His tightly combed-back hair; his small, jaunty lock; the uniform that was too small around his arms and shoulders; his wedding ring that he spun around his finger to hold his impatience at bay. With each conversation Stefan grew weaker and more passive. His strength gradually ebbed out of him. He used his time in the cell to think about the interrogations, and he used his time in the interrogations to think about his quiet time in the cell. Nina wouldn't be able to withstand this pressure. Maybe she'd already told them everything. They claimed that was the case, but could he believe them?

Brank was in a good mood this morning or afternoon—whatever it was, Stefan didn't care anymore. Brank opened a folder, took a pen from the desk, and leaned back in his chair. He smiled, looking more self-assured than ever. The door opened behind Stefan, and a new man entered, the same young man with the air of authority who'd watched from the stairwell as they were arrested. He greeted Brank quickly before turning his attention to Stefan, who was seated in the center of the room. Then he nodded at Brank, and Brank began to speak.

"We know that you and Mrs. Lachner helped your brother escape. We know that you participated in the planning, and we know that you were supposed to follow him later. Is this correct?" Brank looked expectantly at Stefan, who mumbled an unintelligible denial.

"We know that Alexander is in West Berlin—we've had this confirmed—and we know that he fled the same day that we arrested you and your wife. Somehow, he must've discovered that you and Mrs. Lachner were arrested, and that hastened his escape. So your plan worked. Isn't it a shame to sit here knowing that?"

Stefan continued to stare at the floor. Alexander had made it. Hadn't they just said as much?

The new man chimed in. "Planning an escape and maintaining contact with a journalist from *Die Welt*. The first offense *alone* means two to three years in prison for you and your wife. With the other offense thrown in, you're looking at five years in prison. Five years!"

Against his will, tears began to run down Stefan's cheeks.

24

PETER

East Berlin, July 1980

Peter got off the tram at Schönhauser Allee and headed toward home. The sun baked the city, and everyone was suddenly missing the harsh winter of the previous year, when the entire country was frozen in a hard knot of white. They'd all cursed the cold back then, of course, but now it seemed oddly enticing.

He stood for a moment in the cool stairway. Then he went upstairs, pausing in front of the apartment where Jens Rembrandt and Martina had lived. Their relationship had cooled after a few months. Opposites attract, but what had they expected from such a practical person and an artist? Although Martina had tried, tearfully, to get her apartment back, she hadn't been able to do so, for Peter had made sure that the Housing Administration transferred it into his name when she moved out. Rembrandt didn't live in the building anymore, either. A middle-aged couple without kids had moved in.

He didn't know how long he'd been staring at the door. He noticed an eye staring at him through the peephole, so Peter continued to his own place. He put his shoes in the entranceway, removed his tie, and changed his shirt. Then the telephone rang.

At first the line was silent. Then a voice.

"Something terrible has happened, Peter. Will you come?" Without waiting for a response, Sonnenberger added, "At once, please."

A short while later, the major greeted him in his office. Peter's clean shirt was soaked with sweat following another ride in the tram. Sonnenberger apologized, but he had to talk to Peter face-to-face. Sweat pearled on Sonnenberger's forehead, forming small patterns in his eyebrows, which were furrowed in concern. "It's Wolfgang," he said, blowing cigarette smoke from his mouth in little bursts.

Wolfgang had been arrested two weeks earlier. A long prison sentence awaited him, and for what? For having been more than his usual stupid: writing slogans on buildings. Peter had nothing but contempt for such idiocy. He'd consoled Veronika, assuring her that Wolfgang would soon return, though he knew it wasn't true. According to section 215 of the penal code, his brother-in-law was looking at five years in prison. It was a long time, but he deserved it, and Veronika would be better off without him.

"What happened to Wolfgang?"

The major sighed. "There's no easy way to say this, so I might as well be blunt." He paused for a long moment. "I'm afraid I've just learned," Sonnenberger said apologetically, "that Wolfgang committed suicide."

Dead? Wolfgang? Suicide? He was momentarily shocked. That certainly hadn't been Peter's intention when he had Wolfgang arrested. He was shocked that he would do such a thing.

"Why would a man do that?" the major said, removing his glasses and nibbling on the earpiece. Suicide was a form of defeat, Sonnenberger knew. Such deaths tormented him, creasing his forehead with worry, and he wasn't even the one responsible—the one people would point fingers at, the one who would have to write a report and stand at attention, but the state's responsibility was his responsibility. The state became unhappy whenever a prisoner pronounced judgment on himself.

"But how?" Peter asked, trying to come to terms with Wolfgang's death.

"We're looking into that."

Peter knew that he didn't wish to say more but didn't understand how this could happen. In the past, prisoners had committed suicide more frequently, but prisons now took every measure to prevent suicides. Guards zealously monitored the prisoners in their cells, and they'd installed a new, modern alarm system to prevent such things from taking place. Even so, Wolfgang had managed the feat.

Sonnenberger moved on to another topic, as if the matter was closed. "Can you head out to the prison tomorrow? You should interrogate Nina Lachner. You're already interrogating her husband, aren't you? So you're briefed on their situation."

Peter nodded as the news of his brother-in-law's death echoed in his head.

"Take Ms. Majenka with you. A woman might be able to make her talk."

On his way to the prison the next day, he thought about his visit to his sister the night before. Usually, he never arrived unannounced, and she'd been surprised to see him. She'd sobbed through her handkerchief, crying heartrendingly for a long time, when she told him the news, but gradually, her grief gave way to anger, and Peter knew why. Suicide was embarrassing and cowardly, a selfish act, and his action was the ultimate humiliation for her, a final slap in the face.

The prison was at the end of a long, desolate boulevard. Only those who worked in the prison knew of it. The area was so vast that it ought to have had its own city map, but it didn't exist on any cartographical drawings. Every building surrounding the prison was owned by the

Ministry for State Security, so unauthorized visitors didn't have access. It had been built on a military site, and every entrance road was sealed off behind barricades manned by guards. Peter had been here often, and each time he was struck by the same disheartening sight: the thick concrete walls, the barred windows, the dull buildings, the long linoleum corridors, the barbed wire fence, the beaten-down prisoners.

Peter signed in at the front gate. Cell block B and its interrogation rooms were on the second floor. There were 120 interrogation rooms in all. He opened number 56 without knocking. Emil Brank stood by the window, speaking with Ms. Majenka in a hushed voice. In the center of the room was a desk, which was empty except for a slate-gray telephone.

Peter cleared his throat, and the two immediately ended their conversation. With a superior present, Emil Brank suddenly appeared eager. "Operation Dremler," he said, setting the case files on the table.

Brank had interrogated Nina Lachner several times since she had arrived in April: at night, during the day, for a few minutes at a time, sometimes for hours—all in an effort to wear her down. Until now it had just been Brank, Nina, and the same question: How did you help Alexander Lachner escape? He repeated this question over and over, revising it in minor ways. It was of the utmost importance that they find out exactly how he'd escaped. Who had provided the papers? Who had helped them plan it? Were others planning to go as well? Without this information, a hole would remain, a ruined mesh in the net they'd constructed around the Wall, and today she would tell them.

"Maybe she'll be confused by the sight of three of us," Brank said, looking at Peter and Majenka. "It'll put more pressure on her."

"If she still won't reveal how Stefan's brother got away, you and I will leave the room," Peter said to Brank. Then he turned to Majenka. "And you can give it a shot."

He explained that she was to pretend to be a secretary who was writing down the interrogation minutes, and she should make eye contact with the prisoner while Peter and Emil interrogated her. If Nina sensed that Majenka was a sympathetic presence, she might open up to Majenka, who was good at putting prisoners at ease. Once they had a narrow opening, the rest would come.

Meanwhile, Stefan Lachner sat in another cell. Peter had interrogated him several times, but he was just as stubborn as his wife. They were each looking at five-year prison terms, after which they would be stripped of their rights. Concealing information from the interrogator did them no favors. What did they stand to gain from hiding how Alexander Lachner managed to escape?

Brank seemed irritable as he spoke to the guard. "Bring me prisoner number 324."

A guard led Nina Lachner in and guided her into an upholstered chair in front of the desk. Brank nodded at the guard, who immediately left the room. This was the first time Peter had the chance to observe Nina closely. The prisoner who sat before him now was very different from the Nina he'd seen in the photographs. Gone were the meticulous makeup and the bouncy, permed curls. Her hair was now greasy and tousled and even turning gray in places.

"What have you done to my daughter?" She stared at them through her eyeglasses.

"I'm still the one who asks the questions," Brank said, trying to sound patient.

"What have you done with my Petra?"

"Mrs. Lachner, I'm the one who asks the questions."

They began to interrogate her, but Nina didn't respond. Peter heard the irritation growing in Brank's voice and tried to get his attention, but Brank was focused entirely on the woman before him.

"Listen, Mrs. Lachner. We know that you helped your husband's brother flee the country, and once again I ask you: How did you help him?"

She pressed her lips together defiantly.

Peter interjected. "You have a sister, right? And she has three children? Am I correct that she's a teacher?—or, rather, still a teacher, so long as you cooperate?"

Still nothing. Behind her glasses her eyes were dull.

Peter nodded at Brank, who lifted the telephone receiver and spun the dial. "Brank here. I'm interrogating prison number 324. Is it true that we brought her parents in yesterday? Yes. Wonderful." He hung up.

Brank smiled haughtily. "Your mother is sitting in cell 212, your father in 213. Are you sure you don't wish to help us?"

"You're bluffing. My father is dead."

Peter felt a surge of anger. How could Brank make such an amateurish mistake? Peter watched as Brank stood and walked to the other side of the desk. Brank's cheeks flushed scarlet, and he struck Nina on the side of the face with the flat of his hand. Her chair rocked unsteadily, then found its balance. The blow left a hand-shaped welt on her cheek. Peter's mind flashed to a plaster cast of his sister's hand with his smaller handprint just below it. His family had displayed it on the living room wall. He could still recall the way the plaster had oozed between his fingers.

Peter knew that Brank had struck her because he was frustrated by his own mistake. He raised his hand once more in yet another attempt to cover his own incompetence.

"Stop," Peter said sharply, but not before Brank struck Nina across the nose with a clenched fist. She screamed as her chair tipped sideways. Her head struck the edge of the steel desk, and she thumped onto the floor.

Peter glanced over at Ms. Majenka. Her typewriter was quiet now. She was trembling, and the muscles in her jaw quivered slightly. She sniffled. Peter went around her chair and laid his hands on her shoulders. She sighed as he slowly lifted her from her chair and guided her into the corridor. She apologized softly as he returned to the interrogation room, closing the door behind him.

Brank looked at him, furious. "What the hell was that about?"

Peter had no intention of defending Majenka. "Get her up," he said softly, pointing at Nina.

Brank tried to position her on the chair, but her head fell slackly backward. Her face was drained of color, her features already fading. He patted her cheeks, but there was no sign of life.

"Is she breathing?"

Peter held one hand under her nose and leaned forward. With his ear close to her nostrils, he concentrated. Nothing. He put two fingers on her jugular, and then he knew. Nina Lachner was dead.

Brank looked at him hesitantly. "I'm sorry, but I know she helped Alexander!" He picked up her glasses and tried to put them on her. They slid off and landed in her lap.

"You're a specially trained interrogator. How could you let this happen?"

Brank stared at the floor. "What can I say? I'm sorry. I've never struck a prisoner before."

"You're not capable of doing your job if you take it personally."

"My wife asked me for a divorce this morning," he said quietly, clearly seeking to justify his actions.

Peter ignored the remark. "I had the situation under control. If I'd been able to tell her that we'd taken her daughter, she would have talked. You ruined it!"

"I've never heard of anyone dying from striking their head on the edge of a desk." Emil Brank rubbed his knuckles.

The two men regarded Nina Lachner, who sat slumped in the chair. Her nose was broken, and one of her temples was caved in. What would Peter tell Sonnenberger? The woman he'd spent so much time investigating was dead because of an interrogator reeling from the prospect of divorce, and how could she have died from a harmless fall? They called in a prison doctor.

"If the edge of the desk had been soft, a beveled piece of wood, she'd still be alive. What can I tell you? It's dumb luck. Case closed." As if to show his discomfort at this situation, the doctor began furiously packing up his kit.

Peter ran his hand across the sharp edge of the desk; the metal frame felt cold against his fingertips. Hard to believe that so little could do such damage.

When he emerged from the interrogation room, Ms. Majenka was still standing in the corridor. She clutched him pleadingly with both hands.

"I'm sorry. It'll never happen again. I'm sorry, but when she mentioned the child, and the punches . . . I . . ." She tried to regain her composure. "Will you report me?"

"No," Peter replied.

25

ANDREAS

Berlin, January 2007

The cold follows him like a stray dog. At the intersection of Alexanderstrasse and Karl Marx-Allee is an epicenter of biting cold air, which swirls around him as he waits for the lights to turn. The icy wind penetrates his clothes; he isn't wearing enough layers. It's hard to respect winter in a big city; only when the cold reaches down between the buildings is it taken seriously. Maybe his subconscious is just trying to distract him from the appointment he's going to, one he's been dreading ever since he made it.

Bea had explained to him how Stasi kept meticulous records, writing reports about even the most insignificant incidents. After reunification, the truth tore families apart, caused marital rifts, and broke up friendships. People started reading the reports with perhaps a hint of doubt and often finished them with a look of stunned disbelief. Andreas will now have access to all of that information, and he's scared. What if he emerges hating his father, whose genes he shares?

The Stasi Records Agency is located in a gray building only a few minutes from Alexanderplatz. He'd hoped it would be a longer walk; he's not ready. He pauses for a moment and braces himself, but the cold soon gets him moving again. He ascends the stairs slowly, takes a deep breath, and opens the door. He stops just inside the door, trying to get a sense of the place. The silence is striking, almost terrifying. If silence could be measured, this could be described as gigantic. Behind him, on the other side of the door, is Karl Liebknecht Strasse, one of the busiest streets in the city, but inside this building it might as well not exist.

At first glance, the lobby seems deserted. Then a woman wheels a cart filled with colored files past him. The sound of the wheels on the shiny tile floor momentarily breaks the silence. His eyes dart around the room. A pair of eyes catches his and hold his gaze, kindly. Andreas walks to the reception counter.

A man is standing behind the counter, next to a woman who is seated beside him. They're wearing uniforms consisting of a white dress shirt and navy-blue vest. The woman wears an orange scarf that matches the color of the man's tie. They are quiet, their conversation low.

When he speaks to them, Andreas's voice has lost its heft, and he has to clear his throat to explain his business. The man asks to see his passport, then slowly flips through the pages. He turns it sideways and switches to English.

"Just a moment, sir."

He makes a telephone call. A minute later, a middle-aged woman arrives to assist Andreas. After introducing herself as Lena Hofmeister, she asks him to have a seat in a leather chair in the lobby. She sits down opposite him. She reminds him of the undertaker at his father's funeral. She explains the procedures, and as she talks his mind drifts. He thinks of a barrel organ player who keeps playing the same tune over and over yet still can't overcome the melancholic atmosphere. He considers cracking a joke to lighten things up, but he can tell that she wants to maintain a somber tone. Just to say something, he asks whether a lot of people still come to learn about their next of kin.

She tells him that they get more than five thousand inquiries every month. "So we won't be out of a job anytime soon," she says with a practiced smile.

It sounds to Andreas as if she has said this many times before.

"Let's go to the reading room." She rises, then swipes a key card to pass through a turnstile. They head down the hallway and stop next to a door. "Reading Room 01," a sign reads.

In a soft voice, she explains, "You'll find the files you've requested on the table. Take your time, and if you don't finish today, you may return another day. I'll come get you whenever you like. Just let the archivist know."

They enter the room. The carpet absorbs the sound of their footfalls—in fact, the room absorbs all sound. It is very quiet. The tables are numbered, and most are occupied by people reading files. Lena Hofmeister seats him at table 12 and leaves the room.

He looks around, discreetly observing the others. Their faces are solemn. One woman at table 5 carefully wipes tears from behind her eyeglasses. She's no longer reading her files but gazing out the window, probably imagining a distant past, remembering what once was. Maybe she's kissing a bearded man or feeling the wind in her hair on the backseat of a Jawa 350.

A man with a comb-over stares in what looks like disbelief at the papers before him. His thick eyeglasses look like a magnifying glass waiting for the sun to set the old records aflame; they shout at the pages: *It can't be true! It can't be true!* Others turn pages carefully as though the files were rare documents from Bologna's Biblioteca Salaborsa. They flip a few pages, then go back, reading more slowly. Like typewriters, their eyes work their way across the page, left to right, then jump to a new line. Are they reading about themselves? Their family? Or maybe about

Peter's doings? All sound is sucked into the carpet—except for the gentle riffle of pages: swush, swush, swush.

The stack of files on Andreas's table is short. On other tables, he sees two or three stacks. At the far end of the room, deep shelves hold countless files. The numbers correspond to the tables, but the shelf that corresponds to table 12 is empty. All of Peter Körber's files are already in front of him.

He takes a deep breath and grabs the thin light-blue file on top: Reg. No. MfS/1664/83. He opens it and begins to read. Name: Peter Körber, Hauptverwaltung Aufklärung (HVA). Main Directorate for Reconnaissance. Transferred to HVA in 1983 from Department XX/5. There are only three or four pages of information about where and when Peter worked. Dates corresponding to his medals, distinctions, and promotions. There is nothing notable, nothing that makes Andreas any wiser.

He opens a new file, Department XX/5, and browses through it. There's a summary data sheet on top followed by forty-three pages that include a resume of Peter's career in the department and his promotions, bonuses, family members, and health. The level of detail is striking, and it's evident that this department had vast insight not only into the country's citizens but also its own employees. He reads about Peter's successful cases, several of which are marked "OPK Files." He turns more pages, and now they're called "OV Files." Names have been redacted with fat black lines across them.

The first reports are signed by Sergeant Peter Körber. Later, he signs as Second Lieutenant Peter Körber, and beginning in 1980, as lieutenant. On several pages, the name U. Sonnenberger appears next to his signature: *U. Sonnenberger, Department Chief.* Andreas makes a note of this and continues reading. One case is thicker than the others: Operation Dremler. Several surveillance reports are signed by Peter. Many of the files are incomplete. They suddenly stop in the middle of one case or start in the middle of another. It's clear that the Stasi Records Agency has been unable to obtain all of the documentation.

At the end of the folder is one final report. Although the names have been redacted, Andreas senses that the person being interrogated in the report is a woman. It seems that she had planned to flee the GDR with her husband and her husband's brother. Over page after page, she is asked the same question and gives the same response, but then the report takes an unexpected turn. The woman suddenly dies. The cause of death is recorded as pneumonia, and the case is sealed. Three signatures appear at the bottom: Lieutenant Körber, Sergeant Brank, and Sergeant Majenka. A small sheet of paper is stapled to the back of the report, and Andreas recognizes his father's handwriting: *Miss Majenka is unsuited for these types of assignments, and I advise that she be transferred to a less demanding unit.* Andreas jots down the names of Sonnenberger, Brank, and Majenka, then closes the file.

The woman at table 5 sniffles and wipes her eyes behind her glasses.

Andreas nods at the archivist, who makes a phone call. In the hallway Lena Hofmeister awaits his reaction. She knows from experience not to ask questions; he senses that quite clearly. He asks her about the incomplete HVA file. She gives him an apologetic look, then explains that it was all they could find. During the period between the fall of the Wall and the spring of 1990, some HVA departments removed nearly everything from the files. She smiles tentatively. She's not sure whether it's true, but she's heard that employees left their data sheets as documentation that they'd worked for the state and were therefore entitled to a pension.

He inquires about Department XX/5, and she tells him that it was considered the core of Stasi. Department XX/5 was the unit that monitored dissidents, the unit that repressed citizens and decided whether to make their lives miserable. Andreas takes it all in, and she falls silent. As he's leaving the building, he's not sure how he feels about all this. Then he finds himself overwhelmed by a deep disappointment. All he got out of this trip was three names: Sonnenberger, Brank, and Majenka.

He heads straight to Bea's apartment. On his way, he wonders what he'd expected. That it would turn out to be a misunderstanding? That Peter Körber would suddenly turn out to be the father he'd always imagined as a child? It is difficult for Andreas to reconcile the man who was so cold and cruel at work with the man who was so affectionate toward his sister and niece and who helped his brother-in-law, Wolfgang, flee to the West. How many contradictions can one person contain?

Some days he feels that he's wasting time. Why does it matter so much to him anyway? Wasn't his childhood a happy one? But he supposes that it's human nature to seek out one's roots. Life is one long journey of discovery, and maybe that's what's driving him—the fact that he now has a concrete objective for his search: to know his own father.

When Bea opens the door, he's struck by how giddy she seems. It's as though she's forgotten where he's been, but then she seems to remember and adopts a more serious tone.

"How was it?"

Once he shows her the note with the three names, she gets angry. "That's all?"

"I'm afraid so." As he says it though, a thought occurs to him: "Can I apply to see their files? Maybe I can find out something more from them."

"No, you can't. It says on the Stasi Records Agency's website that only relatives can access the files." She reads the names out loud and exclaims in surprise, "U. Sonnenberger. That must be Uwe Sonnenberger, the manager of the security company where Peter worked. He shouldn't be hard to find."

"This could be a significant lead," Andreas says. "Sonnenberger obviously knew Peter both before the Wall came down and afterward."

"So that means we have two things to celebrate then," Bea says. "Come join me at Serene Bar tonight." Andreas notices moving boxes behind her and understands what the *other* thing is. Alice is moving in.

"We haven't known each other very long, but we're in love," she says as though apologizing for her news.

"Okay," he says. He wishes it could be just him and Bea, but he doesn't want to be alone tonight.

As he walks home, he thinks about Lisa. He hadn't been entirely truthful when he told Bea about his relationship with Lisa. At the time, he'd wanted to be in the role of victim. He wanted Bea to take his side, and his account had brought them closer, but the fact was that he and Lisa hadn't gone into a slump together; he'd gone into a slump on his own. Or rather, he'd never really gotten going, while Lisa changed before his very eyes. She'd grown tired of his lack of ambition, she'd told him, but of course that was easy for her to say. Lisa had always known what she wanted to be. He admired her for her determination, her ability to set goals and reach them, and that's how she'd become a journalist. She didn't want to be in a relationship that wasn't going anywhere, but Andreas didn't have anything to give her.

26

PETER

East Berlin, July 1980

Uwe Sonnenberger narrowed his eyes and squashed his cigarette. He pressed it down into the push-down ashtray, sending the cigarette butt into rotation; with a flickering metallic sound, it spun down to the others. He'd begun smoking again, off and on, correlating with his wife's condition: the worse she was, the more he smoked.

The carp in the photograph behind him stared at Peter. In the photo, Sonnenberger was standing on a wooden pier near Lake Balaton. He held the big, glistening fish with both hands, his muscles bursting out of his sleeveless tank top from the weight of it, and wore a huge smile on his face.

The conversation was over, yet Peter remained standing.

Sonnenberger glanced up as though only now realizing that Peter was still in his office. "Was there something else, Peter?"

"We interrogated a woman three days ago."

"Yes, it's most unfortunate," Sonnenberger said and lit a new cigarette.

Peter wondered how much time Sonnenberger's wife had left.

The major looked at him. "The doctor who examined her said it's almost impossible to die that way." Sonnenberger took a deep drag on his cigarette. "If you only knew how much paperwork that death has generated for me." He pointed at a pile of papers on his desk. "But what's done is done."

He tapped his fingertips together, and his facial expression was meant to convey sympathy for Nina Lachner's family.

Peter didn't move. "She had a child."

Sonnenberger raised an eyebrow, and Peter began to explain, but the major seemed uninterested in what he was trying to tell him. Before the words poured out of his mouth, Peter hadn't even realized the scope of what he was proposing, but as he spoke, everything crystalized for him.

"Go ahead and do the necessary paperwork. I don't want to get involved in it." His hand located the knot of his tie and loosened it slightly.

"Thank you," Peter said.

Sonnenberger waved him off, making it clear that it was time for Peter to leave.

The white Lada glided out of the city, its windows wide open; it was going to be a hot day. Peter had brought a driver, Jens Hegeler, who was whistling contentedly behind the great mustache that nearly concealed his mouth. His thick sideburns were already damp with sweat.

Peter noticed smoke billowing over the roofs like a gray-yellow fog and looked over at the nearby towering factory chimneys. They were pulsing like a two-stroke engine, belching gray-white clouds and forming an increasingly dense haze that threatened to cover the entire sky. The sun suddenly burst through a frayed hole in the smoke cloud and blinded him in the mirror.

Hegeler looked at him with a delighted expression. Though Peter didn't share his same passion for cars, he knew that was why Hegeler was so upbeat today. With his foot on the accelerator, his hands on the steering wheel, his back against the warm leather, and the knob of the stick shift in his hand, his joy was written all over his face. A childhood memory flashed through his mind.

They'd waited seven years. Because of Georg's past as a cyclist on the national team, the family got special treatment. Georg had never had a driver's license, and his daily intake of alcohol made him unfit for driving, but he'd ordered a car for his wife's sake. When they were told they'd be getting one, Peter's mother immediately started taking classes in order to obtain her license. The driving instructor was a patient man and, after a great deal of hard work, she got her license. Finally, one day, a sand-colored Trabant 601 was delivered from the factory in Zwickau.

His mother's first trip was to pick up Peter and Veronika from school, after which they planned to surprise Georg at the factory. She drove very slowly, and the car trembled unsteadily as she turned her head in all directions to avoid all the unaccustomed dangers. The children were hooting in the back seat. They reached an intersection, and their mother hit the brake too hard, sending Peter and Veronika bouncing over the imitation leather seat with shrieks of laughter. She found the biting point of the clutch and dropped it into first, and the car lurched forward. She inched cautiously along. As they approached their father's factory, a semi honked right beside them, and they swerved straight into a light pole. The hood was ripped open, blocking the windshield. Thankfully, they were all unharmed.

Their mother sighed in resignation, as if this was what she'd expected all along. She took Peter and Veronika by the hand and marched them to the nearest police station. The officer behind the counter was mystified when she returned her license.

"I'll never need this again. Please confiscate it." The look on her face made it clear that she was serious.

They sold the car, and she never drove again.

As the Lada sliced across the landscape, the distance between the factories grew. The factories were gradually replaced by miles of fields interspersed with old villages of ancient peeling houses clustered around identical churches.

They were on their way to Eisenhüttelstadt—formerly Stalinstadt— where Nina Lachner's mother lived by the Polish border. Some people referred to Eisenhüttelstadt as Schrottgorod, or Scraptown, a combination of the German word for *scrap* and the Russian word for *town*. Peter found Scraptown to be a demeaning nickname. People didn't realize how good they had it. Unlike in the West, no one starved, begged, or loitered around, unemployed. Eisenhüttelstadt was a model city, with lots of attractive new homes and plenty of manufacturing jobs to take pride in, and he wished people understood all the benefits they enjoyed in this country.

They could now make out the large blast furnaces that pierced the sky atop factories that processed iron ore from the Soviet Union. The city was a boiling cauldron of scorching hot iron. Judging by the enormous columns of smoke issuing from the chimneys, production was at its peak. This was the GDR at its best. The people owned the means of production, and they produced for themselves. He smiled.

Hegeler turned down a side street. After a couple miles, they came to a small farm. The Lada's wheels jounced over the bumpy cobblestone driveway.

"This must be it," Hegeler said, cutting the engine.

Peter checked the address. "Yes, this is it." He gazed out the window. It was a typical farmhouse with narrow windows, thick walls, and a tile roof covered in green moss.

"Shouldn't we have brought someone from the local municipality, since it's about a kid and all?"

Peter glanced at his watch. In two minutes she'd be late. What a horrible signal for the authorities to send, being late. He rolled up his window. He cocked his head to study the bicyclist who appeared in the side mirror. The woman leaned her bike against a whitewashed wall, smoothed her skirt, and pulled a purse that seemed too large for her from the bike's basket.

"Take off your sunglasses," Peter told Hegeler.

Hegeler put them down on the dashboard, and they got out of the car. "Give the door a good slam so Grandma hears we're here." There was a loud thump as the car door slammed.

The woman approached them holding a folder in her hands. Her short dark hair was cut close to her ears, and her high-heeled shoes were impractical on the uneven cobblestones.

"Are you from Child Protective Services?"

"Yes, I'm Renate Koch," she said, nodding. Peter handed her the papers, and she scrutinized them. "Seems to check out," she said.

She walked behind the two men as they walked to the front door. Peter inhaled audibly, then knocked.

An elderly woman opened the door. Her dress was decorated with a newly ironed lace collar, and her bosom and hips stretched the material, widening the floral pattern in places. Her hair was the same color as the steel that was processed in town.

"Is Nina Lachner your daughter?"

She nodded cautiously.

"We're with the state. Please let us in." Peter tried to drain all emotion from his voice.

The woman hesitated. Her eyes darted between the three unexpected visitors at her door, which she held only partially open. Peter prodded it, forcing her to take a step backward.

"Where's the child?"

The three of them moved past her into the house. They heard a baby babbling in one of the rooms. A faint voice, barely a voice at all, rose and fell like the sound of a playful young animal.

Peter entered a cramped living room. The television flickered. The volume was turned down, but the images were unmistakable: the Moscow Olympics. In one corner of the room was a playpen. He went to it and peered down at the child, who lay in a crocheted shawl, kicking her legs and flailing her arms. She had wispy blond hair, and her narrow, smiling mouth was moist; a dark stain had formed on the top sheet where she'd dribbled spit.

"Is this Stefan and Nina Lachner's daughter?" Peter asked.

The woman nodded silently, looking fearful. Peter handed her the paperwork. "All you have to do is sign at the bottom."

She was slow to react. Then her face fell, and she whimpered. "You can't take her from me." Her despair caused her chin to quiver.

Renate Koch stood next to the woman. "It's best for the child. She'll be in good hands," she explained in a gentle voice.

The woman hesitated, seeming confused.

"You're not young anymore, and you're lucky that she wasn't placed in an orphanage."

"What happened to Nina?"

"Please go to the kitchen while we take care of this matter." Peter nodded at Renate Koch, signaling that she should go with the woman.

The old woman started to object, but Renate put an arm around her shoulders and guided her to the door. Hegeler, who'd been eyeing the television the entire time, turned up the volume, and the sound boomed from the little wooden box. Just as he sat down in a recliner in front of the television, a couple of vertical lines appeared across the screen.

"Goddamn it." Hegeler leaned forward and gave the television a good whack. The images flickered, then came back. He turned to Peter. "Check out Rica Reinisch," he said enthusiastically. "She set a world record in the hundred-meter backstroke the other day. I'll be damned if she isn't about to set another for two hundred meters."

The camera zoomed in on a woman with very short hair, much like Renate Koch's, and broad shoulders and muscular arms. Her blue swimsuit clung to her flat belly and narrow hips. She smiled in a girlish way and waved at the camera.

Peter leaned over the playpen. The little one babbled happily, trying to catch her own feet. Peter caught himself laughing.

On the screen, the swimmers were now in the water, and Peter whispered, "What are we going to do about the girl? How are we going to take her with us?"

At that instant the starting gun went off, and the swimmers were off.

"Listen up, Hegeler. You've got children, right?"

"Two," he said without taking his eyes off the screen.

Peter started to say something.

"Hang on a sec," Hegeler shushed.

The screen was a blur of arms whipping through the water, leaving a trail in their wakes. Peter tilted his head and studied the little girl. He placed one hand underneath her and scooped her up. He was astonished to discover that he wanted to hold her close. Why this urge? Where did it come from? She was surprisingly light, weighing less than a bag of fuel, he thought, as he rocked her somewhat awkwardly. He heard the grandmother's subdued sobs in the kitchen.

"Goddamn! She did it! Look!" Hegeler shot up from the chair. A news flash appeared on the screen: "Another world record. East Germans sweep medals." He hopped up and down in the low-ceilinged living room, clapping enthusiastically. Suddenly he realized how inappropriate his behavior was under the circumstances and stopped abruptly. He looked at Peter, who held the little girl.

I ought to reprimand him. I can't accept that kind of behavior. I'm the superior, and my reputation is on the line, but . . . Peter couldn't muster the energy. He thought of the girl in his arms, of the joy he felt because of her.

Renate Koch entered the room and hurried over to Peter.

"Haven't you ever held a baby before? How do you plan on bringing a child to Berlin?" she exclaimed as she supported the child's head.

This irritated Peter. How was he supposed to know how to hold a child? He'd never done it before, and this woman from some small town whose name he'd already forgotten had no business correcting him. "We'll take care of that, miss, don't you worry." He turned away.

Renate Koch sighed loudly. "That leaves only a bit of paperwork, then. Please fill out the name and address of the child's new guardian."

Peter filled out the forms as Nina's mother watched from the kitchen door. She was crying softly. Tears rolled down her wrinkly cheeks like melting snow. Peter noticed the handkerchief in her hand, which hung limply at her side.

They let themselves out, and Peter got into the backseat, still holding the girl in his arms.

"Ouch! Goddammit!" Hegeler blurted as he slid into the driver's seat.

"You're frightening her," Peter said quietly, so as not to disturb the girl, who appeared to be falling asleep.

Hegeler laughed apologetically. A glinting, sharp red line cut across the bridge of his nose, reflecting off the sunglasses that he'd left on the dashboard. He adjusted the rearview mirror in order to see the baby, and Peter made eye contact with him. Hegeler gave him a rueful glance.

Hegeler shifted into gear, and they headed back to Berlin. Peter was elated. He felt the warmth of the little body through the blanket. He heard his own voice, calm and gentle, and he thought about Andreas. He was four years old now. He didn't think of him often these days, but the girl had stirred something in him. Tenderness? Love? He already felt a sort of kinship with her, and he was looking forward to passing her on. He knew she was going to a good home.

27

ANDREAS

Berlin, January 2007

Last night it snowed, and now the city is sprinkled with white. He's standing in the window watching the back alley, where the asphalt is covered in soft snow. The tracks from a baby carriage look like the marks left by pioneer wagons in bygone days. There's a set of small footprints next to a spot where the snow has been scraped away by a child making snowballs. Andreas felt it the minute he got up that morning: this day is going to be different, maybe even a turning point. It's in the air. When he steps out onto Kopenhagener Strasse, the winter air is ice cold.

Fragments of last night's telephone conversation swirl in his head. Uwe Sonnenberger had yelled at him over the phone, telling him of the pointlessness of rooting around in the past. Peter was dead, and there was no reason to drag his name through the mud. Besides, neither one of them ever had anything to do with Stasi. Andreas tried to explain that he had no intention of dragging Peter's name through the mud, but by then Sonnenberger had already hung up.

He and Bea have given up on locating Kerstin Hopp, whose voice appears on those tapes. It is apparently a common name, and there are Kerstin Hopps scattered throughout the country. The same is true of Brank. Without a given name, it will be impossible to track him down. Thankfully, Andreas did manage to get a hold of Mrs. Hedwig Majenka. When he called her, she refused to meet with him at first, but after some consideration—once he'd mentioned he was Peter Körber's son—she agreed to see him. Bea promised to go with him. After the visit, Andreas will head back to Copenhagen for Elisabeth's birthday.

Hedwig Majenka is the last person on Andreas's list, and if she cannot help him, he'll have to return to square one.

Mrs. Majenka lives in a village. Not the kind of village that's scattered across the provinces and surrounded by fields and meadows, but the kind that's grown over the years to become part of Berlin. Where there were once fields, there are now concrete towers and big-box stores.

The bus plows through a snowdrift. Andreas gets out, then pulls his hat down over his ears. Veronika told him about the great frost of 1978–1979, and even though the temperature is unlikely to drop that low, the cold bites at his face, and his feet sink into the snow with a squeak. Mrs. Majenka lives in a small apartment complex that also houses an Edeka grocery store. The store's yellow façade lights up against the gray city and dark sky. He waits for Bea outside the building, and she soon shows up on Alice's motorcycle.

"Isn't it icy?" he asks, when she removes her helmet and kicks down the kickstand. *I sound like my mom*, he thinks.

She smiles at him tolerantly.

They walk up the stairs, and Andreas knocks on the door.

"So you're Peter Körber's son?" He senses her curiosity as she opens the door.

He nods.

"You sounded a lot like him on the telephone." The woman shakes their hands. She evidently believes he and Bea are a couple, and he doesn't correct that assumption. *It's as close as I'll get,* he thinks.

They exchange pleasantries, and Mrs. Majenka tells him that she's a widow. She moved here from Lichtenberg after her husband died. Her clothes are plain, and she wears flat, practical shoes like the undertaker at his father's funeral. There's something asymmetrical about her face; it looks heavier on the left side. Her head is big and round, and there's a small goiter growing on her neck.

She drags her leg slightly as she leads Andreas and Bea into the dark living room, which is made even darker by winter. The walls hold decorative plates and framed family portraits. On the wall near the window is a clock in a mahogany case, with gold-leaf numbers and a pendulum that has ceased to function. Noticing Andreas's interest in the clock, she retrieves a big key from a drawer in the shelving unit. There's a metallic click as she winds the clock until it fills the living room once again with its slow, regular ticktock, ticktock.

They sit across from her at the dining table, and he exchanges a glance with Bea as Mrs. Majenka fills their cups with coffee from a carafe. They drink politely, and she begins to speak.

"Well, what can I tell you about Peter?" She considers for a moment. "He was very intelligent, always proper. Exemplary."

It sounds like propaganda, and he knows from Elisabeth's long political career that propaganda and lies are created from the same mold. This isn't what he's come to hear. He makes eye contact with her, and he knows that she's considering how best to proceed.

He'll have to tread cautiously. If he presses too hard, he risks frightening her off. He has come across quite a few cases of sudden-onset amnesia and convenient forgetfulness lately, so he holds back patiently. He smiles at Bea and hopes she understands. Then Mrs. Majenka starts telling them about Peter, the prison, and one particular interrogation that she recalls with remarkable clarity.

"Normally we recorded everything on tape, but because I was a woman, I had to pretend to be a secretary. We were going to interrogate one Nina Lachner, who was under suspicion for planning to escape to the West, and we imagined that she'd be more willing to talk to a woman. We just needed her to admit to planning an escape, that's all. We'd agreed in advance that Peter and Emil Brank were going to leave the interrogation room so I'd get to talk to her on my own, but we never made it that far."

"What happened?" Andreas asks.

"I can't tell you."

Yet it seems as though she wants to tell them something that she's holding back. Should he pressure her or just wait? He hesitates, sensing that she needs to talk to someone, to tell her story.

She looks at him shyly. "I was in love with Peter." She's quiet for a moment. "Until the incident with the child."

"What child?" he asks.

"No . . . I can't, I don't really want to say anything more, but I saw the papers when they transferred me to the central administration. After the interrogation, that is."

She folds her hands in her lap. She hesitates again. Andreas can practically feel her pain. Then she clears her throat. "In some cases, Stasi would take the children of dissidents and place them in good families. It wasn't something anyone ever talked about." She pauses, then goes on to explain that parents who didn't raise their children the way the state saw fit risked losing them. This might include people who fled to the West, as well as those who even considered fleeing or anyone who subverted the state in any way. In some cases, that even included people who'd merely applied for visas to travel abroad. "Mothers were forced to sign the adoption papers, and their children were taken away and given to families who could be trusted to raise them with the proper socialist spirit. Some children were stolen from hospital delivery rooms, and their mothers were told that they'd had a stillbirth." Mrs. Majenka's voice trembles. She's clearly appalled by what she's telling them. "Some children are still looking for their mothers," she says.

"How do you know?"

She shrugs her shoulders. She has said all she wishes to say on the matter.

"Why are you telling us all this?" He tries not to sound irritated, but he's having a hard time understanding where she's going.

She shrugs again, and then, like a child caught in a lie, says, in a slow and emphatic voice, "Peter was a good man, until he stopped being a good man. Until the incident with the girl."

"The girl?"

Mrs. Majenka resumes her account of the interrogation. It seems she has decided to tell them what happened after all. She outlines Nina's unfortunate death in brief, broad strokes and mentions Stefan and Nina Lachner's daughter, Petra. She concludes, saying, "Like I said, I was in love with Peter until what happened with the girl."

"What happened with the girl?"

"Peter gave her to his sister."

Mrs. Majenka pours more coffee, then passes around a small plate of cookies and continues. "It was a special case. Veronika was single; her husband had fled the country. If you ask me, she wasn't one of the good families. It was only because of Peter, but then he was special too, and he lived in Prenzlauer Berg, not with the rest of us. Do you two have children?"

Andreas shakes his head. As she continues to speak, it slowly dawns on him what she is saying. He looks at Bea, who's staring at Mrs. Majenka. Her lips are trembling, and her face is drained of all its color; apart from her lips, she's rigid. He wants to establish eye contact with her, but she's somewhere else, far away. She begins to twirl her cup around on the saucer but doesn't seem to hear the grating sound it makes. He rests his hand on top of hers. She pays no heed and keeps twirling the cup.

"If you had children of your own, you'd understand."

It grows quiet. Andreas wants to say something, but he can't think of anything because there are no words. No words at all. Only empty eyes and thick, impenetrable air. He wants to pull Bea close and tell her that everything's going to be all right, but he's not sure that's true.

"More coffee?" Mrs. Majenka asks.

Bea suddenly stands. For a moment she just stands there, confused and indecisive, her eyes darting around the apartment. The decorative plates on the walls, the embroidered bellpull, a little wood-carved donkey on a shelf with tiny barrels on its back. Then she seems to return to herself. She stares in disbelief at Mrs. Majenka for a moment and rushes out of the apartment. Her footsteps echo in the hallway as he runs after her.

She looks small on Alice's motorcycle. It roars like a rodeo bull under her as she guns the engine. He shouts at the helmet, but she's not in there. The motorcycle hisses, she puts it in gear, and it lurches a little as she races off at full tilt. He holds up his hand to shield his eyes from the blinding snow and watches her fly off across the asphalt and disappear around a bend.

What should he have said to her? What could he have said? His heart is beating so hard he can't think straight. Bea isn't his cousin at all. He stops this train of thought. This isn't about him; it doesn't matter whether she's his cousin. This is about Bea. Her world has been turned upside down. Her childhood memories are lies, and her parents Veronika and Wolfgang are frauds; her biological parents are Nina and Stefan, and Nina is dead, and Peter is partly to blame. Andreas understands why she's in shock. His father was at the center of this all along, but Veronika also played a key role, and he wonders whether Bea ever wants to see her again—after all, she's not actually her mother. On the other hand, Veronika raised her—is it possible to simply throw all that away? And what about Wolfgang? Wolfgang was never Bea's father. The man who sends her postcards from all over the world, the man who writes *I love you*, was never her father. He's writing to keep the lie alive. Veronika must have feared this day would come. Now he understands why she's been so evasive in conversations about Peter. She didn't want him and Bea to discover the truth.

He calls Bea's cell phone. He doesn't expect her to answer it, but he needs to talk to her, to say good-bye. All he manages to do is leave an incoherent voice mail. This afternoon he's taking the train back to Denmark. Elisabeth's birthday couldn't have come at a worse time. She's turning fifty-three. It's not even a big birthday, but he knows she'd be disappointed if he didn't come. He's going to play his role as the dutiful son, and when people ask about his thesis, he'll rattle off his prepared response: "I look forward to finishing my degree and giving back to the society that paid for my opportunity to realize my ambitions." Out of sheer politeness, he'll pay his thesis director a visit at the university. Then he'll have to admit that he hasn't written a single word since they last spoke, and Thomas will patiently tell him that it cannot go on like this. They'll agree to stop working together. He doesn't think there's any point in continuing because this education was really just a means for him to postpone what he fears more than anything: the real world, a steady job, growing up.

Andreas plans to sell his condo while he's home—as quickly as possible. He plans to stay for two weeks and then return to Berlin. He had decided that's where he wants to live—until his visit to Mrs. Majenka caused him to reconsider.

28

PETER

East Berlin, July 1980

"She smells so good!" Veronika looked up from the little bundle in her arms. "What's her name?"

Peter smiled, pleased. "They called her Petra."

"They?"

"Someone who didn't deserve her. Enemies of the state." He didn't wish to tell her more than that, and thankfully Veronika asked no further questions about the girl's parents. Perhaps she was afraid to learn of their fate or worried that the child might one day be taken from her and returned to her rightful parents.

She looked at the girl again, her eyes softening. Gone was her grief over Wolfgang. Peter saw his sister changing before his very eyes. All at once, she'd become a mother. She'd always had a strong maternal instinct, and looking after the child seemed to come naturally to her; she knew exactly what to do. She'd dreamed of having a child for years, but Wolfgang had not wanted one. Too soon, he'd said. Too late, Peter thought.

He told her the girl was four months old. If she didn't like the name Petra, she was free to change it; he'd take care of all the paperwork.

"Beatrice. I want her to be named Beatrice."

Peter helped Veronika procure all the necessary equipment: crib, baby bottles, diapers, and clothes. They painted a bedroom a soft white. They played on the floor with Beatrice, and together watched her crawl for the first time. The joy he felt at seeing his sister so happy kept his ruminations about Wolfgang's death at bay. Peter didn't know whether he'd played a role in his brother-in-law's death. If he hadn't reported him, it wouldn't have happened, but Wolfgang had cheated on Veronika, and surely that justified reporting him, and Wolfgang had denied her what Peter had now given her: a child.

In 1983, Peter was transferred to Hauptverwaltung Aufklärung, the Ministry for State Security's intelligence abroad, which was usually referred to as HVA. Because of his operational experience in Department XX/5 and his tight control over informers, he'd been considered well suited to larger, more comprehensive missions. Sonnenberger comforted himself over the loss of Peter and his wife's worsening health with an ever-growing number of cigarettes, but Peter was excited about his transfer. People like Stefan, Alexander, and Nina Lachner were enemies of the state, but not to the same degree as the West. The external threat was greater than the internal one, and his work in HVA would be directed toward combating the actual enemy.

Colonel Tauber welcomed him to the department, which was located in the same gigantic complex as his previous job. Tauber's hair was coarse, short, and steel-gray. Although his glasses were thin, his body was not. His mustache was the same color as his hair and ran the length of his mouth. He spoke like a soldier, emphasizing every syllable.

"We have no use for people who get here sitting in a lecture hall. It's people like you and me, who work our way up, who really earn our ranks. These are the people we need, the handpicked elite."

Peter was proud of his promotion, and his efforts on behalf of the state were rewarded. Being very dutiful, he adapted quickly to his new job. He didn't question his assignments; he simply fulfilled them—it was as natural and spontaneous a thing to him as breathing. Unlike in the West—where egotistical career ambitions went before the needs of the community—Peter was satisfied to participate in the collective struggle toward a shared goal.

It was around this time that he met the Russian KGB officer Grigor Pamjanov, who was stationed in Berlin. They both knew that each hoped to learn more from the other than they themselves planned to share: Peter wanted to know about the Russian intelligence service, and Pamjanov wanted to know more about the Ministry for State Security, but neither one of them ever revealed anything of real significance. The Russians tended to think that any opponent ought first be defeated verbally, then on the chessboard. Peter didn't offer much resistance in their verbal arguments—he wasn't even trying, and on the chessboard, they were equally mediocre. Once they realized this fact, they brokered a truce, and their mutual distrust grew into a friendship.

He enjoyed listening to the Russian ramble. Peter drank his tea, the Russian drank his vodka; and even when the evening drew to a close, Pamjanov kept right on talking. He prattled on about women, good business deals he'd done, the czar—who got his ass handed to him in a revolution—and the other so-called superpowers who'd been handed a piece of the pie that was Berlin. The Russians had been like the greedy boy at a birthday party, lining their pockets with the best and biggest piece. He laughed at that. "The French have forgotten what they're doing in West Berlin, the English have no clue what's going on, and the Americans treat the city like a shopping mall," he said.

"What about the Russians?" Peter asked, when he could finally get a word in edgewise.

"The Russians are reliably unreliable: we're drunk seventy percent of the time and asleep the rest of the time." He laughed again.

When Peter wasn't at work or with Pamjanov, he visited Veronika and Beatrice. One summer he brought them to the seaside resort town of Warnemünde, where they stayed in the luxurious Hotel Neptune. They swam in the Baltic Sea, built sandcastles, and watched the wakes left by the big ferries as they departed the channel and entered the sea, bound for Denmark. At night they filled their bellies at the buffet, and Beatrice's eyes would grow wide in amazement as empty trays were immediately replaced with full ones. After dinner they ate fruit that was otherwise only available at Christmas: oranges, bananas, pineapple, and strawberries. The following year they went to Bulgaria by train and enjoyed the wonderful beaches along the Black Sea. Beatrice started school, joined the Young Pioneers, and fell in line, repeating the slogan for peace and socialism: *Be prepared!*

Her mother was proud, and Beatrice rarely asked about her father. Initially, Veronika was able to brush aside her questions, but as Beatrice grew older, she was no longer satisfied with vague answers. Unable to bring herself to tell Beatrice about his embarrassing suicide, she fabricated the white lie that Wolfgang had fled to the West. Beatrice was a loyal GDR child, and Veronika was convinced she would come to despise him for leaving—which was tantamount to being a traitor—and that she'd stop asking about him. Though Peter would have liked to come up with a better story, he went along with her version of events.

Peter quickly became a trusted employee in HVA. The service sent agents into West Berlin through secret routes, and when an agent returned from the West, it was Peter's job to debrief him. The agents who were selected to cross the border were those who demonstrated both loyalty and great strength of character. HVA had built a complicated network of agents, primarily in West Germany, but also in other countries. Primarily, they were interested in the government in Bonn and the West German intelligence service, the Ministry of Defense, and the air force. If HVA could place a good informant in one of the enemy's vital organs, the state would be able to shield itself from external surprises.

Having spies in the West was a necessity because the allied powers surely had spies in the GDR. Each side feared the other. NATO had nuclear warheads, the Warsaw Pact had nuclear warheads, and the generals in both alliances were as frightened as the rest of their respective populations that the arms race would end with the destruction of mankind under one giant mushroom cloud.

As the years went by, Peter's workload grew. Peter went in early, as there was no one to keep him in bed in the morning, and no one to come home to at night. He liked coming in early, when the sun painted bright stripes on the office floor, because he occasionally ran into Kerstin Hopp, who also appeared to prefer the quiet hours before the corridors filled with the hustle and bustle of their colleagues.

Like the other women in the operational department, she was a secretary. He observed her while pretending not to: her shiny black hair, her nice rump when she bent to retrieve a coffee mug from the low cabinet, the way she adjusted her skirt. He made certain to have as many errands in her area of the office as possible. She smiled at him, but whether it was out of politeness or because she liked him, he didn't know. He hadn't been with anyone since Martina, and he'd begun to miss being with a woman. He longed for the warmth he found behind an ear, the vanilla scent of a cheek, a gentle kiss, a hot thigh draped across his own. Now his longing had a face: Kerstin Hopp's.

29

ANDREAS

Berlin, February 2007

On the plaza outside Berlin's central station, Andreas hails a cab. While it works its way through the city, he works his way through the past fourteen days. He called Bea several times every day, but she never answered the phone. In the beginning he left voice mails, but eventually he gave up. If only he had Alice's number. He wants to help Bea, but he doesn't know how. He wants to be there for her, but he doesn't know where that is.

The taxi drops him in front of Bea and Alice's building. He knocks. Nobody is home. He knocks again. He lingers awhile, hoping she might come home. Then he takes another taxi to Café Cinema, but the girl behind the counter hasn't seen Bea for some time. He hails another taxi.

Veronika opens the door right away. The dark circles under her eyes have expanded to her cheeks—nearly to the corners of her mouth. Her sweatpants and sweatshirt are covered in stains. She smells of beer and despair. She appears to have aged many years since he last saw her a few weeks ago.

"I've been calling and calling, but she never picks up. I waited at her door for hours. She didn't come home."

He scrambles for his cell phone as if to prove how many times he tried to call her. The sprint up the stairs has winded him, and he stumbles over his words. He has to take a deep breath to ask a simple question: "Where is she?"

Veronika looks at him, wide-eyed. Her eyes are full of tears. The corners of her mouth quiver. With a trembling voice, she says, "Haven't you heard, Andreas?"

He stares at her. Something terrible must have happened, something irreparable. She's ragged, her voice faltering, her face ash-gray, and she begins to sob uncontrollably.

"Haven't you heard?"

"Heard what?"

"Beatrice is dead."

It feels as though his body snaps in two, his spine giving in, and he collapses. In his mind, he shatters on the floor like glass. He sees himself as shards. He doesn't know how long he stares at the floor. A few words can destroy an entire life, and he thinks he's just heard them. Though they are only three words, his head cannot contain them. He wants to run, run until his body aches and bursts open. He wants to get away, but Veronika presses against him. They are both crying. He's not sure who is soothing whom in this tiny hallway. This isn't the way it was when he learned of his father's death. Bea's death is cataclysmic.

His voice sounds like a little boy's when he asks, "What happened?"

She sobs her way through her explanation. He hears fragments, words here and there, nothing cohesive. He pieces together that she died on Alice's motorcycle. The police told her Bea'd caused the accident herself; she'd been speeding. She died, he realizes, the day she discovered that Veronika wasn't her biological mother, the day she learned that she'd been adopted, or rather, forcibly removed or stolen—what can one call it? She'd bolted down the stairs from Mrs. Majenka's apartment, hopped on the motorcycle, and crashed.

"Who is going to take care of me?" Veronika asks, dejected.

He peers through the doorway into the living room. The coffee table is littered with beer bottles. The ashtray is full, and at its edge the little polar bear stares, displeased, at the trash. The air is thick with cigarette smoke that has passed through a pair of damaged lungs, lungs that now cough air up through Veronika's mouth. He looks at her. Tufts of hair stick to her temples, and her hair has thinned in spots. He didn't even know that women could lose their hair, too. He wrenches himself free from her embrace.

"Do you have Martin's telephone number?" She cries softly now. "We have to let him know."

"Martin?" Andreas stares at her, confused.

"Her boyfriend. His name is Martin," she sniffles. "I had looked forward to meeting him, but Beatrice wanted to wait a little longer. Now I'll probably never meet him, and grandchildren—I won't ever have any grandchildren!" She sobs uncontrollably.

Then he finally understands. He is overcome with disgust and rage. Her multicolored jogging suit is cheap and filthy, she reeks of cigarettes and beer, she's monstrous and repulsive, and she lied to Bea for more than twenty-five years. Now she's doing the same to him. Peter had lied and betrayed Bea too, but Peter is dead and gone now. Veronika was the one who built the lie up, who expanded it and stretched it until it burst, driving Bea to her death. All at once he feels his body growing hot with vindictiveness. It roars in his blood, barbed and lasting, and boils under his skull. He wants to hurt Veronika, strike her, break her.

30

STEFAN

Görden, August 1985

"Watch your head," the man said, helping Stefan into the car. The man claimed to be his father.

The man sat behind the wheel and sighed in resignation. He stared straight out the window and down the street, then closed his eyes long and hard as though lost in a difficult thought. He turned to Stefan. "What have they done to you, my son?"

Stefan had served his five years, and it had ruined his mind. All the interrogations emptied it; the many days, weeks, and months alone in his cell wiped out all the thoughts and feelings that had previously filled it. In fact, Stefan didn't even recognize the man who sat beside him in the Trabant.

As they drove slowly toward Berlin, Stefan studied the landscape with a strange mixture of indifference and budding curiosity. They passed fields where clouds of gray dust trailed harvesters. Like broad-jawed beetles, the harvesters inhaled the crops, leaving long rows of bristly stubble behind. Stefan scratched his beard, producing a raspy sound, and stared at the double-wheeled tracks as they vanished in a dust cloud behind the hill. All that expanse made him tremble, made him nervous. He pressed himself more deeply into the seat. The car could serve as his cell until the man beside him stopped driving. Another town emerged. Houses with sharp corners, menacing in appearance, and cars, lots of cars, beside them, in front of them, and behind them. The city pressed in on him like cell walls. They stopped in front of a dull-gray façade.

Up the stairs, a door, a woman. She was crying, and he was pulled into her embrace. For the first time in years, he felt the warmth of another human being, and he surrendered to it. The woman disappeared in his arms. A feeling of something forgotten slipped through him, from his belly into his arms and legs. His entire body shuddered with longing. He didn't want the moment to end. Stefan squeezed so hard that the woman coughed, and the man cautiously loosened Stefan's grip.

The man whispered, "Is the room ready?" She nodded.

The room was small, and he exhaled with a short sigh of relief. He felt better in the cramped space, but he still had to be on alert.

In the cell, there'd only been a bed, table, stool, washbasin, and toilet, but here there were many things. On the bed there were pillows, whose softness was visible to the naked eye; on the wall there was a picture of a buck in a clearing, rays of sunshine like pillars of light in the foliage dotting the forest floor. There were shelves, a table, and a small TV with a rake-like object on top. A frame held a picture of a bride and groom. In it the man was tall, about Stefan's size, and had a thick beard like his. The woman was small, her dress white and puffy like summer clouds, and her hair was wavy, like the waves of his childhood beach.

"Would you like to be alone for a little while, Stefan?" They stood in the doorway and looked at him warily.

He nodded, though he didn't really know what he wanted. They seemed nice, but he wasn't used to people. The prison guards had been like machines, only capable of carrying out a few tasks. They'd had bad intentions, and he was forced to protect himself, but these people seemed different. They smiled, but he nonetheless had to be careful. If there was one thing he had learned in prison, it was that people couldn't be trusted.

They closed the door and left him alone. He was hungry and had to piss, but he didn't know whether the door was locked. He lay down on the bed and let his eyes wander. He couldn't identify the new feeling surging within him. It took him a few moments to realize that what he felt was joy. There were colors everywhere, lots of colors: the city was colorful, the room was colorful. He'd missed green; he'd missed red and blue. Here they all were, and for the first time in years, he could relax, even though his head throbbed and his thoughts were scattered.

Sleep caught up with him, and for a while he hid inside a dream. The dream was hazy, but there was a woman and a child. Images flickered across his mind, like photographs from a time long ago. Small hints, a baby crying, the woman's curly hair.

31

PETER

He'd taken Beatrice to Ernst Thälmann Park that afternoon. They'd tried to build a snowman. They'd packed snow until their fingers were blue from the cold, but the snow had been too powdery. So they'd gone to the Christmas market at Alexanderplatz, where he'd bought her a candied apple. He was going to spend Christmas with her and Veronika, as he always did, and he'd bought her a new dollhouse. It was larger than the shabby plastic house she had, the house whose chimney had broken off. The new one was made out of wood with neat decorative edges along the spine of the roof, a checkered floor in the kitchen, a small fireplace in the living room, and a lamp that lit up both floors when you pressed a small switch on the back. The proportions were wrong. The doors and the window were too big and the rooms too small, but that didn't matter: Beatrice would be ecstatic. She was now eight years old and had grown to be a tall, lanky girl. Veronika didn't have much money, so Peter spoiled her with gifts her mother wasn't able to give her. At least they had a nice home in Ahrensfelde. Everything was new and in order, unlike in Prenzlauer Berg, where the electricity often went out and the water was frequently cut off.

This evening the water was running fine, though. He wet his comb under the faucet and ran it through his hair. He carefully parted his hair and adjusted his tie several times before he left the apartment. Fat snowflakes were falling as he stepped out onto the street, and he thought of Beatrice again. This was good packing snow. They could have built a big old snowman here, and the comb in his back pocket could have served as its mustache. He recalled the small gift box in his pocket and smiled.

People were already drunk when he arrived at the Christmas party. The department director, Colonel Tauber, was wearing an elf's hat and a woolen holiday sweater depicting reindeer that he'd already spilled something on. Peter heard Jan Grebe speak much too loudly at the bar. Peter generally tolerated him well enough, but not when he'd been drinking. A small circle of people had gathered around him as he roared with some boastful story. Peter took up his position, hesitatingly, on the other end of the room. Maybe it had been a mistake to come? He never drank, after all, and actually found drunk people quite unbearable. They were unpredictable and vulgar.

As people drank, danced, and groped, Peter felt increasingly ill at ease. Then Tauber clinked his glass, and the music ground to a halt. A bowl containing slips of paper with everyone's names was passed around; the name you drew was the person you were to exchange gifts with. Tauber walked over to Peter.

"Aren't you going to cut a rug, Körber? You can't hide in this corner all night."

Peter smiled with some effort and drew a slip of paper from the bowl. He opened it, hoping that it would be a man without a mustache or at least not one of the secretaries. The note read *Kerstin*. Tauber laughed lewdly, nudged him in his ribs, and continued on with the bowl. Peter glanced around for Kerstin and discovered that she was standing only a few feet away. Her features were mild, but her big eyes always made her appear slightly startled. He noticed that she'd curled her dark hair so that it framed her face softly.

He'd thought the gift he now had in his pocket was a funny idea, but he suddenly didn't like it anymore. With a male colleague—most of the department—he would have had a good laugh, but no, he'd drawn a woman's name—and Kerstin's to boot. Now he was just embarrassed, but he couldn't *not* give her a gift. He turned to her. She swayed gently to the music. Her beautiful hair fell across her tight-fitting floral shirt, which emphasized her shoulders and breasts. When she noticed she had an audience, she became self-conscious about dancing. He flashed the piece of paper with her name on it, and she smiled. Deflated, he handed her the gift. To his surprise, she smiled broadly. She wore the fake mustache. It was the same color as her hair.

Her gift to him was small and square. Inside was a silver Christmas ornament, and suddenly Peter was taken back to his childhood. He recalled a Christmas in Friedrichshain. Like today, a thick layer of snow covered the city. The apartment smelled of marzipan and dried fruits. His mother was baking Dresdner stollen, which was a treat they enjoyed only during the holidays. On the buffet in the dining room, Veronika had arranged a winter village using cotton balls for snow and a small pocket mirror for a frozen lake. The tiny figures wore elfin hats that she'd sewn herself. The branches of their Christmas tree spread wide in the living room, making the room seem even smaller. The tree sparkled with glass ornaments, braided straw hearts, and glittery tinsel that his mother smoothed out every year so that it wouldn't be creased the following year. She had her heart set on getting a glass ornament made from the finest Thüring glass because it would complete the tree. Peter knew that his father had bought her one, and he knew exactly what the gift box looked like.

He also knew that his mother had sewn a tracksuit for his father. The shiny material had been expensive, and it came only in red, but the needle didn't break once—as it often did with the coarse material she normally used. His mother trembled in expectation as his father began to unpack his gift. As she sat there, she became a child in Peter's eyes, no older than Veronika or himself. Georg impatiently tore the paper and ripped open the box. He stopped in mid-movement and stared disbelieving at the red cloth. Then the veins in his temples began to throb visibly as he held up the clothes, snorting. Peter and Veronika had admired their mother's work before she'd wrapped it, but now neither one of them dared to speak.

Then Georg unleashed a series of profanities. *His color was blue, the club color was blue, how dare she*! He clenched his fists, emitting cascades of spit, and nearly knocked over the tree as he searched for his gift to her. He took it with him as he left, slamming the front door. She never got the ornament.

"Let's sit," Kerstin suggested.

Peter nodded and shoved his gift into his pocket. He held out a chair for her and sat next to her. They talked for a long time. She laughed and innocently brushed his knee, and he casually touched her forearm. The hours flew by as they talked and talked. Behind her somewhat reserved façade was a woman who made him laugh, who gave him gooseflesh, who made him yearn for more.

Peter and Kerstin looked over and watched Jan Grebe making a spectacle of himself on the dance floor; his shirt had come loose, and his pants were falling down, revealing his crack. He danced crazily to a disco tune, while Ursula, a beautiful, big-chested woman from administration, tried to keep up with him, laughing. Jan must have noticed Peter and Kerstin watching him because he pulled Ursula over to their table when the song ended. She was soft and drunk, and her breasts hung over the table. There was no mistaking Jan's intention: he wanted Peter to see that he was leaving the party with the most desirable secretary. Ursula smiled, her lipstick smeared, and her blue eye shadow and the alcohol made her eyes seem dull.

Feeling uncomfortable, Peter stood. "I've got to get going."

Jan laughed as though he'd won some competition and put his arm around Ursula. Peter politely said his good-bye to Kerstin. He was going to shake hands with the flushed and perspiring Tauber, but Tauber instead pressed him into his damp sweater. The colonel tried to persuade him to stay longer, but Peter gave him a friendly, preemptive nod. Then Tauber turned and forgot all about Peter.

In the cloakroom, he ran into Kerstin again. She already held her coat across her arm. Peter wanted to say something nice to her, give her a compliment that might lead somewhere, but he didn't know what to say. She beat him to the punch.

"Come home with me," she said. Then she took a step toward him and embraced him.

Peter got his coat and turned to see if Jan had noticed them, but he wasn't there anymore.

On the street, a taxi pulled up to the curb. It stopped right where they stood, and Ursula leaped out. She tumbled onto the sidewalk, her skirt yanked up to her thighs, and her knees sank into the deep snow. Snowflakes melted on her permed hair as she dropped on all fours and threw up profusely, forming a crater in the snow with her vomit— a mashed-up holiday meal consisting of remnants of sausage, duck, red cabbage, kale, Thüring-style potato buns, and Christmas cake. She sobbed as she threw up, then belched and threw up once more. Jan walked around the car, visibly annoyed. He looked enviously at Peter as Peter helped Kerstin into what had been *his* taxi, the one that was supposed to bring him home to Ursula's naked, hot body.

Kerstin gave the driver her address, and the taxi rolled tentatively through the quiet, snow-covered streets; they had the entire city to themselves. They stopped on a street in Hohenschönhausen. Full of anticipation, he followed her up the narrow back stairs. Her round behind swayed beautifully in front of him, and something stirred in his pants.

Kerstin stood in the door to her living room and laughed because she was still wearing her fake mustache. He was overcome with desire and welcomed the warm feeling that spread through him. It had been absent for far too long. He'd been missing a woman's touch for years, and now his entire body quivered. She walked over to the couch, where he sat like a schoolboy waiting to be called to the principal's office. Then she bent over him and gave him a hesitant kiss. Her mustache tickled his lip. He had an unobstructed view down her shirt. She wasn't wearing a bra, and he saw her breasts, which were small and pointy.

Then they went to the bedroom and stood on either side of the bed, undressing. Peter wasn't looking at Kerstin; he was only listening. He heard the zipper of her skirt, the unbuttoning of her shirt buttons. He unzipped his pants, and his erection slipped free, relieving his pain. He felt exposed with his penis standing at attention, and he hoped she would turn off the light. Just then he heard a click, and the ceiling light went off. Carefully he lay down and saw her shadow leave the room. A moment later, she appeared as a silhouette against the hallway light. He saw the curve of her hips and the gentle movement of her breasts. She crawled into bed next to him. The bed was narrow, and they were close, suddenly so close. She was naked, and her pubic hair tickled his thigh. She was warm and soft. Slowly she leaned over him, her forearm resting on his chest. Her mouth drew near, and he moistened his lips. She tasted sweet and warm. Her hand glided from his chest down to his belly—sending shivers down his spine—and then continued downward. The hairs on his arms and legs stood as her hand found his penis and carefully rubbed it up and down. He closed his eyes. Her fingertips played with him. Everything in him contracted, and before he could stop her, he came on her hand in thick spurts. He nearly cried in shame over his lack of self-control. What should have been something special was about to turn into a pathetic disaster. What would she think of him now? What would she do? He turned away from her, holding his breath.

Then he heard her voice and felt her arms around him. She practically rocked him back and forth, whispering to him so softly that he couldn't make out the words. He said nothing, lying still, almost petrified. A short time later, she fell asleep.

The next morning, Peter woke to Kerstin humming in the bathroom. She emerged with a towel wrapped around her waist. Her wet hair was glistening, her face beaming, and below her towel her knees shone. In the light of the morning, freckles were visible on her cheeks and forehead. He recalled last night's disaster, but felt a kind of lump inside, happiness perhaps. He didn't say anything and just looked at her, smiling. He thought of a riddle and asked her, "What gets wetter the more it dries?"

She shook her head. She didn't know.

He pointed at the towel.

She let it fall to the floor, tore back the duvet, and lay down on top of him.

Two months later, Kerstin moved into Peter's apartment on Kopenhagener Strasse. Unlike Martina, she wasn't interested in interior design. Other than her clothes, she brought only a few things, including a conch, some letters Peter had written her, and some cassette tapes by the American singer Patsy Cline.

It had been Kerstin's idea that they move in together, but Peter was easily persuaded. Although he hadn't really been looking for a girlfriend, since his job took up all his time, she was everything he could have dreamed of. For the first time ever, he was truly in love, and he surrendered to it completely. He thought about Kerstin constantly. She'd fallen in love too, and together they were frisky, sometimes forgetting their age and acting like teenagers. They kissed each other in public simply because they couldn't help it, and he was delighted that everyone could see that she was his.

32

ANDREAS

Berlin, February 2007

Back on the street, his throat burns, and his knuckles are throbbing. The fresh wind that sweeps through the complex of buildings wakes him from the peculiar trance he's been in for the past few minutes. He knows he's been yelling—that's clear from the pain in his throat and the rush of blood to his head, and he knows he left Veronika crying on the floor when he exited the apartment.

For a moment he imagines himself beating her furiously. His fists work like pistons against her soft body, which fights back at first but then simply absorbs the pounding. She is a repulsive, awful person—a fraud.

His desire for revenge had threatened to overwhelm him, but now he feels only relief because he left before it was too late. Though it had taken all his willpower, he'd suppressed his urge to pummel her and instead just yelled at her until his throat nearly burst. The wall of the stairwell had received his enraged pounding instead.

What she and Peter did is unforgivable. Criminal, but only then does he realize that she had no way of knowing that he and Bea had discovered the truth. He pictures her lying on the floor with her sweatshirt hoisted up on her fat belly, sobbing and pleading without understanding the reason for his angry explosion, but he can't go back, not now, not ever. He starts toward the train station. Although Veronika has most likely given Bea everything she was capable of giving her, he can't imagine that he'll ever want to see her again. She's of no consequence. She means nothing—only Bea means anything. Or meant anything.

He tries to imagine her in a coffin: lacerated by the collision, her legs broken, her head twisted—and her peeling nail polish. She deserved better. What was she thinking when it happened? Was she thinking about her biological parents?

He takes the train and gets off at a random station. He looks around for a tavern. Not a café, not a bar, but a tavern, where he can sit in a corner and hide in the cigarette smoke and disappear. He finds what he's looking for. No one pays attention to him when he enters. He orders a beer. The bartender is the jovial type, but Andreas can't be bothered to talk to the man and crawls onto a chair in a corner.

He hears the sound of dice rolling on another table. A man and a woman, perhaps a married couple, look like they are about to have a fight over the game.

Andreas drinks from his pint. There are burn marks along the edge of his table—traces of long-forgotten cigarettes. He reads a rune carved by a man name Rudi, who sat here with his knife in 1995.

A dwarf approaches his table. Andreas just wishes to be left alone, but the man wants to play pool. An unlit cigarette dangles from the corner of his mouth, and he has a scar from a botched harelip operation underneath his nose. He holds the cue out to Andreas, who raises his hands to signal he's not interested, then sets his face to show that he wants to be alone. The dwarf wobbles back to the pool table, rests his chin on the edge of the table, and breaks so hard the balls clink loudly around the table.

The first beer tastes good, but it takes too long to get drunk with beer. He wants to get drunk fast; he wants a rush in his blood, a ticking in his head, now. He wants to hold his grief at bay and drink his sorrows away. He orders two whiskeys. They sting his sore throat, but he doesn't care.

The man rolling the dice bangs the two squashed dice cups onto the table, rises in anger, and heads for the door. The woman tries to pry apart the two dice cups. When she succeeds, the dice fall to the floor. She picks them up and looks quizzically at Andreas as she holds up the cup. He turns away.

Another man plants himself in front of Andreas. There's something ominous about him. His legs are spread, and his arms are covered in faded tattoos. Andreas instinctively scoots his chair back as the man leans across the table. He has no idea what the man wants. Frightened, he stares at the man's giant hands splayed on the table. With his index finger, the man taps on the name carved into the table. A quick hand gesture indicates to Andreas that he should get up. He turns to the bartender, who shrugs and points to a vacant table. Andreas empties his glass and leaves the tavern.

He goes from one dive to the next, letting the alcohol do its job. Slowly he feels himself going numb. He has a sniffling conversation with some girl. His compliments make him sound horny and despondent, and she walks away. A group of people in jerseys displaying a roaring polar bear drink with him. At first he thinks he's run into a cult that worships arctic wildlife, but the jerseys appear to be sports related.

Ice hockey fans, the bartender explains, and asks him were he's from.

"The Netherlands," he replies, for some reason.

It's dark outside, and he has no idea where he is. The streets all look alike. The city seems different at night—strangely enticing, like a circus, a freak show, a pirate ship. Pirates, dwarves, and bearded women swarm from the ship's hold, knives between their yellow-brown teeth. They trundle down the sidewalk, and he stumbles. He flops around as this mad world rumbles past him. A motorcycle accelerates, causing the flagstones to vibrate, but it's not Bea.

A jukebox brings him to his feet. It's the same music as the one on Peter's tapes. The woman singer.

He sways at a new bar counter, orders a couple of shots, and immediately drains them. He maneuvers onto a stool and orders a refill. He listens to Patsy Cline's song, "I Fall to Pieces," and wishes he were someone else, with someone else's thoughts and someone else's problems.

"Buy me a drink, young man?"

The woman's question reveals her age. He considers what it might be while unabashedly sizing her up. She's probably around fifty. The low cut of her shirt pulls at him, and though every other part of her sags, her breasts still appear firm under her shirt. There's lipstick on her teeth, and her forehead and cheeks are caked with foundation.

"So, what's it gonna be, love?" She leans lasciviously forward and gropes his thigh.

When she speaks, the caked foundation shifts like continental plates and, suddenly, there's a tectonic displacement right in front of him, an earthquake rocking her painted face. She smiles, and he feels the heat of her body, and something in his pants feels tempted. He stands and staggers to the bathroom.

His face looks wrong in the mirror, distorted. He speaks to his reflection, but it doesn't seem to understand. His voice is impure and hoarse. It's not his voice but a strange, creaking sound. The alcohol has acquired its own voice. It's the whiskey, the blue shots he doesn't know the name of, the beers—all of it has passed through him into the urinal, and they are the voice speaking. The voice speaks of Bea, and he tells it to shut up. After he accidentally pisses on one of his pant legs, he feels pathetic and begins to cry.

Jesper Bugge Kold

He fumbles his way back to the bar. He feels as though he's been locked up. People are standing too close to him, much too close. They rub themselves against him, he needs to get out, get away . . .

The woman helps him into his jacket. One arm gets stuck in the sleeve, but she's patient. He cries as his arm keeps getting stuck; he doesn't have any energy left, but then he's in a taxi, and she taps the window and waves, and his head slams into the window as the taxi pulls out onto the street.

The taxi stops. He looks for a good place to keel over, but then he recognizes the street. His feet are heavy with booze. Useless. Like an animal, he creeps across the sidewalk. The old lady's still up. She peeks out from behind the curtain.

His keys are gone. He's locked out, out of luck. He paws through his pockets with the slow desperation of drunkenness. Wrinkled chestnuts, chewing gum that's fallen out of a packet, coins, a slip of paper. It's the woman's phone number. Then he feels a slice of cold metal in his back pocket. He kisses the little saw-toothed blade and fumbles to insert it into the lock.

He begins the ascent on all fours, his hands moving against the dirty linoleum, step by step. Will his legs hold him? He gives it a go. The railing holds him up. Another half floor. He falls and hits his shoulder against the railing. He expects pain but feels nothing. He's soft, a lump of kneaded dough that takes the shape of the stairs. He might stay here, might sleep here. He doesn't have the strength to get up. He doesn't care. He's comfortable. His brain is empty, freed from all thought.

A thought flashes across his mind: he needs to get in touch with Volker Dietmaier, the doctor who received his father's dead body. He needs to call him right away, but his cell phone seems to be missing. He crawls onward and finally reaches his door. The key doesn't work, or maybe it's the lock. They no longer fit together; they've lost their mutual justification for their existence. Now they're just two pieces of metal in a jam. A key and a lock that prevent him from entering his home.

He laughs stupidly: *home!* Home, what does that even mean? But he needs to get inside and make his phone call. He's forgotten whom he needs to call, but it's important. He knows that much. Is it Lisa? Maybe he still loves her.

He sits down with his back against the door, sleeps a little. He fumbles for the door handle in order to get to his feet. Finally he clutches the handle. The door opens, and he drops into the hallway. He stares at the ceiling as it begins to spin. Or as he spins. He's a roulette wheel. Everything spins faster and faster, and he disappears.

33

PETER

East Berlin, October 1989

"Colonel Tauber wishes to speak with you."

Like Sonnenberger's office, Tauber's was decorated with photos of trophy fish, as though all officers were members of the same fishing club. Maybe they earned their stripes based on the size of their catch, Peter thought, as Tauber's fishes surpassed anything found in Sonnenberger's office.

Tauber laid the palms of his hands on the table and began to speak as he studied his hands. "Peter, you're one of our most trusted employees," he said, looking up. "And now I need you on the other side."

There was a lull in the conversation as Peter let the words sink in. Then he slowly shook his head as though he didn't believe Tauber.

The colonel held his gaze. "I'm serious, Peter."

"Why me?"

Tauber explained how the entire web of informers had become unstable. The unrest that had swept through the country meant that Peter would have to meet, quite extraordinarily, with his own contacts in the field.

"You'll tell the informers that all's well, and you'll assure them that we haven't forgotten them, that we're still protecting them. You're always one hundred percent professional. Somebody like Jan"—he gestured with his arm, exasperated—"I can't send him over. He'll try to screw anyone in a short skirt." He laughed at his own remark. "We need to act fast, because this is a highly unusual situation. We'll send Kerstin Hopp with you to make your travel look less suspicious and to create a better alibi for you. Since you're already a couple, it'll be easier. You know each other well, and we know you both."

"Yes, sir."

"Kerstin Hopp is already on board with the mission." Tauber sighed. "These are strange times, but we have to continue our work. Without us, the entire edifice will fall apart."

The colonel explained the exact nature of the mission. Peter would spend the next three weeks in West Berlin, convincing his informants that the unrest was only temporary and that they must continue their work without hesitation. Then he and Kerstin would come home.

Before they left, they'd be issued new identities. They were to study up on the history, politics, culture, and traditions of West Germany, and they were to learn about everything—from the local cuisine to which team was ahead in the Bundesliga standings. In addition, they'd be taught everything about how the border patrol operated so that they'd be less nervous when confronting West German guards. These types of assignments were given only to party loyalists who displayed the proper values, character, and mental resistance.

East Berlin, November 1989

They walked past Friedrichstadt-Palast and across Weidendammer Bridge, the river Spree shimmering beneath them. The cast iron railing of the bridge felt cold against Peter's hand. In the other, he held Kerstin's hand. The closer they got to Friedrichstrasse Station, the more clammy and moist hers became. Her shoes clacked against the cobblestones with the precision of a clock.

A glass-and-steel building appeared ahead of them. Its unofficial name was the Palace of Tears, because this was where people said their good-byes whenever they'd had a visit from relatives on the other side of the Wall, their tears dripping onto the cobblestones.

They glanced into the huge glass lobby. The rays of the winter sun were reflected in the many windows, reminding him of the television tower. In 1969, when its construction was complete, an optical phenomenon occurred that the architect hadn't anticipated. When the sun shone on the polygonal cupola, a glowing cross appeared. People began to speak of it as the pope's revenge, as a form of divine retribution, because the state had required the churches to remove all crosses. In an attempt to remove the reflection, large mirrors were placed on the ground beneath the tower; another attempt involved painting over the glass. In the People's Chamber, there was even talk of tearing the building down. Finally, a solution was devised: the reflection was to be regarded not as a cross but as a plus sign, a plus for socialism.

Thinking of this story calmed him. He squeezed Kerstin's hand and smiled at her as they walked past the long, unmoving line. He could tell from the way people shifted on their feet that the atmosphere in the hall was depressed. The waiting made people nervous, and though no one had any reason to be afraid, the mere presence of the border guards made them feel guilty; it showed in their lackluster faces and their sagging shoulders. Everyone inched toward the border patrol, where men examined their luggage, then nodded and sent them into another line, and more guards peered down at them from wooden booths. Behind the guards' glass windows, there were telephones, monitors, cameras, and hats held in place solely by furrowed foreheads.

They continued past the Palace of Tears down Friedrichstrasse, under the station where the kiosks displayed Russian fashion magazines with long-limbed models on the front pages. On the south side of the station, they went down a flight of stairs and, next to a hair salon, they found the entrance used by employees of the national train service. This was where the Ministry for State Security could send its people into West Berlin unhindered.

An officer in a gray uniform received them. Kerstin clutched Peter's hand. The officer gave them a brief nod, then scrutinized their papers before stamping them with a metallic clonk. They passed through a control room filled with television screens then down several corridors, and finally to another guard at another counter. The second guard studied the stamp and turned the passports ninety degrees. When he pushed a button, the lock in an electronic door buzzed, and Peter and Kerstin headed into a tile-covered tunnel and disappeared among a crowd of passengers on their way to platform B and line U6 toward Tegel.

Massive steel walls between platforms B and C kept people from sneaking onto the train to West Berlin, and cameras positioned throughout the platforms kept an eye on everyone. Guards dressed as civilians walked among the passengers or stood beside them with feigned nonchalance, but Peter easily recognized them.

The train was already waiting. Peter and Kerstin boarded. He heard her exhale. Neither of them had any reason to be nervous, yet he felt her anxiety. He took her hand. Through the window they watched soldiers with their guns strapped over their soldiers and German shepherds sniffing under the trains. Using mirrors attached to long metal rods, the guards inspected underneath the carriages.

The train began to move, rattling and clanking, and they looked at each other gravely. The train slowed as it rolled past the shuttered stations. The stations looked ghostlike, and even the guards from the transportation police appeared faded in the platform's dim light. The train slowed. They had arrived in West Berlin.

Kerstin started beaming from the minute they got off the train. She suddenly looked like a Westerner, like she'd been a Westerner all her life. She moved with the self-assuredness of a Westerner and spoke with the arrogance of a Westerner. He noticed with pride that men on the street turned around to check her out.

The hotel was shabby. They put their luggage in their room and asked the overweight manager who smelled of alcohol where they might find a good restaurant. When they found it, the waiter showed them to a table. Kerstin seemed ecstatic and spoke with the eager enthusiasm of a child about how they would see the entire city. How they would stroll on the Kurfürstendamm, eat chocolate at Kaufhaus des Westens, kiss in the Tiergarten. In a low voice, he reminded her of their mission. She fell silent for a moment. Then she spoke again. At first he thought she was joking; her tone had been lighthearted after all, as though wanting to gauge his reaction before sounding too committed. She blinked as though afraid her eyes would dry out.

"Let's stay here," she repeated.

"Please be serious," Peter replied, trying to contain his shock.

"Let's get married and stay." Her voice was tense.

He tried to smile indulgently, uncertain how to respond.

She laid her hand on his. The warmth spread from her touch. "We can travel the entire world. You and me. We can go to the United States, to a Patsy Cline concert. You'd like that, wouldn't you?"

Some small part of him admired her for having dared to speak so candidly, because she knew his work essentially involved suppressing those very desires in others. In fact, his first thought was that he'd have to report her, but he knew he'd never be able to.

"I don't want to go back." Tears appeared in her eyes. "I'm afraid. Who knows? Maybe we're in danger? You've seen the demonstrations in front of our offices; more people are joining them every day. Who knows what they'll do? Aren't you afraid that we'll lose our jobs—that everything we have will be taken from us?"

Peter shook his head. "Everything's going to be all right!" he cried earnestly, but he was startled to discover that he had to convince himself that that was indeed the case.

They returned to the hotel and brushed their teeth in silence, her words ricocheting through his head; once in bed, he couldn't sleep, and he could tell she couldn't, either. Was Kerstin more important to him than East Germany? Was he willing to betray the state for a woman? Without Kerstin his life would be meaningless; he knew he couldn't let her go. Until this moment in this hotel room in enemy territory, their love had been the best thing that had ever happened to him, and now this. No East German could honestly say they'd never contemplated what it would be like to live in the West, but it appeared that Kerstin had let herself be seduced by it.

The events of the last few months had frightened him too, but he didn't want to justify Kerstin's fears by sharing his concerns with her.

"The shit is hitting the fan," Pamjanov had said in his typically blunt manner the last time they'd met. "Moscow's got a soft guy at the top, and that'll never lead to anything good. The Central Committee shouldn't listen to Gorbachev. He's aligned with the West." He'd shaken his big heavy head in resignation. "The whole structure's going to come toppling down soon."

Maybe he was right. Hungary had unsealed its border to Austria just a couple of months earlier, and East Germans now went on "vacation" in Hungary and were pouring through the hole in the Iron Curtain. Tadeusz Mazowiecki had become the leader of the first anti-communist government in Poland in more than forty years, and anti-communist demonstrations had been taking place in the larger cities in Czechoslovakia. There were a growing number of demonstrations in Leipzig as well, and every Monday people took to the street following the weekly prayer meeting in St. Nicholas church. Unrest was spreading like the plague. Across the country, people were demanding freedom and democracy and protesting the scarcity of everyday goods and the ban against leaving the country. In Leipzig, two days after the GDR celebrated its fortieth anniversary on October 7 with grand parades on Karl Marx-Allee, some seventy thousand people took to the streets with torches and candles. The crowd had quickly ballooned to three hundred thousand, and they'd demonstrated in front of the State Security complex.

Tauber had urged his staff to remain calm. "It'll pass," he assured them.

In the middle of October, Erich Honecker had been deposed and was replaced by Egon Krenz. The unrest that had been smoldering had burst into flames on November 4, when half a million people gathered on Alexanderplatz to demand freedom, but freedom for what? No one was starving, and everyone had work and access to health care. Everyone was taken care of. Hopefully, by the time he and Kerstin returned, things would be calmer.

Kerstin writhed in the bed beside him.

He put one hand on her smooth cheek. "You know we have to return, don't you?

"Yes," she sighed. "I know."

34

ANDREAS

Berlin, February 2007

The toilet bowl is an echo chamber. He hears the hollow roar of his own guts. From its depths comes yet another outpouring of thin vomit. The pain is amplified, and his ears fill with the sound of puking, ringing through his entire body. His head throbs. The yellow freshener on the edge of the bowl radiates its nauseating, perfumed freshness, but it can't cover up the stench of his own insides. He leans his head against his arm, which is draped across the toilet. If his arm slips, he'll fall, and he'll crash through the tiled floors, to never stop falling. His arm fails him, and he loses his grip; he whimpers as he glides down the side of the bowl. He fights to control his rolling guts. He's lying on the floor, and the pain in his temples has reached its peak. It can't possibly get any worse. He just needs to get through today without dying.

Light slants through the small window. "Let the damn day come," he says aloud, and as he does so, he realizes that he's become Peter. He's pissed his pants and crawled home on all fours, and who knows but maybe that's only the beginning. He and his father are one and the same person, though his father's body has perished and his is still alive—or rather lying on a cold floor fighting for—or against—his own existence. If the pain wasn't thundering through his head, he'd shake it in resignation.

Then Bea appears. He's filled with sadness at the thought that he'll never see her again, never speak to her, never study her broad mouth or fine blond eyebrows, or see her spit nicotine gum into her palm. It's an unbearable thought, but one so strong and malignant that it'll plague him for the rest of his life. He wishes he could change the timeline so that he might nullify the line that runs through his life. Remove Peter, forget Veronika, save Bea.

He thinks of Coca-Cola. There's one in the fridge that probably doesn't have much fizz left, but it's cold. The fridge is miles away. First he has to cross the hallway, and to get there he has to stand up. He gives up.

He vomits, forcing the last of it from his body. He finally stands. His belly is empty and his head heavy. He tries to avoid seeing his reflection; he knows how his face appears: puffy, wrenched up, dead flesh on a skull, glossy-eyed, lips swollen.

The sink is littered with glass shards. He sees himself in the shards, his face in tatters, like his state of mind. He doesn't recall smashing the mirror. It must have happened during the night. He washes his face, wipes his eyes, and attempts to rinse the night away as the water swirls down between the shards and becomes a kind of abstract art. He scrutinizes the rest of the smashed mirror above the sink; he glances at his knuckles and figures out the connection. That means seven years bad luck in addition to the already insurmountable crosswind he's facing. He hocks in the sink, and that's when he sees it—behind the glinting shards of glass still attached to the wall. A compartment.

He inserts his hand cautiously. He feels around, making sure not to cut his arm on the mirror, and touches something metal: a cold, square box. He pulls it out. It's a small, dented tin box the size of a child's lunch box. The red paint is peeling, and he thinks of Bea's nail polish. His curiosity is piqued. The box rattles as he opens it. On top is a sheet of paper folded up several times. He removes it, then sees several medallions underneath.

He unfolds the paper and reads.

This medal is awarded to Peter Körber in recognition of his honest, conscientious, and dutiful work for the Ministry for State Security.

It is signed by Erich Mielke, Ministry for State Security.

He removes the medallions one by one, studies them, and puts them back in the box. Medals of honor, prizes, and distinctions from the Free German Youth, Felix Dzerzhinsky Guards Regiment, and Ministry for State Security. Some of them are shiny, while others are dull.

He sticks his hand in the compartment again and feels a strange object made of metal. He pulls out a pistol. The shaft feels good against his palm, and it scares him to suddenly have a weapon in his hand. Alarmed, he hurries to return it. His wrist brushes against some pieces of paper, and he pulls out three envelopes, two brown and one white.

Dear Kerstin, the white envelope reads. As he opens it, he realizes it must have been opened many times, because the glue is no longer tacky. It's a letter from his father to Kerstin Hopp. The language is simple and yet expressive, too. Peter declares his love to her, and judging by Peter's language, he clearly didn't doubt that Kerstin had feelings for him as well. He writes about how happy he is that she'll soon be moving in with him. Andreas feels a surge of sadness, because he knows that Kerstin left his father. Peter must have saved the letter, venerating it as a memory of a woman he'd loved. Maybe he sat with it pressed against his chest while thinking of her? Maybe his pining for her was what caused him to drink? But even the thought of alcohol makes him nauseous again.

Then he flips over the brown envelopes. They're both addressed to Grigor Pamjanov. He stares at them in wonder. His first inclination is to mail them to the Russian. It's none of his business what two old friends wrote to each other, but then again, why were they hidden?

He gets the soda from the fridge and sits down with the two brown envelopes. When he unscrews the cap, the bottle makes a faint whoosh. As the liquid cascades down into his belly, he immediately feels better. His hangover yields to curiosity.

He tears open one of the envelopes. He doesn't owe Pamjanov anything. There's a postcard inside. He stares at an image of the pyramids.

Welcome to lovely Egypt appears in red letters across the desert sand. There's a note on the reverse side, and the writing is the same as on the envelope, but it's not addressed to Grigor. He begins to read.

Dear Beatrice,

My work has now brought me to Cairo, where I'm sitting at a café and writing this postcard. The sun is hot today, and Egyptian beer doesn't slake your thirst like German beer. I've ordered food from the menu, but I don't know what it is I've ordered, and while I'm waiting I'm writing to you, my daughter. I miss you and promise that we will meet one day. I'll write again soon.

I love you.
Your father, Wolfgang

Andreas sets the postcard down on the coffee table. His hangover returns with renewed vigor, and he begins to tremble. Now he realizes that Wolfgang didn't flee. He concludes that he never existed. He was a figment of the imagination, a construction that Peter and Veronika created with Pamjanov as messenger, but why?

Now he hears Pamjanov's words to Bea: "I was supposed to send these postcards. They were for you."

It makes sense now. Bea had wondered what the Russian had meant, but Pamjanov had just acted as if it was all some joke. A new city, a new postcard for Bea, no questions asked.

Andreas pulls his legs up underneath him and crouches in a fetal position, even though doing so hurts his diaphragm. He's overcome with a sense of helplessness. They are a family of liars. Peter, Veronika— even Bea, who'd told her mother she was a dating a guy named Martin because she didn't have the courage to tell her she was a lesbian. Even Andreas is lying, if only to himself, since he refuses to admit that he can't go on like this.

It's time for him to go home, time to forget Berlin. His apartment in Denmark hasn't been sold yet. Lasse—a stylish, cocky real estate agent—keeps claiming that he's finally found the right buyer, but maybe there's no longer a seller.

He understands now that Peter maybe wasn't a victim. Of all that he's learned about his father, multiple things point to him being an unscrupulous man: stealing Bea, Nina Lachner's death, his mistreatment of Ejner, his fabrication of Wolfgang. Andreas thought his father had been killed by a cold-blooded murderer, but now he realizes that many people may have had good reason to kill him.

35

PETER

West Berlin, November 1989

Peter glanced at his watch again. Kerstin must be returning from her walk soon. She'd promised him that she wouldn't be gone long. A half hour, no more. He should have gone with her, but her gentle, insistent voice had convinced him to stay: "I'll be back soon." Those words still reverberated in his head.

He lay on his bed in their shabby hotel room, staring up at the multitude of small cracks in the ceiling. A rust-speckled pipe ran along the wall into the adjoining room, the radiator thumped loudly, and the bathroom smelled thickly of corrosion. The bed was too hard, and the sheets were no longer white. The only positive thing he had to say concerned the toilet paper; it was soft, layered, and ornamented with butterfly patterns. The November sun made a bright stripe across the wall where there was a gap in the wallpaper, not much of a gap, but enough to recognize the difference in the pattern. He didn't like those kinds of mistakes. They were a sign of shoddy morale among workers. The painter had been either sloppy or incapable of carrying out a simple piece of work, though it ought to have been child's play. That was the West in a nutshell. Laziness or incompetence—or both.

Where had she gone? It occurred to him that she might run away, but then she would have taken a duffel as well as all the Deutschmarks in his coat pocket.

To pass the time, in the hotel lobby he'd bought a faded post-card with images of the city's attractions: Wilhelm Memorial Church, Charlottenburg Palace, the Victory Column, Brandenburg Gate. He flipped the card over and began to write. *Dear Bea*. He described the city using the same language he'd just read in a brochure that now lay on the nightstand. *I love you. Your father, Wolfgang*. He got up and stuffed the postcard into the liner pocket of his coat. He would send it when he had the chance. For the next few weeks, he wouldn't need Grigor as a go-between. Why did he even write these postcards? To protect her from the truth? To give her hope? Maybe a mixture of both—or maybe it was for his own sake. Without even being consciously aware of it, he'd dreamed of faraway places. With every new postcard, he'd experienced a new place, or at least that's how it felt.

He stood by the window, looking for her. It was afternoon now, and the street below teemed with people bustling up and down the sidewalk, their breaths visible in the cold like empty speech bubbles. He noticed a billboard with three erect penises for something called Dildoking. He shook his head in despair. What was he doing here? What the *hell* was he doing here? He was already looking forward to going home.

In the distance, a radio was playing soft and catchy pop music. It sounded like pastel-colored plastic, drums like cotton balls and guitar and bass run through a distortion filter. He watched the building across the street, but the windows in the gray, concrete structure simply stared back. The city was one big advertisement for Coca-Cola, Mercedes, and Kodak. A glimmering world where people were pampered. They had the same products in the GDR—they just went by other names: Coca-Cola was Vita Cola or Club Cola, Bounty was called Bon, Milky Way was Fetzer, and Nutella was Nudossi.

She would *have* to return soon. He lay back down on the bed, thinking the time might pass more quickly if he slept a little. Perhaps in her excitement she'd wandered off and lost track of time. If he fell asleep, he'd wake up to her soft lips kissing him.

Tomorrow, he would find a better hotel for them, a hotel without grime and mildew. The hotel here in Wedding was cheap and ugly.

He couldn't sleep. He went back to the window and peered out at the darkness. He was so close to the glass that his reflection disappeared.

When he awoke the next morning, the place beside him in bed was still empty. He waited another day. By the time the streetlamps came on again that night, he was certain: Kerstin wasn't coming back.

It was like a punch in the gut. The truth cracked the walls, made his head pound. It was unbearable. Had she been plotting her escape from the moment Tauber asked her to go to West Berlin? Or did she only get the idea when they arrived at the hotel?

Either way, she had deceived him; she had used him and exploited her position. For a moment, he worried that something had happened to her, but he knew that wasn't the case. She'd dreamed of all this, even if it meant living without him.

He sat on the edge of the bed and tried to hold back his tears as he tied his shoelaces with trembling hands. He snatched his coat from the hook behind the door, then went out. Not to search for Kerstin, just to walk. He'd been at the hotel for two days now; he'd tramped down the stairs and dined in the smoky restaurant only to return to his room and wait. For two days he'd not spoken to anyone. For two days he'd only thought of Kerstin. Two days alone with his thoughts.

The air was cool, and the sky was heavy with clouds, but there was no rain. Now he saw the city as it really was. Their ostentatious Mercedes-Benzes, their BMWs, their Audis spinning around the city's streets mocked everyone who could afford only the tram or the sidewalk. Behind the scent of aftershave, it was a false and brutal place. No one turned a sharp eye on the wealthy when they exploited others, because it was the right of the wealthy to exploit others. So they grew richer and the masses grew poorer, and their greed slowly gobbled up the world. He cursed his own blindness. He'd believed that he would be able to work in West Berlin, if only Kerstin was with him. He cursed again.

Though he had nowhere to go, he walked on, from one neighborhood to another, walking until his feet and knees ached. Then he turned around to head back to the revolting hotel room in Wedding. He saw a street sign, Brunnenstrasse, and turned down it—even though the street name only made him more homesick—and there he found it, at the far end of the street.

The evening was illuminated by the floodlights along the Wall, a blinding streak, like daylight cutting into the darkness. The floodlights sliced holes in the sky. The cones of light and their luminous darts drifted across the city, and above the Wall, he recognized the TV tower in the distance. He walked toward the Wall, right up to it. On the West Berlin side, it had been desecrated, painted with ugly drawings, crude slogans, and defamations of the GDR. For West Berliners the Wall was a source of amusement, but for East Berliners it was a shield against the very people who'd mocked it. Their lack of respect simply underscored its legitimacy. He set his palm against the cold concrete. For his whole life, when he'd stood on the other side of the Wall, this part of the city hadn't existed. Now the other side was unreal. He was so close to home and yet so far.

He was overwhelmed by sadness at the thought that he couldn't return for three weeks. He lived right there on the other side. So close, but he had to turn around and finish his job without Kerstin.

He followed the Wall eastward along Bernauer Strasse, grazing his fingertips across its coarse surface. A younger couple looked at him curiously, and he quickly shoved his hand in his pocket. He followed the Wall as far as he could, but he had to veer around the train tracks in several places. He knew there was a border crossing close by. Although he couldn't go across, he could longingly glance home.

On Bornholmerstrasse he turned toward the border crossing, where Bösebrücke crossed the tracks. The border ran between the rails. He heard loud voices and figured there must be a party going on somewhere. Partying on a Thursday was typical of West Berliners. There was something shameless about being so carefree. No respect.

He walked slowly toward Bösebrücke. The bridge was a heavy steel construction that resembled curved train tracks arching into the sky on either side of the broad boulevard. The center was divided by tramlines. The bridge was stitched together and bolted into the ground. When everything else was gone, it would still be standing, like the Wall.

He glanced at his watch. Quarter past nine. It was time to return to the hotel. He stared across the bridge; the security on this side was pathetic. He realized now that the shouting he'd heard was coming from the eastern side of the Wall. He stood for a moment, suddenly hesitant. He thought he could see something on the bridge, figures approaching. He looked left and right; there was no one else around. They came closer, waving their hands above their heads, beckoning. He wanted to turn and leave, since he was uncomfortable at this demonstration. They were cheering, some were crying, and others laughing loudly. Probably some drunken West Berliners, but what were they doing on the bridge?

He *had* to get back now, but a young woman suddenly ran toward him, her arms spread wide to embrace him. He stiffened as she fell into him. When she let go, she gave him a big, wet kiss on the lips. She held out her ID card. She was an East German. At that moment he realized they were all waving ID cards.

She ran on, skipping, beaming with joy, and Peter stood stock still, confused. The bridge was once again empty, but the shouts continued to echo. His tired legs and his curiosity carried him out to the middle of the bridge. On the other side of the barrier, hundreds of people had gathered, maybe thousands. They were the ones who were shouting. Bellies pressed against the barrier, faces against the chain-link fence, screaming mouths, eyes filled with hope. The border guards stood facing the throng, their broad backs to Peter. It made no sense. What were all these people doing here? They didn't actually believe they would be allowed to cross the border, did they? But what about that woman—and the others—who'd already crossed the bridge? He began to sweat under his winter coat.

Something was happening, but he had no idea what. He'd been gone for only a few days, and already it seemed as though he didn't understand his own country. He was exhausted, but he had to stay to see what was going on.

He watched the border guards conferring. The superior officers walked back and forth; a new officer arrived, and another conversation followed. Peter looked at his watch again. It was 9:30 p.m. This would have to wait—it was time for bed. Tomorrow he would buy a newspaper and learn what this strange demonstration was all about. Western media loved to write sarcastic articles about his country, of course, those know-it-all journalists who believed they knew everything.

Then it happened.

The guards pushed the barrier aside. Peter raised his hands to his face as the crowd poured through the opening like a gushing torrent. Dumbstruck, Peter watched the inexplicable scene unfolding before him. Faces radiated joy and cheers filled the air. Smiling and laughing, the crowd spread out across the entire width of the street, singing, shouting, drinking from bottles they'd brought with them, toasting, grinning, and calling out hoarsely. Some cried. From the other side of the bridge, West Berliners streamed out to greet the newcomers. Peter was thunderstruck. The barrier had been set aside, and the guards were doing nothing. The two groups had now merged in the middle of the border crossing, and people had begun to embrace one another. He felt a surge of terror—nothing would ever be the same. Quivering with excitement, his countrymen and countrywomen were pouring into the very city he wished so desperately to leave, but nothing could stop them now. He watched as they poured in by the thousands.

The nightmare was *not* a dream; it was all too real. The tears were real, as were the laughter and the overjoyed faces, and yet it couldn't be real. He would have to wake up soon; it *had* to be a dream. Maybe he would find Kerstin back at the hotel room, or even better: they would wake up together in their apartment back on Kopenhagener Strasse.

Gripped by panic, Peter wanted only to get away from it all, so he started to walk toward home. Several people hugged him along the way. A man in denim with a bushy mustache made the peace sign right in Peter's face; another waved a flag over Peter's head. The center of the flag, where the GDR emblem had once been displayed, had been cut out.

The growing hordes seemed impenetrable, but he fought his way through. The guards watched in resignation, their hands clasped behind their backs, lipstick smeared on their cheeks. Some wore flowers in their buttonholes. People laughed at Peter as they danced across the border crossing. Some shouted at him, saying that freedom was the other way. They tried tugging him along with them, but he clung to the barrier and resisted the mass of people. He felt like a swimmer fighting for his life. The waves crashed against him, ripped and tore at his clothes. His coat disappeared, and he lost one of his shoes, which was kicked away by hundreds of tromping feet. On tired, unsteady legs, he finally made it across the border.

A guard scrutinized him. "You coming home already?"

Peter continued on without replying. The entire city was out, and the euphoria was a communal shout that reverberated. "The Wall has fallen! The Wall has fallen!" Tears formed in his eyes as he let himself into his building as his neighbor Irene Krause disappeared behind her curtain. The celebrations carried on straight through to morning. As the sun rose, he knew that nothing would ever be the same.

36

STEFAN

Berlin, October 1990

Stefan didn't understand the television that day. On every channel he heard talk of reunification, but it didn't concern him. Every station featured smiling faces, as if they had just won an important soccer match. Though they spoke in German, what they were saying was incomprehensible to him, almost ramblingly euphoric. It irritated him that their foolish joy filled all of his channels, because *Dempsey and Makepeace* was on every Wednesday. That's how he knew what day it was.

He could hear his parents toasting in the living room. They'd asked him if he wanted to celebrate with them, but he didn't know what they had to celebrate. They tried to explain something about a wall, but he didn't understand and didn't care. Maybe they had told him that he'd once been a mason, he wasn't sure. All he knew was that he'd once been something other than what he was now.

Stefan watched TV all the time. He could no longer read, because his eyes had been ruined by the bright lights in his cell. He watched crime shows, lifestyle programs, documentary films, series—anything that could keep him from thinking. Sports calmed him, animal programs made him affectionate, cooking shows made him hungry, and porn gave him erections.

He occasionally trudged around the apartment. He tried all the doorknobs, just to be sure that no doors were locked. Even the front door was open, and he began to go out. Often he went with his mother, but when she didn't go with him, she would supply him with a note with their address and some money for a cab. On his strolls, he gradually relearned the neighborhood. He spent hours sitting on a bench and observing the children on the playground near the apartment block.

Whenever his mother went shopping, she always forced Stefan to come along. She said that he would need to learn to take care of himself someday. So she taught him how to shop, prepare food, and wash clothes, and she taught him how to find his way around the city by himself. He enjoyed his walks around the city, because no one told him where to go. He walked on and on, as if he were searching for something—he didn't know what. Maybe the person he'd once been? Though they'd tried, his parents hadn't been able to conceal from him that he was not like others. They talked to him often about his childhood and his brother, Alexander, who now lived in Australia but never visited them; it seemed that he wanted to forget everything and everyone from his past. They talked about Nina, but he recalled nothing except for the cries of an infant and a woman with curly hair. "Yes, that's her," they said, but when he asked what happened to her, they fell silent.

Stefan's father died in 1996, and his mother followed two years later. A man from the authorities visited him. Stefan didn't understand what he said, but they gave him money every month. He did what he'd learned: he shopped, made dinner, and washed clothes. One day, a letter arrived from the real estate company. Due to missed payments and repeatedly ignored reminders, his lease was being terminated. He packed his duffel and moved out, but he didn't know where to go.

37

ANDREAS

Frederikssund, April 2007

They park at the fried chicken joint. It's still completely dark when they walk out onto the bridge. They're not the first ones there. A man raps his pipe on the guardrail, and it vibrates against the metal. Then he blows a solid puff of air into it, and it whistles a shrill note as if it were a wind instrument. Already he has two garfish in his bucket. Aerodynamic darts, with wide-open eyes and needle-sharp teeth glisten a blue-green.

It's almost seven o'clock, and the sun is on its way up over Frederikssund, sluggish and lazy. Many sport fishermen prefer to fish at a place called the Broken Teeth, the long headland where the remains of the old train trestle are planted in the bottom of the fjord. The water is deep there, and during the late summer months, they pull in sea trout as they're swimming into their spawning areas. Andreas and Thorkild prefer Crown Prince Frederick's Bridge. He doesn't recall why, but it's a tradition. Year after year they stand on the bridge on a Sunday in April and watch garfish shoot up the fjord in enormous schools, looking like organic torpedoes. Late in the afternoon, when their bucket is full, they go home to Vanløse. In the evening, Thorkild pan fries the fish and prepares a thick parsley sauce. He brings a bottle of sauvignon blanc up from the basement, or a Riesling, and if Elisabeth doesn't have a meeting, she'll eat with them. Afterward, Andreas will ride his bicycle back to the city, feeling like he's still a child.

Thorkild hasn't seen Andreas since he returned home from Berlin a few weeks ago. He dozed in the car while Thorkild hummed softly along with Joni Mitchell's album, *Blue*. Out on the bridge, they prepare their carbon fiber poles. Thorkild finds a few lures in his tackle box, which smells of bait, saltwater, and Nescafé. The old Jensen Tobis lures are worn down from all the times they've been dragged through saltwater, but they still work.

The garfish's long mouth makes it nearly impossible to hook, so Thorkild binds a three-inch piece of fishing twine between the lure and the hook. Every year, he explains to Andreas that he devised this technique when *he'd* learned to fish with his grandfather. Three inches is the most humane length of hook for the fish, he says every time he hands Andreas a lure.

They fasten the lures to the line and cast. The only thing they hear is the soft click of their reels spinning like newly oiled racing bikes. Otherwise the morning is quiet. The sun glistens on the water, and the stillness is shattered by a school of garfish swimming close to the surface. The fish pass by an early-rising pleasure boater. His boat, a rundown carbon fiber model with a tarnished blue great sail, glides slowly toward the bridge. Two blinking red lights indicate that the bridge will open for through-sailing from the north. Rattling heavily, the two halves of the road begin to rise in the air, breaking the silence for a moment.

A light breeze brushes Andreas's face, and he remembers to enjoy it, the fresh air that softly waves his worries away, like a docking station filling him up. He sucks it in, all the way down into his lungs, then pushes it out again. The morning breeze is gentle, like the bristles of a soft broom or a piece of fabric.

Thorkild is silent. He always is on such mornings. Not until the first fish is pulled from the water does he begin to talk.

Andreas's pole vibrates in his hand. The garfish is toying with him, tugging at the lure with its mouth. He reels in a little. A few more tiny nips. He's the old man in Hemingway's novella, he's Santiago, and his streak of eighty-four days without a fish on his hook seems to be coming to an end. The pole vibrates again. The boy, Manolin, mustn't sail with him any longer, and all that remains is the lonely struggle between a man and a fish. He drags the lure through the water—quickly but not too quickly—so that it planes the surface. He pauses. Then he spins the reel once more and pauses again. Spins. Then he jerks on the line and begins to haul the fish in. As it leaps from the water, he can tell that it's hooked perfectly; it struggles, writhes, and tries to break free. Andreas yanks it out of the water, and Thorkild hauls it over the guardrail with his net.

When the garfish is in the bucket, Thorkild nods, acknowledging its size. He clears his throat, "So, how was Berlin?"

Andreas thinks of his mother. She'd asked what Andreas had learned about his father, but by her tone he could tell that she didn't really want to know. Maybe it was just him, but he thought he heard sarcasm in her voice. Lagging behind the question was another sentence waiting to emerge. Once Andreas muttered some vague reply, she was ready with, "What did I tell you?"

Something made him want to shield Peter from her. So he said nothing about Stasi, nothing about the interrogation and Nina Lachner's death or Bea's forced adoption. Once upon a time, he would have wanted nothing more in the world than to talk about Peter with her, but not anymore. Not after what he'd learned about him.

Sometimes he's not even sure just *what* he knows. Ever since Bea told him that Peter worked for Stasi, he's questioned everything, but Peter had been more than just a Stasi man. In his relationships with Veronika and Bea and in the letter to Kerstin, Andreas had met a completely different person, a man who'd been considered good, even loving. It's as if countless identities resided within Peter: evil, ambitious, loving, cynical, good, heartless, lovable. Little by little he begins to recognize himself in his father. Andreas can't accept all of Peter's actions, but he tries to accept the fact that his own father was as much a composite as he himself is. So he feels a shift inside him, almost a physical change. It occurs to him that not only has he been trying to find his father, he's also been trying to find himself.

But for some reason, Andreas decides to confide in Thorkild. Standing on the bridge, he tells him the entire story of Peter, Bea, and Veronika.

38

STEFAN

Berlin, October 2006

Though the heel of his hand was bleeding, he felt no pain. It was an open, oblong slice from a broken bottle. Stefan found a napkin smeared with dressing and wiped his hand with its cleanest corner. Now he had a fresh wound to go along with all the encrusted scabs that covered his hands. Using his other hand, he continued digging for his dinner in the garbage bin, though more carefully this time. Someone had tossed out a half-eaten döner kebab. It looked fine except for some unidentifiable black flakes and a single shard from the glass bottle, easily removable.

He didn't have a regular place to sleep. Usually he found a back alley, but he had to be careful about urine streams. If he was lucky, he found a dry piece of cardboard to sleep on. Sometimes he slept in parks, in abandoned buildings, or on the hot-air vents—if they weren't already occupied. Some people lived on them and didn't give them up without a fight. He often recalled his time in the factory. The best time of his life. He smiled at the thought—at the fact that he could remember, which was new to him, but he still remembered nothing from *before* his time in prison. His parents had shown him old photographs and told him about his life, but it was as though they were speaking about someone else. He did remember the cell, the interrogations, Emil Brank, and more and more about his life after prison.

After he was forced out of the apartment, he'd traversed every inch of the city, every sidewalk, every section of asphalt, and then one day he'd found himself in front of the train station. Suddenly he'd recognized something, though he wasn't sure *what* it was that had caught his attention. His legs had taken him up the stairs, onto the platform, and onto the train. He'd gotten off at another station and then walked on. Only his feet knew where to go. Then he stopped and simply looked around.

They poked the sky like two naked trees, but they were taller. At least two hundred feet, maybe three hundred. Slender columns that stretched up into the clouds, spitting smoke into the air. He suddenly recalled the approving way he and his colleagues had looked at them as they crossed Langerhans Canal in their overalls on their way to work. Yes, this was where he'd worked.

What was left of his porous memory had brought him there. As he gazed at the abandoned factory through the wire fence, he recalled the large production facilities that echoed when you sang, the ovens that belched smoke into the chimneys, the administration buildings where Bernd Müller had once hung calendars with photos of scantily clad women, and the cafeteria where he'd once attended someone's wedding. He saw the enormous, cylinder-shaped cisterns with the steel ladders that had once held sulfuric acid. They weren't allowed to fill the cisterns completely, because the acid expanded as the temperature rose in the tanks. He pictured himself in rubber boots, gloves, and safety goggles, and he remembered the mild prick he felt on his skin at the end of the working day. They made animal feed and fertilizer, and he remembered the distinct smell of phosphates.

He walked along the fence. Someone had cut a hole in one spot. He squeezed through the hole and entered the vast expanse of the plant. The buildings were now useless behemoths, corpses of concrete dinosaurs. Everything had been abandoned. The production halls were hollow, resoundingly empty; all the windows were smashed, and the floor was littered with empty plastic jugs and pill bottles with skull and crossbones symbols on their disintegrating labels. A few birds fluttered around the ceiling, flying in and out of the gaping windows. The offices were a mess of papers, handwritten notes, broken furniture, and cat excrement. Poisonous green puddles fizzed, and weeds had begun pushing up through the rust-red soil. A sharp chemical smell hung in all the rooms and stung his lungs. There was graffiti on the walls, large cursive lettering that he couldn't read and a riot of colorful drawings of faces like those in comic books.

He looked around for a place to sleep and for any curtains that he could use as blankets. A skinny cat with large, curious eyes followed him. He named it Petra, not knowing why; it just seemed to fit the gray-striped kitty. When he lay down on his makeshift bed, he tried filling in the blank spaces in his memory but could only summon images of himself in the factory. Through the tall windows, he saw the night sky full of stars, like seeds blown from a hand. There was hardly room for all of them. Some of the stars fell, a sparkling tail of light trailing behind them. Each night he fell asleep to the creaking sound of rust and decay, with warm little Petra in his arms.

During the day, he went downtown to forage through the trash bins. He jumped off the train whenever he spotted a train conductor's uniform.

One morning he was woken up with a kick. He sat up, confused, drowsy. A guard was staring at him and kicked his legs again. Stefan winced, and the cat jumped off.

"You can't sleep here. Get out."

Another guard appeared. "Come on, Jan. I think he got the message."

"I want to kick him to pieces, goddamn it. Look how scared he is."

"Come on."

Stefan stared at him. The voice seemed familiar, and he felt as though he was about to remember the face. That hadn't happened before. They dragged him to the fence. He crawled through the hole and scrutinized the two men, who both seemed to puff themselves up in their navy-blue uniforms. He was more and more certain that he'd seen one of them before.

"Get lost!" they yelled.

39

ANDREAS

As they walk up the flagstone path, Andreas spots his mother through the kitchen window. She sets down the potato peeler when they enter the house, dries her hands on her apron, and kisses Andreas on both cheeks. Thorkild proudly holds up the bucket with their catch, so she can see the fish.

"Would you mind preparing them on the patio? Otherwise the kitchen will smell of fish."

She puts the pot filled with potatoes on the stove and snaps off the radio. Andreas follows her into the living room. She pours wine for them and hands him a glass. They sit on opposite ends of the sofa.

"It's lovely to see you, dear," she says as she sips her white wine. "I love this tradition. It's just like when you were a boy. Do you remember when you and Thorkild came home after the car had hit one hundred thousand miles? Do you remember how excited you were?"

He nods and instantly feels himself getting defensive. He has no energy for talk. He decides it's time to ask some questions.

"Why are you pretending that I never went to Berlin?"

"I'm not." She smiles, unperturbed.

"Why didn't ever tell me anything about Peter?" As he speaks, he hears an echo of all the times he has asked this question.

He sees her hesitate. In a minute she'll begin her classic evasive maneuver: pour more wine and change topics. Through the patio doors, they see Thorkild cleaning the fish, slicing them from the anus to the ventral fins. When he's removed the entrails, he cuts off the heads and tails and tosses those parts back in the bucket.

Elisabeth fills their glasses, though they've yet to empty them.

"Andreas," she says, her voice soft. She pauses. "You probably discovered something in Berlin, something I ought to have told you about years ago." She sips her wine and shifts apprehensively in her chair.

"I had this friend, Ejner Madsen. We talked pretty regularly until he moved to East Germany. He worked for Peter and confided in me that Peter worked for Stasi. Peter *was* the Stasi."

"I know." Andreas looks at her earnestly, surprised that she'd known all along. "But why didn't you tell me?"

"To protect you, but maybe that was wrong of me. I just wanted to spare you." Elisabeth bites her lip. "It wasn't easy for me, you know." She sighs. "I really believed in communism, but when I learned what Stasi was doing—and that Peter was part of it—suddenly I was no longer proud of it. After the Wall fell and all the skeletons came out of the closet, all my friends back here were quick to distance themselves from Stasi. I just tried to forget about Peter, and I didn't see any reason that you should know about him."

Andreas regards his wine glass pensively as she speaks. If he'd known all that before his trip to Berlin, Bea might still be alive. He might never have felt compelled to learn more about Peter—he would never have gone to see Mrs. Majenka, would never have learned the truth. What right had he to interfere with her life?

Elisabeth looks at him as though waiting for an indication that he'll forgive her. He nods slowly, but only to make her turn away from him. They sit in silence for what seems like an eternity. Finally Thorkild enters with the grilled garfish on a plate. "You haven't drunk all the wine, have you?"

"I have to go." Andreas gets up quickly. He doesn't want to leave, but he doesn't want to stay, either.

Thorkild looks at him, puzzled. His raises his eyebrows and turns to Elisabeth. She shakes her head, her expression resigned.

"Well, more fish for me then," Thorkild says, trying to cover up his disappointment by sounding jovial.

As Andreas bicycles back to the city, he considers how little Elisabeth has told him about Peter. Now he knows why she was so taciturn. His instinct is to be angry and let her have it, but he forgives her. All at once her reluctance to talk about Peter during his childhood makes sense: she didn't withhold information out of malice but to shield him. Nonetheless, he had to get out of there. He just couldn't sit there, thinking about Bea and pretending nothing had happened.

Some memories are good for you, while others grow distorted with time. Andreas has made it a habit of clinging to the latter. Throughout his life he has viewed himself as a victim because he didn't have a father. All this time he's been looking for excuses for his own failures. He has always blamed others, never himself.

It's as though he awakens right there on the bike path on Hillerødgade. He must act; if he doesn't, he'll be stuck forever. Either he must become an active participant in life, or he'll wind up a hermit living in some forest with a limping dog. He's got to get on with his life, put an end to all those years of hibernation, face reality. Face himself.

He realizes that in putting his memories of his father to rest, he's buried his longing for him as well. It's as though he's suddenly free. It's as though a chain has been removed from his ankle. He feels lighter, and everything that has held him back is now propelling him forward. He'll have to start over, but where to begin?

His apartment on Frederikssundsvej is like new, as though he's never been there. He's reinvigorated, brand-new. He punches a number on his cell phone.

"Hi, Lisa. It's me, Andreas."

40

PETER

Berlin, October 2006

Peter looked at the others around the table. In a way, their faces were similar, all furrowed by loss, despondency, and disillusion. They weren't all from East Germany, but their collision with the city had marked them all; their souls were battered by the many beatings the city had doled out. Now their hopes could be found at the bottom of every bottle of beer they drank. The same men, another afternoon. The casualties of reunification. The unemployment that plagued West Germany, which they'd once mocked, had now become their own. A common "good" for half the people. Only a single industry seemed unaffected by the crisis that had befallen East Berlin: the pubs.

Peter and one other man were the only ones with jobs. Peter worked for Sonnenberger Security, a security firm that patrolled the city's malls, factories, and warehouses. Most of the employees were former colleagues. Jan Grebe and Peter were partners. It was their job to keep shopping centers orderly and to make sure that thieves, teens, and other unruly elements didn't disturb the customers, who'd come to send their

Deutschmarks into circulation. Goods practically fell into shopping carts, and the security company now defended everything that he'd despised and fought against.

And that wasn't even the biggest problem. Now his company was being pushed out by other companies—tough Turks, broad-shouldered Poles, and Russians with facial tattoos who looked like members of a death cult. Sonnenberger had lost interest in his firm after his wife died in 1995, and he didn't have the energy to fight the new competition. Little by little, they were forced out of the larger shopping centers and had to be content with factories, warehouses, and strip malls on the outskirts of the city where the local drunks held court on benches, counting their coins for another beer.

Peter had begun to resemble those drunks. When he removed his uniform each night, he felt old. Not old in the sense that his bones creaked and his joints hurt, but old inside, in his head. All he wanted was another beer, and that's what he got every day in this pub. He was only fifty-four, but he had no energy left for anything. What was there to muster energy for? How was he supposed to come to terms with the fact that his future was behind him? Did he have any hope left? The answer was simple and even more depressing than the question: no. Because no one even *noticed* him anymore. He meant nothing to anyone who meant something to him. He didn't exist.

Martina had left him, Kerstin had left him, and his country had crumbled around him. It had been a long time since he'd had any kind of influence, and loss of control made him feel empty. Once when he was very young, he had gotten drunk and the lightness of the intoxication was, briefly, uplifting. His sense of giddiness almost unreal, but then he'd vomited, which had been disgusting, and his self-recriminations the next day were even harsher. Since then, he'd never wanted to lose control of himself, his thoughts, or his body, but that loss of control was a daily goal now—a relief that made his life's failures bearable.

If he told anyone about what he used to do for a living, they sneered or spat at him, so he kept it to himself.

He'd believed in the state, but it no longer believed in him, and he was just someone people pissed on, someone who could point you in the direction of the nearest McDonald's, and when it was time for last call at the pub, he was more alone than alone, more lonely than lonely. No man should ever have to feel that sense of isolation, and certainly not a man of his caliber. Behind the mirror in his bathroom, where he kept the postcards for Bea, he also kept a gun, a nine-millimeter Makarov. It was a way out, and it was no longer a strange idea to him. Wolfgang's suicide had been an embarrassment to the family, and Peter didn't want to end up that way. That fact—coupled with his own cowardice—was what kept him alive.

He still carried inside the pain of Kerstin leaving him, and where was she? He tried to find comfort in the possibility that her heart had also been broken, though he wasn't entirely successful. Her beloved Patsy Cline had died in a plane crash in 1963. He always felt a certain sense of joy when thinking about that: Kerstin's idol had been dead for over twenty-five years when Peter and Kerstin met, and she hadn't known, but it was a pathetic revenge.

"Understandable," Tauber had said in response to Peter's return from West Berlin, but Kerstin Hopp was branded a traitor just before there was no longer a GDR to betray. Tauber blathered about how they had to make the most of the new situation, as though he completely failed to understand that everything would change, that everything *before* the Wall had come down was a beginning, and everything after was a conclusion.

The years had passed, and he didn't quite understand how. Perhaps life merely consisted of a set of points, moments that one could recall, and the rest, all the rest, was insignificant, and what did he remember? Only the good remained. How was he so able to distort his memories? He'd remember something one way even though he knew it hadn't happened that way, but that was how he wanted to remember it. The more he told it, or the more he thought about it, the more it seemed like the truth. His truth.

His son lived in Denmark, his own flesh and blood. Peter wondered what he was like, had always wanted to meet him, and it would be so easy. A train ticket to Denmark, but where others saw the Wall's collapse as an opportunity, Peter saw the opposite. Anyway, what did he have to offer his son, who would probably be ashamed of what his own father had done?

The best thing he could do was to stay away and never contact Andreas, because a wall still existed between them, or rather, a chasm, and there was no reason to attempt to scale it. In his mind, he'd written to his son often, but Andreas had never received the postcards because they'd been addressed to Beatrice. Everything he had written to her—including his parting words—*I love you, Dad*—he'd written for Andreas.

Of course he loved Beatrice too, but she knew that. He didn't have to write it to her. His one regret was that he'd deceived her with the lie about Wolfgang. He no longer recalled why Veronika had concocted the story of him fleeing. She'd had no reason to do so. Yet they'd maintained the story, and it eventually became the truth: Wolfgang had fled to the West, and the postcards Peter sent made the story credible. That had been his idea, and he'd enjoyed writing them, but Peter and Beatrice hardly spoke these days. Once she'd grown up, she drifted away. To love her wasn't the same thing as to understand her. She wasn't a child of the GDR like he was. She had been able to put the past behind her. He couldn't.

GDR was like an organ that had failed and now, following a transplant, the body had rejected the new organ. The West Germans were arrogant and condescending, because they were paying for everything. They called them *eastwhiners*, but they weren't the ones forced to rummage in trashcans for food, and when a guy from Cologne or Munich spoke of his earliest memories, he called them simply childhood memories, but if he was from Leipzig or Dresden, it was contemptuously dismissed as *eastalgia*. Some East Germans were ashamed, some evolved, and many became turncoats. They edited their past, revising their personal history to suit the times. Those who had once been party men now claimed they'd fought state suppression of the people. That's what they called it. Some put on their Sunday best and got good jobs somewhere with these sketchy memories, while others, like the men gathered around this table, put up with jobs not even Turkish immigrants wanted.

The six men sat shoulder to shoulder in the cramped wooden booth. The frosted glass windows with their lace curtains allowed them to forget that it was still daytime, and the beer helped them to forget all else. Hartmut drained his bottle. Peter could tell by his darting eyes that he was about to let out his daily gripe, and that usually meant Hartmut had to take a leak.

"When capitalism fails and all the economies have been eaten up by greed, when common sense prevails, my time will come again." He stood up and staggered toward the bathroom.

At least Hartmut still had hope. That was more than you could say for the others. Peter doubted that common sense would ever prevail. Pornographic magazines were displayed in storefronts and cheap vodka sat on the shelves at a height any child could reach; young people sniffed glue and lighter fluid in the back alleys, and teenage prostitutes from the Baltics lowered the prices for a blow job. He lived his life in full recognition that nothing would get better tomorrow or the day after. The future was no longer something he'd been promised and that he looked forward to but something he feared. It hung before him like a heavy shadow, black as night. It was still difficult to grasp that he could speak of a country in the past tense. It was supposed to be a reunification, the *merging* of two countries, but instead, one country had been destroyed, its inhabitants forced to live in the other. Those who'd been discarded sat around this table—the new migrants in Germany.

41

ANDREAS

Copenhagen, March 2008

It's been almost one year since Andreas called Lisa. After he'd picked up the phone that night, they'd met in a café, on neutral ground, and had a cup of coffee. Then two days later, she'd called him. She had sensed what he too had recognized when he called her. He knew what he wanted, she said. She'd sensed an energy and ambition that had been absent before. So right there in the café, she'd met a new Andreas, one whom she once again felt attracted to.

And now they're lying in bed, the first rays of morning sun beaming through the blinds, drawing stripes on Lisa's naked skin. His hands had not forgotten her body. They recalled her curves and the tickling sensation in his fingertips whenever he slid them along the small peaks of her spine.

He drew letters on her back with his finger.

"What are you writing?" Lisa's voice is faint from exhaustion.

"You'll have to guess." The letters vanish in her soft skin, but she already knows everything the words are meant to say.

"Not now." She turns over and pulls him near. "Are you nervous?" she asks as their lips part. Her breath is sour and warm.

He shrugs. "Are you going to the paper after?"

"No, I took the day off."

"But don't you have to go wrap up your work, or whatever you do when you quit?"

"Not today."

Lisa gives his shoulder a squeeze as he climbs out of bed. His foot gets tangled up in her panties on the floor. She rolls over in bed and appears to go back to sleep. For a moment he stands there, enjoying the sight of her back. Then he heads to the living room. He looks around, his eyes settling on the spot where the TV used to be. They've sold it.

He hears Lisa moving around in the bedroom. He loves her sounds, loves the feeling of knowing she's there. Close.

He stands by the window, glances across the street, and suddenly she's right behind him. She puts her arms around him.

"I never gave my wonderful boyfriend a proper good-bye." She speaks close to his ear, tickling it. Whether it's her words or her proximity doesn't matter. In the beginning she'd called him her new boyfriend, and he'd also felt the change.

"Dear Andreas, you've done it. Congratulations on your master's degree."

As Thomas, his thesis advisor, tells him how he's always had faith in Andreas's abilities and how easy it was to be such a diligent student's advisor, Thorkild begins opening champagne bottles. One of the corks escapes his grasp and smacks the ceiling; particles of plaster land on those sitting directly under it. Elisabeth gives Thorkild a chiding look.

Andreas finished his thesis in six months. He dug into the work with a new sense of resolution, working around the clock, and today is his reward.

Elisabeth has brought glasses in a little picnic basket, and she hands them out as Thomas continues to talk. As they toast Andreas, his mother smiles proudly and gives him a peck on the cheek.

"There's a house for sale down the road. You'd love it," she says.

He nods absentmindedly. He has yet to tell her that he and Lisa are moving to Berlin, and he intends to wait a little longer.

Elisabeth clinks her glass with a spoon and begins to speak. He looks at Lisa. She looks lovely. He forgets to listen and just enjoys the sight of her in the tight black dress. She's only fifteen weeks along, but they've both noticed the little bump, the slight arch of her dress, which others will notice only later. When the baby arrives, it's going to be cramped in the apartment on Kopenhagener Strasse. He smiles without realizing he's doing so, and the others mistake this for pride at Elisabeth's words.

42

PETER

Berlin, October 2006

He feels the eight beers in his blood as he gets to his feet. The door is his point of orientation, and he staggers toward it. The smokers are standing outside, covering the sidewalk with their cigarette butts. He mumbles, "See you later," and heads home.

On the sidewalk lies another victim of life's beatings, a homeless man propped against a storefront, his legs forming a barrier to Peter's section of sidewalk. The homeless man glances up at Peter with blood-shot eyes, and Peter stops. The man's eyes are glazed over, like his own. He holds out a plastic bucket, one of those ice cream tubs you buy at the supermarket. There's some change inside. Peter turns away, studies the window display, and pulls out his wallet. The homeless man's eyes light up, but Peter gets a different idea. On a whim, he decides to buy a new coffee maker, one that's less noisy. He steps over the man's legs and enters the store.

He walks through aisle after aisle of dinnerware and silverware, toasters, and potato peelers with flexible handles. He considers turning around, but then he spots the aisle with thermoses, which means he must be getting close. All the models are made of stainless steel, with lit displays, indicator lights, and buttons. He feels overwhelmed. He reads the signs but doesn't see the word *coffee* anywhere. They're called names like Mocha Master and espresso-something-or-other. He wants to ask the shop assistant, but he knows how ridiculous it will sound if he asks whether they carry a coffee maker with only *one* button, two at most. He gives up and just wants to go home.

He turns and sees the homeless man making his way toward him. Peter holds his breath to avoid the man's stench, then steps back to let him pass, but the man just stops and stands there, staring, forcing Peter to exhale. A rancid smell emanates from the man's clothes, and Peter senses that the man may have recognized him. Have they seen one another before? Suddenly he's frightened; the fear creeps into him, spreads under his skin. Does he know that face hiding beneath the dirt and the beard? The man's eyes are accusatory. The stench is nauseating. Peter spins on his heels and heads down the silverware aisle, past the kitchen utensils and carving sets. He looks back. The man is following him. The homeless man removes a chef's knife from a shelf.

Peter rushes out of the store and nearly trips over the plastic bucket. Coins roll out onto the sidewalk, scattering everywhere. An elderly woman offers to help him gather them up, but he shakes his head and hurries off, taking long, fast strides. Halfway down Kopenhagener Strasse, he glances over his shoulder. The man hasn't followed him. He's trembling. It's not the first time he's felt stalked without reason, but this time feels different.

He rummages through his pocket for his keys. He feels the buzz of alcohol, which makes him sleepy. He thinks of coffee and how nice it would be to have a new coffeemaker. He hears the heavy wooden gate that's covered in graffiti. He hears footsteps. The stench has returned.

He turns and spots the homeless man. He sees the beard, long and gray, and the pulsating vein in the man's neck. He sees his dilated pupils and the broken blood vessels in his eyes. Then he sees the knife, and he sees the man raise the knife. Between this moment and the knife's entry in his belly, Peter remembers who the man is.

He remembers the man's name and he remembers the prison and he remembers the interrogations and he remembers the man's proclamations of innocence. He remembers the man's wife and the sound of her head when it struck the edge of the table, and he remembers that Stefan served a year in Hohenschönhausen and four years in Görden. He remembers the broken man who was released in 1985, without his wife or daughter, without his memory, unable to put two coherent thoughts together.

After reunification, he erased any trace that might lead Stefan back to him. He redacted his name from all the files, as well as from Renate Koch's file on Beatrice in the registry at Child Protective Services. He thinks how paradoxical it is, because Stefan Lachner couldn't possibly know about all that. He doesn't know that Peter was present when Nina was killed, and he doesn't know that Beatrice grew up with Veronika. Yet Peter can tell from his mad eyes that he knows something. Stefan Lachner wants revenge. Peter knows he destroyed Stefan's life, and now Stefan is going to destroy his. Peter knows why he must die.

He knows why the knife violently lifts his body off the ground and toward the heavens—a heaven that he doesn't believe in. Maybe it's time to start believing. The knife seems to beg him to regret his actions, but he did what he had to do, and he'd do it again. A glimmer of light blinds him, and he hears his mother's voice, loving and gentle, "You mustn't stare at the sun. You'll ruin your eyesight." The last thing he sees before his head slams against the asphalt is the outline of Irene Krause disappearing behind the curtain.

ACKNOWLEDGMENTS

I owe a huge thanks to Thomas Wegener Friis, a historian who specializes in the history of the secret service, for all his help; Dagmar Hovestädt and Elmar Kramer from the Stasi Records Agency; professor Helmut Müller-Enbergs; writer Jesper Clemmensen; Anne Marie Nielsen; Allan Nielsen; Helle Rabøl Hansen; Clemens Flämig; Mette Jensen Hayles; Thorbjørn Haslund; Rasmus Boe Hermansen; Mathilde Hermansen; Niels Rosenkvist; Anne Behr; Katrine Rastad; Ulla Therese Kræmer; Jess Dalsgaard; Søren Lind; Nanna Ask; Nicole Jessen; Simon Papousek; Marie Brocks Larsen; and Anne Krogh Hørning.

Finally, I would like to thank copyediting's answer to Jacques Cousteau, my editor, Henrik Okkels, for diving down through the darkness and into the depths of this novel.

Any errors that may have crept into the story are entirely my own.

ABOUT THE AUTHOR

Photo © 2016 Peter Clausen

Jesper Bugge Kold was born in Copenhagen, Denmark, and worked as a journalist before becoming a librarian and website designer. His previous novel, *Winter Men*, was nominated for the Debutant Prize at Denmark's Book Forum in 2014. He lives in South Funen with his wife and two children.

ABOUT THE TRANSLATOR

Photo © Eric Druxman

K. E. Semmel is a writer and translator. In addition to previously trans-lating Jesper Bugge Kold's *Winter Men*, his translations include books by Naja Marie Aidt, Karin Fossum, Erik Valeur, Jussi Adler-Olsen, and Simon Fruelund. He is a recipient of numerous grants from the Danish Arts Foundation and is a 2016 NEA Literary Translation Fellow. He lives in Rochester, New York, where he is the executive director of Writers & Books.